Tales from Grace Chapel Inn

The Pipe Organ

Jane Orcutt

Guideposts

CARMEL, NEW YORK

Acknowledgments

All Scripture quotations are taken from
The Holy Bible, New International Version. Copyright © 1973,
1978, 1984 International Bible Society. Used by permission
of Zondervan Bible Publishers.

Published in association with the literary agency of
Janet Kobobel Grant, Books & Such, 4788 Carissa Avenue,
Santa Rosa, CA 95405.

www.guidepostsbooks.com
1-800-431-2344
Guideposts Books & Inspirational Media Division
Series Editors: Regina Hersey and Leo Grant
Cover art by Edgar Jerins
Cover design by Wendy Bass
Interior design by Cindy LaBreacht
Typeset by Nancy Tardi
Printed in the United States of America

Chapter One

"This year you're ready for something new. It may be more difficult than what you've already studied. Are you eager for a challenge?" Louise Howard Smith smiled at her preteen piano student.

Seated at the baby grand in the Grace Chapel Inn parlor, Ashley Moore clasped her hands together in her lap. "Yes, Mrs. Smith."

"Good." Louise lifted her wire-rimmed glasses from the chain around her neck to the bridge of her nose, ready to get down to serious business. She pulled up one of the Victorian chairs next to the piano bench and sat down. Some of her students took off the summer from piano lessons, but young Ashley persisted during her vacation from school. Louise knew that it was the girl's decision, not her parents', and each year Louise rewarded the girl for her determination, providing her with ever more challenging music.

Ashley had already warmed up her technical skills with repetitive exercises from her *A Dozen a Day* book, and now they were ready to make some real music.

Whack! Wham!

Ashley turned to Louise. "What was that noise, Mrs. Smith?"

Louise grimaced. Thank goodness it was only a few small holes in the shingles that needed repairs. "Just a roofer, dear. He should be finished soon. I had hoped that his work wouldn't bother us since he's several stories overhead. Can you ignore him while you're practicing?"

Ashley nodded, and Louise smiled. She placed a shiny, red music book against the stand and opened it to the first song. "This will be your first cross-hand piece. If you like it and do well with it, we should consider having you play it at our concert."

"Yes, Mrs. Smith." Ashley sat up straight, her expression serious.

Louise smiled to herself. She knew that many of her students were somewhat in awe of her. As the oldest of the three Howard sisters, Louise could be intimidating with her disciplined, orderly ways. Her students didn't joke and play with her the way they did with Louise's sisters Alice, who worked with the ANGELs middle school group of Grace Chapel, or Jane, who loved her gardening and cooking chores at the inn.

But it was those disciplined and orderly qualities that made Louise such an effective piano teacher. If her students' awe compelled them to practice regularly and to be prepared for her scrutiny, then she welcomed it.

Still, she didn't want them to fear her. "You'll do well with this, dear," she said. "You're more than ready for a little challenge. You performed so well last year at our spring concert."

"Really?" Ashley smiled. She flexed her fingers and poised her hands over the ivory keys.

Thump!

Louise gritted her teething, nodding. "Let's give this a brief run-through, shall we? The cross-hand part is not until the second line. Stop when you get there, and we will go over it together."

Ashley launched slowly into "Nobody Knows the Trouble I've Seen," while Louise patiently counted out the time. "One-and-two-and. One-and-two-and. Don't worry about the pedal, Ashley. We will work that in later."

Louise had been teaching from this same music book for nearly forty of her sixty-five years. The publisher had altered the cover from time to time, but the music inside remained the same. Teaching it over and over again felt comfortable and right to Louise, like easing into a favorite cardigan.

Ashley's fingers slipped on the last measure, and the keys plunked discordantly. She looked sheepishly at Louise. "I'm sorry, Mrs. Smith."

"That's quite all right," Louise smiled encouragingly. "It's a good place to stop, anyway. Let me show you how to handle that cross-hand portion. It's really quite easy, once you know how."

Thwack! Whack!

Once Louise had demonstrated the proper method for crossing her left hand over—never under—her right, Ashley continued to pick her way carefully through the piece. Louise subconsciously kept an eye and ear on the music, but she found herself more than once gazing through the open window to the green leaves dancing on a handsome maple. A mockingbird sang contentedly from a branch, and other birds chirped in unintentional harmony.

Louise could well understand why some of her students chose to skip piano lessons during the summer. She loved this time of year, when the warm weather and bright sun meant freedom from being cooped up indoors as the cold chill of winter often dictated. Her late husband Eliot had always loved summer, and he often took a leave of absence from teaching music at the conservatory in Philadelphia so that they could travel to New York City, to Hilton Head or to Boston, the home of their only daughter Cynthia.

After the death of their father, Rev. Daniel Howard, Louise and her younger sisters had decided to fix up their Victorian family home into a bed-and-breakfast. With Eliot gone and Cynthia grown and moved away, Louise felt that she now had a new life here in the small town of Acorn Hill, Pennsylvania. She loved meeting the guests at Grace Chapel Inn, and she loved teaching her young students.

Ashley sounded the last note of the song, let out a sigh of relief and retired her hands to her lap. She sat back and let her shoulders slump. "I don't think I'm ever going to be very good at this, Mrs. Smith. Not by the recital, anyway."

"Of course you will, dear."

"How did you get better at playing, Mrs. Smith?"

"Lots and lots of practice. I still have to play a lot. Music is like exercise. You have to practice to stay in shape. Especially if you want to perform in front of other people."

"Do you get that jumpy feeling in your stomach when you perform, Mrs. Smith?"

"Almost every time."

Ashley's eyes widened. "Even every Sunday?"

Louise smiled patiently. "Maybe not *every* Sunday, but a good number of them. I usually ignore my nervousness, however, because it gives me so much joy to share the talents that God has given me. Shall we try that again?"

Louise played the organ in Grace Chapel for the Sunday worship service. Her father had been the minister there for over sixty years. Coming together at his funeral had made the far-flung Howard sisters renew their bond of sisterly devotion. Establishing their inn had involved a lot of hard work, patience and love, but they were pleased with the result of their efforts.

The rest of the lesson proceeded smoothly, with only a few more noises from the roof. Louise was surprised when the antique, brass-faced mantel clock chimed the hour. She rose, smoothing her light green skirt. "Goodness, Ashley. Time has truly gotten away from us. You have done a wonderful job, and we will work some more next week."

"Yes, ma'am." Ashley rose and headed toward the door.

"Take the book with you, dear," Louise said, handing it to her young student. She escorted her out of the parlor and toward the front door of the old Victorian. "Is your mother picking you up?"

"Yes, and I see her now." Ashley waved toward a maroon minivan that pulled up at the curb. "Good-bye, Mrs. Smith. See you at church tomorrow," she said as she raced down the steps and along the long walkway to the street.

"Good-bye," Louise called after her. "Don't run!"

"How could anyone not think of running on such a lovely day?"

Startled, Louise whirled to her left. "Jane Howard! You gave me such a fright."

Jane laughed. At fifty, she was the youngest Howard sister and Louise's opposite in so many ways. The impression made by Louise's neat sweater and skirt was so different from that of Jane's baggy overalls, which made her appear even younger than the fifteen-year difference between the sisters. Her blue eyes twinkled with delight at frightening the older, staid Louise.

She held out a basket of fresh-cut, long-stemmed, red and yellow roses. "These will make a nice bouquet for Walter and Kathleen Haverty's room. I thought the red and yellow of these blooms will look well in the Sunset Room, where they will be staying." She paused. "You don't have another lesson scheduled for the day, do you? You know how tough it is getting guests settled when your students are whacking and pounding on the keys." Her blue eyes twinkled with mischief.

Louise bristled. "That was the roofer, Jane. Not my student."

"Of course it was," Jane said cheerfully, putting her arm around her sister to lead her back into the house. "Just the same, I'd rather the guests heard *your* lovely music . . . something like Debussy's 'Claire de Lune' or Beethoven's 'Moonlight Sonata.'"

Louise stopped short in the foyer. "Since when have you become a music lover?"

"Justin and I occasionally went to the symphony when we lived in San Francisco," she said. Her smile wavered for a moment as she recalled the husband from whom she had been divorced. "It was hard for us to get away from the restaurant business, but we managed to get some 'cul-chah' a time or two."

Louise sniffed.

"Oh, come on, Louie. I'm just joking with you. You know I don't know beans about music compared to you, but then you don't have my cooking or gardening or artist's skill."

Louise softened. "That's true. It's part of the reason why this bed-and-breakfast runs so well. You, Alice and I have our own special gifts to contribute."

"Speaking of sharing, I'd better get these flowers into a vase and upstairs right away," Jane said. "Otherwise ... are we ready to check in the Havertys?"

Louise, who handled most of the Grace Chapel Inn business affairs, nodded. "All the paperwork is ready. It's nice to have returning guests."

"I'm going to make a special breakfast for them tomorrow morning: *huevos rancheros*, smoked sausage and chili corn bread."

Louise raised an eyebrow. "What did you just say? Whey-who, ranch-*what*?" She put a hand over her heart. "And a chili item—for breakfast?" *What kind of people did Jane remember the Havertys to be?*

"*Wave*-ohs ran-*chair*-ohs. Eggs served over warm tortillas, smothered with cheese. I like to add some avocado and a dollop of sour cream too."

"Oh." Louise was at a loss for words, still mystified at Jane's choice of menu.

"Relax, Louise. This is what a lot of people eat for breakfast in Texas. The last time they visited, Mr. Haverty said that his wife is from South Texas, near the Mexican border. I thought it would be a nice surprise for them."

Louise hoped that the Havertys would be exceptionally hungry for the special breakfast that Jane was preparing. She didn't think her stomach could handle spicy food so early in the morning, especially on a Sunday when she would be playing the organ. The ancient pipe organ was difficult enough to play these days without the added worry of an upset stomach.

"Don't despair. I'll fix you a plain cheese omelet," Jane said, winking at her sister. She headed toward the kitchen. "I hope that cat hasn't managed to knock down the crystal vase I left on the counter for these flowers. In fact, if I even catch Wendell trying to jump up on anything in my kitchen, I may use him as a pot holder."

Louise smiled as her sister disappeared into the dining room. Jane would never do anything unkind to the cat. She adored the gray tabby as much as everyone else, even if he did like to hide small items occasionally—like Jane's vegetable scrub brush. She was forever having to buy a new one in town.

Louise was halfway up the staircase, heading to her room to check her hair, when she heard the front door open. She put a smile on her face to welcome their guests, but saw that it was Alice, her younger sister. Dressed in her nurse's uniform, Alice closed the door and leaned against it, catching her breath. She had been called in to work an extra shift that morning. "Whew! I wanted to be here before the Havertys arrived."

Louise descended the stairs to greet her sister. "They should be here soon, but it looks as though you have made it with time to spare."

"Good. Then maybe I have time to change," Alice said, gesturing at her nurse's uniform.

"I was just heading up to my room myself," Louise confessed. "I wanted to make sure I looked presentable too."

"You already do." Alice started up the stairs alongside Louise. "You look perfect as always. Your pearls are gleaming, your sweater and skirt are neatly pressed, and not a strand of hair dares to be out of place."

Louise patted her short silver hair, feeling pleased. Then she remembered that pride went before a fall and dropped her hand. Alice did look less tidy than Louise, but she had just gotten off duty at Potterston Hospital. As usual when she returned from a difficult shift, her bobbed, reddish-brown hair was mussed and her uniform was a bit wrinkled.

"Did you have a busy morning?" Louise said, concerned. Alice was never one to complain, but Louise often worried about her sister. She and Jane sometimes debated the idea of coaxing Alice into retiring, especially now that the inn was thriving. But they knew that their sister still had much valuable medical knowledge and compassion to share with her patients.

"No busier than usual," Alice replied.

The sisters reached the landing of the second story. They could hear Jane bustling around the Sunset Room, arranging the rose bouquet, no doubt in a perfect spot. The Havertys had specifically requested that room, with its warm colors and impressionist prints. The Sunrise Room, the Symphony Room and the Garden Room rounded out the guest bedrooms, and all of them were welcoming, cozy and comfy.

Louise and Alice headed up a second flight of stairs to their own rooms on the third floor. Each of the sisters' rooms was cozy, too, and each was decorated in its owner's individual style. Jane, the artist, had decorated hers in bold contemporary colors, Danish furniture and her own artwork. Alice's room was more folksy and homey, with its soft yellow walls and multicolored antique patchwork quilt. Louise's room, with flowered wallpaper and green woodwork, was classic and dignified, just like her personality.

Alice paused at her door. "Remind me to talk to you about the church organ later, Louise. I ran into some of the church board members during my lunch break, and I need to tell you something when we have more time to talk."

"All right," Louise said. She knew that the board had planned for quite a while to discuss the state of the dying old organ. Maybe at last they had decided to put it out of its misery.

Chapter Two

The Havertys were every bit as kind and friendly as the sisters remembered from their last visit. Walter Haverty was tall, robust and white-haired, including a neatly trimmed goatee. His blue eyes sparkled with delight at everything in life, it seemed, but particularly at his wife. Kathleen Haverty was probably a foot and a half shorter than her husband, at just under five feet. Where he was jovial and outgoing, she was quiet and serious. Still, anyone could tell she adored her husband. Her dark hair was flecked with gray, and she wore it in a long braid pinned all around her head.

While the Havertys relaxed in the library, Louise helped Jane in the kitchen by washing tomatoes for the sisters' dinner. As she gently turned the green tomatoes under the running water of the kitchen faucet, she wondered why Jane had picked them so early. She was about to ask her sister when she heard a loud noise behind her.

Whack! Whack! Whack!

Wielding a culinary mallet, Jane pounded some sort of meat on a butcher block countertop. Louise flinched with every stroke of the mallet, wondering if Jane intended to beat whatever it was to a fine pulp. Between Jane and the roofer, there seemed to be no peace at the inn lately.

Jane finally laid aside her instrument of torment and drew a deep breath. "Whew!" She smiled at Louise. "That's hard work."

"What on earth are you making that requires you to treat the meat so violently?" Louise said.

"Chicken fried steak. The meat has to be really tender."

"I don't believe that I've heard of that dish," Louise said, drawing her eyebrows together.

Jane bustled around the kitchen to gather flour and spices. "It's a Texas specialty. Thinking of the special breakfast for Mrs. Haverty put me in mind of a Texas dinner for us."

"Whatever in the world is a fried chicken steak?" Louise asked.

"Chicken fried steak," Jane corrected. "It's not chicken at all. Just round steak that's battered and deep fried. In the South it's generally referred to as country fried steak. It's very tasty. I'm also cooking mashed potatoes, cream gravy, fried green tomatoes and pecan pie for dessert."

Louise carefully dried the tomatoes with a clean dishtowel. At least that explained why Jane wanted unripened tomatoes for dinner. Though she didn't often go to movies or watch them at home, Louise thought she remembered hearing about a popular film named after the famous Southern dish. She couldn't imagine fried tomatoes to be palatable, but she would reserve comment until she tasted Jane's efforts for herself. Her youngest sister seldom cooked a dish that Louise didn't like.

Yet the thought of cream gravy *and* fried meat and tomatoes made her wonder. She hated to think of the cholesterol content of such a meal. Fortunately, none of the sisters had a major problem with weight, and Jane usually did try to keep their meals on the healthy side. Tonight, however, they were apparently splurging.

Jane took the tomatoes from Louise and laid them on a

clean cutting board. "I'll bet that Kathleen Haverty is an artist," she said as she began to slice the tomatoes. "You can tell by her long, slender fingers."

"Maybe she is a pianist," Louise said thoughtfully. She dried her hands on the dishtowel and laid it carefully beside the sink. Jane didn't mind assistance in her kitchen occasionally, but like all masters of craft, she preferred to work alone. "I'll leave you to work your magic, while I make sure the Havertys have everything they need."

"Thanks for the help," Jane said, already turning into a culinary whirling dervish as she gathered pans, whisks and eggs into her prep area.

Louise headed for the library. She paused to glance at the sign on the door, THE DANIEL HOWARD LIBRARY, as she so often did when she entered. She smiled at the memory of her father and how he had warmly welcomed the guests who visited his home.

The Havertys were seated in the library's russet-colored chairs, talking with Alice. She stood behind Daniel Howard's desk, pointing at various framed family photos hanging against the mossy-green, tweed-patterned wallpaper.

Mrs. Haverty smiled when she saw Louise, and Mr. Haverty rose. "Your sister was just explaining the photos to us," he said. "Kathleen and I have an interest in older photos such as these."

"They are not the original photos, of course," Louise said. "Even the sepia-toned one of Father as a boy. We had all the originals enlarged at a professional's shop."

"They look wonderful in that grouping," Mrs. Haverty said. "They're a lovely chronicle of your father's life."

"Kathleen knows what she's talking about. She's a professional photographer," Walter said, putting his arm around his wife. "She often has her work displayed in galleries."

Kathleen Haverty smiled. "I think family photos make a home feel so cozy. I'd rather see them in frames than hidden away in photo albums. I'm sure your father must have been very proud of his daughters."

Louise saw Alice swallow. Their father's death had been especially hard for her middle sister because she had lived with him in his final years. "We like to think that his love lives on in our home and in the hospitality of this inn, Mrs. Haverty," Louise said.

"It does. And please call me Kathleen. I feel as if I know you three sisters. We were only here for one night the last time we stayed, and we didn't get much of a chance to chat, but Alice has been telling us not only about your father's life, but about your lives as well."

Mr. Haverty stepped forward, his eyes twinkling beneath bushy, white eyebrows. His goatee bobbed when he talked. "I hear you're quite the musician," he said.

"I teach piano here at the inn. Before I moved back to Acorn Hill, I taught in Philadelphia. Before that . . . well, *long* before that . . . I received a music education degree from the conservatory in Philadelphia."

"Really?" Mr. Haverty stroked his goatee. "I recall hearing you play the organ at Grace Chapel the last time we visited. Lovely music. Lovely performance."

"Thank you, Mr. Haverty."

"Walter," he corrected, smiling at both sisters. "You're quite talented, Louise."

"Thank you again . . . Walter," Louise said. "I enjoy playing for the chapel, but I'm afraid our organ has seen better days."

"What's the problem? I've toyed around with a musical instrument or two in my life."

"Well . . ." Louise wavered, then decided that since she was speaking to a kindred musical spirit, he would surely understand her dissatisfaction with, if not the technicalities of, the old organ's problems. "It has a limited number of stops and lacks solo stops as well. The air support comes from a single blower in the basement, below the pipes. Over the years there has been a leakage in the delivery of the air supply, which gives the music a wavering sound. The old leathers have also become dry and brittle, which makes the organ unreliable. And that's just for starters," she said, warming to the discussion.

Suddenly she realized that she was dominating the conversation. "But for an old organ, it really could be worse," she finished in a rush, hoping that it didn't sound as though she was critical of Grace Chapel or its care for its organ. There was only so much church money to go around for property maintenance, and she owed loyalty to the other church members.

An awkward pause ensued. "Perhaps the organ can be repaired," Kathleen said kindly, trying to help.

"I'm sure you're right," Alice said. "Louise played that organ when she was in high school and knows it better than anyone else in Acorn Hill."

"Sounds to me like the old beast needs to be hauled off to the dump," Walter said cheerfully.

Louise secretly feared that might be true, but it certainly wouldn't do for her to voice her opinion out loud. She had already said too much. She loved Grace Chapel and its members, and she would never want to be responsible for any criticism directed at either. "I must say they don't make pipe organs like they used to," she said, laughing lightly. "But please, Kathleen . . . Walter. Tell us about your professions."

"Walt's already mentioned that I'm a photographer," Kathleen said. "But he was being modest when he said he's 'toyed' around with a musical instrument or two. He's a professional musician."

"How wonderful," Alice said. "What do you play, Walter?"

"I play the guitar a bit, and I've been known to sing, though some folks compare it to a hen scratching in its feed. Mostly I play the fiddle."

"Walt's part of a country-western band that's popular in the Southwest, though you may not have heard of them here in Pennsylvania," Kathleen said proudly.

"We play a lot of good, old-fashioned country-western music. Swing music too. Not the crossover, pop-country music that a lot of young folks like these days," Walter said.

"I like some of that music," Kathleen said playfully. "You and your band should give it a try sometime. You might draw a younger audience."

Walter leaned toward Alice and Louise. "We like our audience just fine," he said in a stage whisper.

Louise, who didn't care for country music, whether crossover, pop or swing, smiled politely. Fortunately, Alice was more interested in the genre. "I like some of Bob Wills's music. Do you play anything like his?"

"He's one of our favorites," he said. "We also have a great gal who's one of our lead singers. She does a pretty fair imitation of Patsy Cline and Loretta Lynn."

"I'd love to hear you sometime," Alice said. "Do you ever play in our area?"

Walter shook his head. "Haven't so far, but we've been looking into the possibility. The band likes the idea of traveling more, so you never know."

"You could send them a CD," Kathleen said. "They cut one several years ago."

"Why, that's a right smart idea," Walter said. "It's a cryin' shame I don't have one with me, but I've got a whole mess of them back in Texas, where we live."

"What brings you to this area?" Louise asked.

"We're on our way to visit our son and daughter-in-law," Kathleen said. "They live in Rhode Island."

"We're staying with them for a few days. Then we hope to stay with you ladies again on our return trip home," Walter said.

"Do you normally drive all the way from Texas to Rhode Island?" Alice asked.

Walter nodded. "Can't stand airplanes. All that security and fuss, not to mention the air pressure changes and claustrophobia."

"Walter and I like to see the countryside of America up close and personal," Kathleen said.

Walter took her hand. "This fall we're going to head out west for a spell. Maybe listen in on some of the music out Las Vegas and California way."

"If you plan to go as far as San Francisco, you might want to check with our sister Jane," Louise said. "She lived there for a number of years."

Walter nodded. "Thanks for the tip. We'll have to do that."

After Jane had finished her prep work for dinner, it was still only mid-afternoon. The Havertys were heading into Potterston for the evening, so the sisters were free to go their own ways. Jane considered puttering in the garden for a while. She had had trouble with moles in the past and was ever on guard against the pesky creatures. Besides that, there was always weeding and pruning, not to mention picking the fruits of her labors in the vegetable garden or the lovely blooms in her flower garden.

Instead, however, she remembered that she wanted to check on Craig Tracy. She hadn't seen Acorn Hill's only florist in weeks, and she thought it odd that she hadn't at least bumped into him at the Coffee Shop. She headed out of the inn and down the road to town, where she hoped to find Craig in his florist shop.

Jane enjoyed learning about flowers, plants, landscaping and floral arranging from him. When she had a spare moment, which wasn't often, she liked to check on the progress of his efforts. Craig was a relative newcomer to

Acorn Hill. He had arrived in town to set up a florist shop, Wild Things, which had proved to be quite successful. He often provided flowers for the sisters at Grace Chapel Inn, and more than once guests had commented on the loveliness of his floral displays. He was always interested in keeping up with the latest innovations with flowers and other plants. Jane secretly wished she had more time to study on her own, but until then, Craig was a good mentor.

Jane's life had been blessed with knowledgeable teachers, and Craig was the latest. He was probably five to ten years younger than Jane, but she felt that age was no indicator of a person's abilities to mentor. Jane had never seen a drooping flower he couldn't coax back to life nor a seedling that he couldn't nurture into growth. The man didn't merely have a green thumb; he had a green hand.

When she finally reached Wild Things, Jane found that instead of working on plants, Craig was dusting the counter. "Jane, I'm so glad to see you," he said, setting down his cloth. "I need a good reason to stop cleaning."

"Ah, the mundane work of running your own business," Jane said, laughing. "If you can tear yourself away, I stopped to see what was new at Wild Things."

Craig stuffed the cloth under the counter. "Now you're talking. I've got something to show you, but I haven't had much chance lately."

He turned on the answering machine, flipped the shop sign to CLOSED and shepherded her out the door. Bewildered, she watched as he locked up. It wasn't like Craig to close in the middle of the day. "Are we going somewhere?" she asked.

Craig smiled, nodded and pocketed the shop key. "Do you have some time?"

"Sure."

"We'll have to take my van."

"Then it can't be a trip to the Coffee Shop," Jane said,

filling with excitement. She loved adventure and surprises, and she had a feeling that wherever Craig was taking her involved both.

Craig unlocked the door to the delivery van that he used for the florist shop. The van had WILD THINGS written on the side alongside a bold graphic of vibrant flowers. He helped her into the van, then started the engine and headed out of town.

"Are you going to give me a hint?" Jane asked.

Craig smiled, lightly gripping the steering wheel as he turned the van down a country road. "We're almost there, so I guess I can tell you now. I've decided to expand my business."

"Really?" Jane's heart beat a little faster. She liked to see not only the creative, but also the entrepreneurial side of her friends.

Craig nodded. "I've decided to expand my business and my personal interest in horticulture by starting my own nursery. Instead of merely selling flowers, floral arrangements and plants that I've purchased from wholesalers, I'm going to invest time and money in growing my own to sell."

Jane clapped her hands, as though she were eight years old again. "That's wonderful, Craig!"

"I've bought some land just out of town, and I've been working for the past few weeks on building a nursery. Keep in mind it's nothing fancy, and it's just enough to last through this year until I can build a better one next spring. But it's a start. Here we are. Welcome to the Wild Things Nursery."

Jane eagerly got out of the van. In the middle of a bare field stood what she believed was referred to as a shade house: wooden columns with a skeleton of a roof, covered by a screen. Individually potted plants grew in precise rows on the ground cloth under the shade.

Seeing all the lined-up, living greenery excited her like Christmas morning. "Can you show me what you're growing?" she asked.

"I was hoping you'd ask," Craig said. He led the way to the shaded area and walked down the first row.

Jane walked behind him a short distance, then knelt to examine some of the plants. "I don't recognize any of these. What are they?"

Craig knelt beside her. "I plan to grow all kinds of flowers and plants, but I decided to specialize in native Pennsylvania plants first. That one's a Jack-in-the-pulpit, there's a wild columbine, and down the row there is a summer phlox."

Jane pointed a few rows over. "At least I recognize that over there. It's a sunflower."

"Right. Know what this is?" Craig gestured to a plant by Jane's knee.

She shook her head.

"Goat's-beard."

"Interesting name." Jane smiled. "Everything looks healthy, Craig. How did you get started with these?"

"I grew them from seeds. Eventually, I hope to propagate them myself."

Jane surveyed the rows. He must easily have had a hundred pots, which amazed her. "All these are native Pennsylvania plants?"

He nodded. "Some of them are suited for wet soil, some for dry. Some attract butterflies, some birds. Some are good for sunny areas, some for shade."

"In short, something for everybody." Jane rose, brushing her hands against her thighs. "You never said a word about this, Craig. This is a pretty big undertaking. What made you decide to start?"

He didn't say anything, and she felt a rush of embarrassment. Maybe business at Wild Things was not as good as she had thought, and he was hoping to supplement the florist shop's revenue. "I'm sorry if I asked a personal question," she added hastily.

"Not at all," Craig said. "I was just wondering if you thought I was foolish for following a dream. I'm not a pup anymore, Jane. It's been over twenty years since I got a bachelor's degree in plant and soil science and my advanced degrees in horticulture. Since then I've been a botany teacher, a greenhouse manager and a florist. I love working with flowers, but lately I've dreamed about going back to my first love."

"Which is?"

Craig gestured at the plants. "This. My family ran a nursery and sold plants and seeds through mail order while I was growing up. I miss that life, especially working with seeds and with plants other than those that get jammed in a fancy vase or have ribbons around them. I thought I might dabble in the nursery business again, starting with my latest interest in working with native plants."

"I think it's a wonderful idea," Jane said. "I wish we had more native plants in the garden at Grace Chapel Inn. But Craig, how have you been able to work out here and at Wild Things? This shade building alone must have taken a lot of time."

"It hasn't been easy. Actually, I'm thinking about hiring some summer help. I have more plants and seedlings at Wild Things that I need to move out here. I also want to build a greenhouse before the winter. Do you have any suggestions for someone I could hire?"

Jane shook her head. "Maybe there's a college student home for the summer. Or a high school student."

Craig stroked his chin. "Somebody who's interested in botany or horticulture would be ideal."

Jane looked at the building with all its lumber and screening, then glanced at the long rows of plants. "With all the building and plant lugging the person would have to do, I'd say you're better off looking for a serious weight lifter."

Craig grinned. "Who needs a gym rat? Lifting and toting is how we florists and nurserymen stay in shape. Just find me a ninety-pound weakling with the desire to learn, and the muscle will take care of itself."

Louise finished a late Saturday afternoon piano lesson. Once she had seen her young student safely into her mother's waiting car, she headed to the kitchen. Perusing the inside of Jane's top-of-the-line refrigerator, she pushed aside pickle, olive and condiment jars in search of something cool to drink.

Ah! Her secret treat, and it had been the previous summer since she last indulged. Glancing around to make sure neither Jane nor Alice was watching, she withdrew the carton of buttermilk. Jane purchased it only for coating chicken for frying or for making her special salad dressing. She and Alice had never understood why Louise liked to drink the rich milk, and they would give her a mountain of grief if they knew she was drinking it now.

Louise hurriedly retrieved a drinking glass from the cupboard, filled it with buttermilk, and returned the carton to the refrigerator. Feeling confident that she wouldn't be discovered, she took the luxury of sprinkling salt and pepper into the glass, then stirring with a teaspoon.

Cautiously making her way through the house, she kept an eye out for Jane and Alice as she headed for the sunroom. Not encountering anyone, she sank into a wicker chair, feeling at peace in the sun's warmth in the plant-filled room.

Louise knew it was ridiculous to worry about what her sisters thought of her buttermilk habit, but she had been sensitive about it since she was a teenager. Long ago, they had visited distant family relatives in western Pennsylvania during a summer trip. The matriarch of the family had a penchant for buttermilk, and she insisted that the Howard sisters try it. Alice and Jane had nearly choked, but Louise discovered that she liked its buttery taste.

For some reason that endeared her to the matriarch, who doted on Louise for the rest of the visit. Thereafter, Louise associated the taste of buttermilk with summertime, trying new things and being a young girl. Through the years, however, Jane and Alice had teased her, albeit gently, about having old women's tastes, and ever since Louise reacted sensitively to the accusation.

She sipped from the glass slowly, smiling as she appreciated its contents. Eliot had been a buttermilk drinker, too, and it was he who had introduced her to the refined addition of salt and pepper. Thinking of him made her smile as she leaned back in the chair and let sunshine and memories wash over her.

"Having a secret beverage?"

Louise straightened, trying to hide her half-empty glass as a child might hide a forbidden cookie. "I, uh . . ."

"It's all right," Alice said, taking a chair beside Louise. "That's the only teasing you'll get out of me today or from now on. Have you ever heard that poem about the woman who says that when she is old, she will wear a purple dress and a red hat?"

Louise nodded. "Are you saying that I've earned the right to drink my buttermilk in peace?"

Alice smiled. "I believe so, Louise. After all, I'm only a little younger than you, so I'm more willing to share the niceties of our age than Jane is."

"She does have the audacity to be more than a decade younger," Louise said dryly, sipping gratefully from her glass again. "Some day she will understand."

"I don't know about that," Alice said, laughing gently. "I think our Jane will always be rather young and wild at heart."

Louise laughed with her, for they both loved Jane dearly. Though her personality was sometimes quite different from their own, they wouldn't trade her ways for anyone else's. She was not only multitalented and creative, but also full of concern for others. Moreover, she possessed a zest for living that inspired them and often made them feel much younger than their years.

"While I have you here," Alice said, "I wanted to let you know that the chapel board is planning to meet tomorrow night."

That was not unusual. The board met on a regular basis to keep the chapel humming and running. It was unusual, however, that the board would call a meeting on only one day's notice, as well as scheduling the meeting for a Sunday night. "I suspect that there's something special on the agenda," Louise said.

Alice picked at a thread in her cotton pants. "They want to discuss the organ, Louise. They're inviting you to meet with them so that its future can be decided."

Louise didn't care for the sound of that. She knew that Florence Simpson, one of the board members, had frequently made snide comments about the organ to other chapel members. She had never confronted Louise directly, but Louise sensed that Florence wanted her to get the message all the same.

"I'll be glad to meet with them," Louise said grimly.

"Wonderful," Alice said. "Meanwhile, I'll leave you to your buttermilk. I'm going to go see Carlene. I thought she might be interested in interviewing Walter Haverty or Kathleen. They're both accomplished people, and the *Nutshell* readers might be interested in learning about their professions."

"I don't know how interested readers will be in a country-western musician," Louise said, "but I suppose there are some fans of the genre in Acorn Hill."

"I certainly hope so," Alice said, smiling at Louise. She rose to head for the walk into town. "Because I'm one of them."

Chapter ☗ Three

A lice enjoyed the walk down the hill to town, and she waved at several town members as they shopped or worked in their stores. She was surprised to see the "Closed" sign hanging in the door of Wild Things but decided that Craig Tracy must be on a delivery.

Nia Komonos, the town librarian, was helping a young patron carry a huge stack of books out the library door. Alice smiled fondly, remembering how many times as a young girl she, too, had checked out too many books to carry. She still loved reading.

"Hi, Alice," Nia called, glancing up as she headed back inside the library. "Are you coming to get some books?"

Alice shook her head. "Another time, Nia. I have to see Carlene."

"See you later then." Nia waved good-bye, and the tall young woman in her customary tailored suit disappeared back inside.

Across the street from the library was the Acorn Hill *Acorn Nutshell*, the weekly newspaper that Carlene Moss put out by herself for the citizens of the town. Besides selling the advertising, she did all the interviewing, writing and layout. After that she e-mailed the content to a printing business in Potterston to print and deliver back to her for distribution in

Acorn Hill. The *Nutshell* had been published without interruption for over ninety years. Carlene's father had started there as a copy boy and had risen to become chief typesetter. Carlene proudly carried on the family tradition when her father retired after sixty years of service.

Alice glanced briefly at the old-style black letters with gilt edging that spelled out THE ACORN NUTSHELL on the frosted glass door, then entered the aging brown brick building. As always, she paused to wonder why Carlene didn't get the county historical preservation society to come out and look at the building. Chances were that they would want to designate it as a historical landmark. This was the *Nutshell*'s original building.

"Hi, Alice," Carlene said, looking up from her desk by the door. Her heart-shaped face lit up in a smile, showing two dimples. She waved a brief greeting, then went back to whatever she was typing into her desktop computer. "Almost finished . . . and . . . there!" she said triumphantly, hitting the save button, then rising to greet her friend. She tossed back a shoulder-length strand of gray-flecked brown hair that fell in her face. "What brings you here?"

"Hi, Carlene," Alice said. She shut the door behind her and stepped over to the desk. "I had an idea for an article that I thought you might be interested in."

"Lay it on me," Carlene said. "I'm always looking for news."

"It's about a couple of our guests," Alice said, then proceeded to tell Carlene about the Havertys. "I thought you might like to interview them for an article about interesting people who have passed through Acorn Hill."

"They do sound like people the town would be pleased to read about. I could run a photo alongside the article too. Maybe Walter Haverty has a publicity photo with him of his band. Or maybe Kathleen Haverty has a sample of her photography work." Carlene scribbled notes on a white legal pad.

"Thanks for the tip, Alice. Hang on for a second while I make a few notes to myself. I just had some great ideas for questions, and I want to write them down while they're fresh."

While Carlene continued to scribble, Alice glanced around the room. On the large L-shaped desk sat pages of printed copy, dictionaries, stylebooks and almanacs. Next to a terracotta pot filled with ivy sat a bowl with several fresh-water fish.

Toward the back of the room was an ancient printing press and more current, but still outdated, typesetting equipment. Carlene dusted them off occasionally for school field trips, particularly Vera Humbert's yearly visit with her fifth-grade class.

The building held many fond memories for Alice, who herself had attended a field trip several times as a young girl when Carlene's father had been in charge. Change didn't come quickly to Acorn Hill, but life, as always, moved on.

She loved having her sisters living at home again. She wouldn't trade that for anything, but sometimes she missed her father and grew lonesome for him. Sometimes, if she was honest with herself, she missed the easy life of being a girl again too. If she squinted her eyes just right, even now, the walls of the shop looked slightly newer, and she could pretend that she was that girl on a field trip.

Carlene set down her pencil. "Thanks for waiting, Alice." She looked at her friend, who didn't respond. "Earth to Alice. Hello?"

Alice shook her head, trying to clear away the cobwebs of memory. "Sorry, Carlene. I was woolgathering about old times, I suppose." She paused. "I know you keep busy with the *Nutshell* and don't have much time, but would you mind if I contacted Irene Watts?"

Carlene frowned, going back to her note taking as she thought of a new question for the Havertys. "Remind me who Irene Watts is?"

"She's with the county historical preservation society. If you remember, she was the one who helped us when we first remodeled Grace Chapel Inn. I thought she might like to take a look at the *Nutshell*'s building here. I wouldn't be surprised if she would want to look into having it designated a historic landmark. It's one of Acorn Hill's older buildings, and it's still in good shape. It would be nice for you and the town."

Carlene shrugged. "That would be great, Alice, but I don't know that it would ever happen. Or that it would help the newspaper. It might just be a lot of work for nothing."

Alice thought for a moment. "If the *Nutshell* building got a historic designation, it would make for an interesting article," she said, appealing to the reporter in her friend.

Carlene looked up from the pad. "It would at that, wouldn't it? It might even get us some publicity in Potterston and elsewhere." She set down her pencil. "You might be on to something, Alice."

Alice grinned. "Great. I'll contact her as soon as I can."

"And if it's all right, I'll stop by after church tomorrow and see if I can talk to the Havertys," Carlene said. "If they don't have time to talk to me then, we can always talk by phone after they're finished with their vacation, or we can conduct an interview by e-mail."

"It certainly must be easier to be a reporter in this day and age when we have so many different methods of communication," Alice commented.

"Until they come up with something better, I still have to type the interview." Carlene held her fingers in the air and wiggled them. "Good thing God gave me ten of these."

When Alice got back to Grace Chapel Inn, she looked up the number in the inn's address book and found the county historical preservation society. She decided to call right away, even though it was Saturday, and leave a message. To her surprise, someone answered the phone.

"Irene Watts, please," she said, thinking that the person sounded familiar.

"Speaking," a chipper voice said in reply.

"Irene, this is Alice Howard from Acorn Hill. You may remember my sisters and me or our—"

"Why, yes. The Howard sisters with the Grace Chapel Inn. Of course I remember. What a lovely old house you have. I was delighted to visit it. What can I help you with?"

"Actually, I'm calling about a friend," Alice said. "Her name is Carlene Moss, and she's the publisher of the Acorn Hill *Acorn Nutshell*. The paper's been in operation for over ninety years and is still in its original building, which was built in the early twentieth century. I was wondering if you'd be interested in taking a look at it to see if it would qualify for a historic designation."

"I'd love to, Alice. That building does have a lot of character and charm, not to mention history." Alice heard her flip through paper on her desk. "I'm glad you caught me at work today. My calendar is free on Monday . . . can I meet you then?" Irene asked.

"I'm working at the Potterston Hospital on Monday, but Carlene should be available to show you around. You may want to call first to make sure she's not out on an assignment, though," Alice said, then gave the *Nutshell*'s phone number.

Irene thanked her and promised to keep in touch. Alice hung up the phone, feeling as though she had done two good deeds for the day by giving Carlene the tip about the Havertys and by passing along the information about the *Nutshell* to the preservation society.

The next day, the Havertys attended the service at Grace Chapel, looking forward to hearing Louise play the organ. She was mortified, however, as the aging instrument gasped and wheezed during almost the entire service, and she cut short the music she normally played at the end of the service to spare the members' musical sensibilities.

Afterward, the Havertys met her in the parlor at Grace Chapel Inn to say good-bye before they continued their journey to visit their son.

"You're very gifted," Walter said. "I'm glad you're not only sharing your music but your knowledge, by teaching those youngsters how to play the piano."

"Do you give organ lessons too?" Kathleen asked.

Louise shook her head. "No one has expressed an interest in taking lessons. There are few people in Acorn Hill who even own an organ. It seems as though it has lost its popularity for home entertainment."

"Well, churches will always be in need of a good organist, that's for certain," Walter said, "and Grace Chapel is right fortunate to have you working their keyboard."

"It's a pleasure to serve," Louise said, "though to be honest, I'm not sure about the future of the organ. I'm meeting with the church board tonight." Louise paused, not wanting to sound as though she were trying to blame the discordant service music on the instrument, even though it was the truth. "Being a musician yourself, Walter, I'm sure you recognized some of the music today as being rather, er . . ."

"Noisy?" Kathleen offered gently.

"Downright awful?" Walter suggested, laughing. "Don't worry, Miz Louise. We knew it wasn't you. We agreed that instrument does need some improvements, and we hope you and the board can reach a consensus on the best thing to do."

"I'm sure we will," Louise said. "Meanwhile, thank you for your kind words. I hope you'll have time to attend Grace Chapel next Sunday, on your return trip through Acorn Hill."

Walter shook his head. "I wish we could, but we'll only be here Friday night. We have to leave Saturday morning to get back to Texas in time for my band's gig."

"I understand," Louise said. "My sisters and I will at least look forward to your company next Friday then."

"As will we," Kathleen said. "And now I must find Jane to tell her how much we enjoyed the *huevos rancheros*."

Carlene arrived just as the Havertys were upstairs packing their bags. "I'm so glad I caught them," she said. "Do you mind if I wait in the library so that I can talk to them alone?"

"Not at all," Alice said, noticing that Carlene carried the same legal pad she had taken notes on when Alice first gave her the information about the Havertys. She ushered Carlene into the library to wait for them.

When the Havertys descended the stairs, luggage in hand, they saw Alice. "Thank you so much for welcoming us at your lovely inn again," Kathleen said. "We look forward to rejoining you soon."

"I know you're in a hurry," Alice said, "but a friend of mine would like to speak with you for just a moment. I promise she won't take but a minute of your time."

Curious, the Havertys followed her into the library. "Kathleen and Walter, this is Carlene Moss. She runs Acorn Hill's newspaper, the *Acorn Nutshell*. Carlene, meet Kathleen and Walter Haverty."

"How do you do?" Carlene said, smiling as she extended a hand.

Walter frowned, but he shook her hand. Kathleen's brow furrowed, and she bit her lip.

Alice felt a small wave of apprehension and quickly excused herself. She retreated to the small reception area near the bottom of the stairs, where she found Louise finishing up the paperwork for the Havertys.

"Why, whatever is wrong, Alice?" Louise asked. "You look perplexed."

Alice quickly explained the situation in a tense whisper, then concluded with, "Why do you think they would react that way to Carlene?"

Before Louise could respond, the library door opened.

The Havertys exited first, quickly retrieving their luggage from where they had left it by the stairs.

Carlene was close at their heels. "Are you sure I can't change your minds? Acorn Hill may not be a large town, but I think folks would be interested in learning about your photography, Mrs. Haverty. And about you and your band, Mr. Haverty."

Kathleen smiled, but to Alice her smile looked forced. "I'm afraid not, Ms. Moss. Just the same, we wish you all the best with your newspaper."

Walter placed a Stetson on his head, then immediately tipped it in Louise and Alice's direction. "Ladies, thank you kindly for your hospitality."

"Yes, of course," Alice murmured, dazed. She wanted to apologize to the Havertys if she had upset them, but the front door banged shut behind them faster than she could form the words on her lips. Louise followed after them, along with Jane, but Alice stayed behind to talk with Carlene.

"Do you think I offended them in some way?" Alice asked.

"I doubt it," the newspaperwoman answered. "You were just trying to help. Most people are flattered when you say you want to interview them, but these folks clammed up like I'd asked them each to donate a kidney. Well, some folks just don't like publicity, even if it's free."

"That's strange, isn't it?" Alice said. "You would think that Walter Haverty would like to give his band a little recognition."

Carlene shrugged. "To each his own."

Louise and Jane re-entered the house after seeing the Havertys out to their car. They were chatting with one another, brows furrowed. Seldom one to internalize her concerns, Jane spoke her mind directly. "The Havertys certainly looked strange when they left. Do either of you know what was wrong with them?"

Alice sighed. "I told Carlene she might want to interview them for the *Nutshell*, and apparently they took offense."

"It sure isn't Alice's fault that they're too sensitive," Carlene said, sticking up for her friend. "She was only trying to help me."

Louise's expression softened. "Indeed she was. It's difficult to believe that's why the Havertys were in such a rush to leave, however."

"Was I out of line for asking?" Alice said. "I always try to respect the privacy of our guests, but perhaps I stuck my nose too far into their business."

"My stars, Alice," Carlene said. "You make it sound as though you and I were conducting a muckraking operation. You gave me a good tip, they weren't interested in cooperating, and that's that. I appreciate your effort on behalf of the *Nutshell*, though."

She sighed, tucking the legal pad under her arm. "I'd better get back to the office."

"On a Sunday?" Louise asked.

Carlene nodded. "I wish it weren't so, but this job requires work to be done when I least welcome it, even on the Sabbath."

"I know you feel you have to work," Louise said, "but I wish you didn't have to. The Bible says the Lord made the Sabbath for man. You would be surprised how a day of rest can refresh."

"And you'd be surprised how difficult it is to put out a newspaper pretty much by yourself," Carlene said good-naturedly. "Ladies, if you'll excuse me, I'll get out of your hair." She headed for the front door, giving Alice an affectionate tap. "Chin up."

Alice smiled. Carlene was right. Whatever reason the Havertys had for guarding their privacy was not something to worry over. No doubt when they returned, the whole situation would have been forgotten.

Chapter Four

That evening Louise walked the short distance to Grace Chapel alone for the board meeting. As a board member, Alice would also be present, and she seemed to understand when Louise mentioned that she wanted to walk alone and arrive early for the meeting. Louise needed a few moments to collect her thoughts before she had to meet with the board. She sensed that she should have some sort of speech prepared when called upon to account for the organ's current state.

That it was in want of repairs wasn't because of lack of attention, but lack of funds. Several years before she had mentioned to the board that the organ was showing signs of wear. It was, after all, at least seventy years old. It had been well established when she played it for Sunday services when she was in high school.

Louise had learned to play from the aging organist, Hezekiah Watkins, a kindly old gentleman who, to her then-girlish sensibilities, had seemingly been around as long as Grace Chapel itself. Perhaps he had been, for he seemed to know everyone in and everything about Acorn Hill. She wished now that she had talked with Hez Watkins more about the history of Grace Chapel and, in particular, the organ. Since she had returned to Acorn Hill and taken over the organ-playing duties again, she regretted that when he had died, he had carried off much knowledge with him that could never be regained.

At the chapel, she automatically turned on the lights and drifted to the back, where the organ was located. She sat down on the well-worn seat and caressed the toneless keys. There had been several organists between the time she had played while in high school and her return to Acorn Hill. Who else had once had the privilege of coaxing music from the aging instrument, even back before Hez Watkins?

"I thought I heard someone in here," a voice said.

Louise looked up to see Rev. Kenneth Thompson walking down the aisle toward her. He had taken over the permanent role of pastor after Daniel Howard's death, and he had endeared himself to the congregation. As usual, he was dressed conservatively, tonight in a button-down dress shirt and khaki pants. The signet ring that he had inherited from his grandfather glistened as he braced his hands on the organ.

"May I let you in on a little secret?" he asked Louise.

"Why, I suppose," she said, her curiosity piqued.

"Many members have told me how blessed we are to have you as our organist," he said.

"That's very kind of you to share with me," Louise said, feeling warmed by the compliment. "Thank you."

Rev. Thompson smiled. "I feel the same way, Louise. You bring not only talent but also love when you play on Sundays for us. I appreciate your sharing your gift with the members of Grace Chapel. Thank you."

Louise didn't know how to respond to such praise. "I . . . you're welcome," she said.

"There you two are," Florence Simpson said, strutting down the aisle toward them. "The board is assembled downstairs, and we only need you two to begin." Although Rev. Thompson was not a member of the board, he often attended board meetings as an adviser. He was especially interested in the meeting tonight since it concerned the organ, a longtime fixture in the church.

Louise touched the organ, as though bidding good-bye to a friend, then followed Rev. Thompson back up the aisle. As they descended to the lower level of the chapel, he paused to offer his arm, ostensibly to help her negotiate the stairs.

"Don't worry," he whispered, so that Florence couldn't hear. "You have many champions on the board, and we are all eager to hear your opinion."

Instead of encouraging her, as she was sure that his words were intended to do, she felt dread that perhaps she had more reason to fear the meeting than she had suspected.

Seated in a circle in the Assembly Room was the board. Some of the members looked as ill at ease as Louise felt. Associate Pastor Henry Ley, Florence Simpson and seamstress Sylvia Songer looked decidedly uncomfortable. Hardware store owner Fred Humbert, Coffee Shop owner June Carter, and the elderly Cyril Overstreet were expressionless. That left Mayor Lloyd Tynan, Alice and the Howard sisters' aunt, Ethel Buckley, who all smiled their encouragement at Louise. Patsy Ley, Pastor Ley's wife, had her hand poised above her pad to take the minutes, a task for which she volunteered as a service to the board.

Lloyd pulled up a chair for her next to Alice. Louise had no sooner sat down than Florence Simpson leaned forward. "Let's get right to the point, shall we? Something has to be done about that old organ, and we all know it."

"I realize it is in poor condition," she said calmly. "What do you board members propose?"

"I say we get rid of the old thing," Florence said. "It sounds like a dying emphysema patient Sunday after Sunday, and I just can't stand it anymore. All that squawking and bellowing. Why, I never know if the right keys are being played or not. For all I can tell, Grace Chapel could have brought in a trained chimpanzee."

Louise didn't embarrass easily, but she was certain that her face burned. Alice covered her hand and said quietly, but calmly, "Well, Louise's playing is lovely. We have no question about that."

"We would like to know, Louise, what you think we should do about that old organ," Sylvia said. "Forgive me, but I think we should look into buying a new one."

"I like to think the organ has historical significance to Grace Chapel," Louise said. "And perhaps even to Acorn Hill. It would be a shame to get rid of it without considering that."

"Or the c-cost of what a new organ w-would be," added Pastor Ley, who often stuttered when speaking in public.

"Is there anyone who might know the history of the organ?" Fred asked.

"It's been here as long as I can remember," Aunt Ethel said, "and I'm with Louise. That organ's a part of Grace Chapel. It should stay." She glared at Florence.

"*Hmmph*," Florence said. "It's wretched sounding."

"It *has* sounded better," Sylvia said mildly, with an apologetic glance at Louise. "I brought some friends to service a couple of weeks ago, and it didn't sound very good. They all asked me what was wrong with it."

Louise sighed. "It's old. It needs repairs."

"It needs to be hauled to the junk yard," Florence said.

"It *would* be nice to have something newer and more modern sounding," Sylvia said.

"It's an *organ*, not an electric guitar," Aunt Ethel said.

"Now now," Fred said, raising his hands to restore calm. It was part of Fred's job as chairman of the church board to keep the meetings orderly. "No one's arguing that it's seen better days. But perhaps it can be fixed for a reasonable cost. Louise, do you know anyone who could evaluate it for us?"

"One of the inn guests once gave me a business card for a friend who repairs old organs. He lives in Maryland," she said.

"Do you think he would come to Acorn Hill without his appraisal costing us an arm and leg?" Fred asked.

"I can contact him to find out," Louise said. "If I call him tomorrow, do I have the board's authority to allow him to appraise the organ for us?"

The members glanced at each other, then nodded. Louise felt a wave of relief. Round one, if not an outright win, was at least a draw.

Walking home together, Alice slipped her arm around her sister. "Cheer up," she said. "Nobody's taken a hatchet to it yet."

"No, but some of them would like to," Louise said with a trace of bitterness. "Florence was certainly getting out her whetstone."

Alice chuckled. "Aunt Ethel and I will support whatever you think is best. We know that you won't spend the church's funds carelessly. Others will be behind you too."

Louise sighed. "One way or another, I hope the appraiser makes the decision easy for the board."

Back at the inn, she located the business card that Ray Roswell had given her. Ray was a music minister, and when he and his family had visited Grace Chapel Inn, he gave Louise the business card of Myron Apodaca, a pipe organ repair specialist.

On Monday morning Louise called the phone number on the business card, and Mr. Apodaca agreed to drive up the next day to look at Grace Chapel's organ. When Louise hung up the receiver, she didn't know whether to feel anxious or relieved.

Early that afternoon Jane decided to look up Craig Tracy at the florist shop. Since their visit to his nursery two days before, she had been thinking about his new business.

"Things are kind of slow right now," Craig said. "Would you like to ride out to the nursery? I put in some more plants, and I need to carry out a load of herbs today, as a matter of fact."

"Herbs?" Jane asked, as they got into the delivery van. "I thought you were just going to work with native plants."

"I'd like to do herbs too," he said. "I'll probably sell the native plants to wholesalers from the nursery location, but the herbs I can sell in my shop year round. I'm already producing them now, but I'll be able to grow more with the extra space at the nursery. Not to mention when I finally get the greenhouse built."

"You know I'm always good to buy herbs for cooking," Jane said. "And so would all your other regular customers, especially the chefs."

When they got to the nursery location, Jane could see that he had indeed set out at least another twenty pots within the shade building.

"I found someone to help me this summer at the nursery," Craig said.

"Already? It was just two days ago that we were talking about your hiring someone."

Craig shrugged. "I asked around, and just like you suggested, I found a football player from Franklin High who was looking for a summer job. It also helps that he wants to study botany or horticulture when he graduates from high school."

"So he'll not only be toting plants for you but learning about the trade at the same time," Jane said. "Perfect. Is he anyone I know?"

Craig shook his head. "I doubt it. He doesn't come to Acorn Hill very often. His name is Trevor Walker. He was supposed to be here today." Craig shaded his eyes against the sun and studied the land. "There he is," he said, pointing to a vehicle in the distance.

A dirty white pickup truck lumbered down the dirt road,

rock music blaring out the window. As it pulled closer, Jane recognized the tune as a popular Christian rock band. She saw that the bed of the truck was filled with plants. The truck braked to a stop, the music cut off, and a handsome young man with a dark tan and a wide smile emerged from the driver's side.

"Hi ya, Mr. T," he called. "I must have just missed you in town. I made a swing by the store and picked up these plants."

"Thanks," Craig said. "Trevor, this is Ms. Jane Howard. She's one of the Howard sisters I was telling you about. The sisters who run Grace Chapel Inn."

"Hi there," Trevor said, extending a hand.

Jane stuck hers out in response, and her hand was engulfed in his. She had to lean back to look at his face because he was so tall.

"Let me guess," she said. "You must be a defensive tackle for Franklin High."

He laughed, a nice easy sound. "How did you know? Say, I've heard a lot about you and your sisters. I'm glad to finally meet you. A couple of my friends were either in your sister's ANGELs group when they were younger, or they've been involved with the youth group at Grace Chapel."

"And I hear that Franklin is going to have a great football team this year," Jane said. "Now I know why."

Trevor laughed. "I enjoy football, but I don't want to make a career out of it like I do working with plants. I'm looking forward to learning from Mr. Tracy."

"It's a win-win situation," Craig said.

"I'd like a little education myself," Jane said. "Would you gentlemen care to show me some of the plants you have in stock, so that I can start learning about native Pennsylvania flora?"

"I thought you'd never ask," Craig said. "Step right this way, under the big top."

All three walked under the screened roof of the building, and Craig led them to the middle. "These are perennials best suited for shade."

"There's a maidenhair fern," Jane said, recognizing the green leafy plant.

"That's right," Craig said.

"That pink one looks like a geranium," she said.

"*Geranium maculatum,*" Trevor said. "A wild geranium."

"Very good, Trevor," Craig said.

"What kind of plants do you have for sunny areas?" Jane asked.

"I'm glad you asked," Craig said, his voice sounding like a carnival barker's. "Step right this way, little lady, and see the rest of the native plants. Over here is—"

"Coneflowers," Jane said, bending over separate plants, each a different color.

"*Echinacea pallida* and *echinacea purpurea,*" Trevor said, "Pale and purple."

"Echinacea? I think Aunt Ethel takes that when she feels a cold coming on."

"Good for her," Craig said. "And yes, that's where echinacea comes from . . . coneflowers. That's one of the reasons I advocate native plants. They can be good for treating ailments. They're also better adapted to our soil and climate, so they require less fertilizer, pesticide and watering than nonnatives."

Jane put a hand over her heart in pretend shock. "Goodness, Craig. I think you have a passion for this subject."

Craig drew a deep breath, looking abashed. "I'm sorry, Jane. I do feel quite strongly about this topic. I didn't mean to bore you."

"I'm not bored in the least," she said. "I think it's great. I wish more of us could share in your knowledge. Speaking of which, when do you plan to announce this new aspect of your business to your current customers?"

"Soon," he said. "First I'm trying to get established with retail nurseries. That's where I plan to enlarge my client base. If my Acorn Hill customers want some native plants, I'll be delighted to sell to them. But I plan to sell most of these beauties to other retailers."

"It's great to see someone working at a business he loves," Trevor said, then grinned. "Particularly when it's something that interests me too."

"Count me in as interested," Jane said. "This project of yours, Craig, has me more and more intrigued.

Chapter ▦ Five

On Monday, Alice worked her shift at the hospital. She had many patients to tend to, and it seemed that she no sooner started one task than another one came to her attention. Unfortunately, nursing meant more than caring for people; it also meant an enormous amount of paperwork to be filled out, filed or discussed with other health-care personnel.

By the time she got home late that afternoon, Alice was ready for a few moments' rest. She had just set foot through the door, however, when Louise greeted her. "I know you're tired from working, Alice, but Carlene Moss called and asked if you would meet her at the *Nutshell*. She apparently has something urgent she wants to talk to you about."

"Oh dear. Did she sound upset?"

"Quite the opposite," Louise said. "She sounded elated."

Alice's feet were aching after her long day. "I wonder if I could just phone her."

Louise shook her head. "She was explicit about your meeting her at her office."

Alice sighed. "All right, I'll drive into town then."

Once she found a parking space and headed up the sidewalk to the *Nutshell*, she found a note taped to the front door: *Alice. Meet me at the Coffee Shop. Carlene.*

Alice trudged back to her car. She sat in the driver's seat and rested her head for a moment against the steering wheel. She would be delighted to go home and soak in a warm tub with therapeutic bath salts. Carlene was a dear friend, however, and wanted to see her, for whatever reason. The bath would have to wait.

Hope Collins, the waitress, greeted her when she entered the Coffee Shop. "Hi, Alice. Carlene's waiting for you in the back booth."

Carlene was chatting with an older woman whom Alice recognized as Irene Watts. She had short, salt-and-pepper hair and was wearing a chic red tailored suit. When she saw her friend, Carlene waved. "Alice, I'm so glad you've come."

"I was worried when I got your message, but you look pretty happy." Alice nodded at the other woman, who smiled back.

"Hello, Alice. How are you?" Irene extended a hand, and Alice shook it.

"Hello, Irene. I'm fine. How nice to see you again."

"Have a seat, Alice, and I'll tell you why I'm, well actually, extremely happy."

Alice settled herself next to Carlene in the red vinyl seat.

Carlene smiled broadly. "Let me buy you something to eat or drink, Alice. I know you're tired after working all day."

Weariness seemed to lift from her shoulders at her friend's concern. "I'm always glad to see you," Alice answered truthfully. "And there's no need to buy me anything."

"Nonsense! A cup of tea for Alice," Carlene said to Hope Collins, who appeared at the table to take their order. "This isn't a social visit," Carlene said, turning back to Alice. "I wanted to tell you about my meeting with Irene."

"I figured this was about that," Alice said, looking from Carlene to Irene. "How did it go?"

Carlene leaned back, the dimples in her heart-shaped face prominent as she smiled broadly. Irene smiled too, clasping her long, thin hands over each other on the table. "I looked at every nook and cranny of the building. Carlene showed me all the old papers about the architecture and structure of the place, as well as her father's memoirs about all his years of working there."

"What do you think? Is it worthy of a county historical designation?"

"She thinks it's worthy of a *state* historic designation," Carlene said, leaning forward. "She wants to take all the information to the state commission to see if it could be listed in the state register of historic places. If so, they'll put a plaque on the front of the building."

"That's wonderful!" Alice said, then turned to Irene. "I had hoped you'd be interested. It's truly a piece of Acorn Hill history."

"It's also a piece of Pennsylvania history," Irene said.

"It would be the first state-designated building in Acorn Hill. Isn't that exciting? And I have you, Alice, to thank," Carlene said.

Hope brought Alice's tea and a cup of coffee each for Carlene and Irene. They all sipped silently for a while. Finally, Irene set down her cup. "I had a good look around the office, and I was also fascinated by all the old printing and typesetting equipment."

"I've always loved the old machinery," Alice said. "It reminds me of your father, Carlene."

"Me too." Carlene's face softened. "Printing was so much more labor intensive and time consuming way back when, but sometimes I really miss the old ways. It seems so cold now, laying out the newspaper on a computer, then e-mailing it to Potterston. It's only when I'm holding the finished product in my hands that I feel like things are really right."

"I can remember smelling the ink and hearing the rattle of the typesetter's trays when I used to walk in the door," Alice said.

"Carlene tells me that she still gives field trips to show students the equipment," Irene said.

"Yes, but that's all I do with it," Carlene said, her voice tinged with sadness. "It's a dying trade."

"It's more of an art form now," Irene said, then smiled. "That is one of the reasons I love my job with the historical society. We make the past come to life, or at least pause it for a while so that we can study it and remember. And by remembering, perhaps we can bring the best of the past into the future."

"Hear! Hear!" Carlene lifted her coffee cup. "To celebrating the past."

"To the past," Alice and Irene echoed, lightly clinking their mugs with Carlene's.

That night the sisters gathered at the dinner table over the salmon that Jane had grilled with lemon and spices on their small charcoal grill, which she tried to use as often as possible during the summer. Alongside the salmon she served fresh green bean bundles and a leafy salad tossed with orange slices and a sprinkle of coconut.

"I love every meal you cook," Louise said, "but I especially love your summer dishes. They're so light and fresh."

"Summer is a great time for produce," Alice said, between bites of green beans.

"Speaking of which," Jane said, "we have fresh watermelon for dessert. I bought one at a roadside stand on the way back from Craig's nursery."

Louise wrinkled her brow. "I'm proud of his endeavors, but I hope that he doesn't decide to abandon the florist shop in favor of growing all these landscape plants."

"He does provide Acorn Hill with the prettiest flowers," Alice agreed. "For years we had to drive over to Potterston if we wanted a floral arrangement or even a fresh-cut stem or two."

"I don't think there's any chance of his abandoning Wild Things," Jane said, "although . . ."

She leaned her elbows on the table and stared into the distance, sighing.

"Although . . . ?" Louise prompted her to finish the sentence.

"What? Oh, I'm sorry. I drifted off there, didn't I? I was just thinking about Craig and how he's pursuing his dream of growing his own flowers and plants, as well as working with native plants." She sighed. "Of course, Craig doesn't have any family he has to care for, so he's free to do what he wants, when he wants."

"You sound a bit wistful," Alice said softly. She laid her hand over Jane's. "Is anything wrong?"

"No, not really," Jane said. "But I must confess that sometimes I do feel the need to learn something new."

"Why, Jane Howard," Louise said. "Of the three of us, you're the one who's always doing something new."

"You supervised the renovation of this house," Louise said. "You cook a different meal nearly every night of the year. And you're always updating your wardrobe."

"Exactly. I don't like to stagnate."

"So it's not that you have . . . what was that line from the poem by Langston Hughes?" Alice asked. "It goes something like 'What happens to a dream deferred?' Unfortunately, I can't remember what the answer is."

"Me neither." Jane looked lovingly at her sisters. "But *my* lifelong dream is to be here at Grace Chapel Inn with you two. And I bet the dreams of many don't often get fulfilled. I'm glad to see that Craig is following his dream."

The next morning, Louise anxiously awaited the arrival of Myron Apodaca, the organ repair specialist. She had taught a piano lesson at nine o'clock, and she had become distracted every time a car door shut outside. Her student had left, and Jane had already served a light lunch, however, by the time the doorbell rang.

Louise opened it to find a short, middle-aged man in a rumpled suit, topped by a baggy trench coat. He wore a battered fedora, which he lifted as he squinted at Louise through thick eyeglasses. "Mrs. Howard-Smith?"

Louise nodded, slightly taken aback. "Yes, but I'm simply Mrs. Smith. My name is not hyphenated."

"Sorry about that." He lifted the fedora again. "I'm Myron Apodaca. Ray Roswell's friend. You called me about the organ?"

"Please come in," Louise said, opening the door wider. "The organ is in the chapel across the way." She glanced outside and saw not a cloud in the sky nor felt a chill in the air. *Odd summer apparel*, she thought. "Would you, ah, like me to take your coat?"

"This?" He glanced down at the trench coat, as though he were surprised to be wearing it. "Oh no, no. Wouldn't dream of it."

"Oh," Louise said, puzzled. "Would you at least like a glass of something cold to drink? Some lemonade, perhaps? It's a rather warm day."

"No, thank you," he said. "I prefer to get right to work. Where is your little beauty?"

Louise frowned. "I beg your pardon?"

"The pipe organ," he said, blinking behind the thick lenses. "Where is the organ?"

"Oh." Louise laid her hand over her heart. "As I said, it's next door in the chapel. Follow me, please."

After Louise had left, Alice helped Jane tidy up around the house, both of them silent as they worked diligently. A guest was due to check in that afternoon, and though they were not expecting anyone else until the weekend, they wanted the inn to be spotless.

They were nearly finished and were dusting in the library when Jane said, "You were awfully quiet last night when we talked about dreams, Alice. Any reason?"

Alice swiped at any dust that might have settled on a row of books. "I was thinking about what you said, I guess."

"Are there any dreams of your own that you want fulfilled?"

Alice thought fleetingly of Mark Graves, her gentleman friend with whom she had renewed a relationship after years of separation. She blushed. "I'm not sure, Jane. I just know that what you said is true. I've lived in Acorn Hill all my life and can't imagine living anywhere else. And yet sometimes . . ." she trailed off, afraid that she had said too much.

"And yet sometimes you wonder what life would be like somewhere else. Or if you had made different choices in the past. Am I right?" Jane asked.

Alice nodded, then smiled. "I don't mean to sound maudlin about my life. The truth is that I doubt I could be happier anywhere else but with you and Louise and helping to run this inn. I don't know what I'd do if I couldn't be a nurse, either, but sometimes I wonder if I might have aspired to do more in my past."

"I can relate to that," Jane said, leaning against the desk with a sigh of relief. "I'm so glad you understand. I was sure Louise would give me a lecture about being grateful for a good life or something like that. Watching Craig take off with his lifelong dream has made me happy. Great things happen in Acorn Hill."

Alice eased into a chair. "If you had the freedom right now to do anything in the world, choose any life you wanted, would you really want to be here at Grace Chapel Inn?"

Jane thought for a long time. "There are so many things

I'd like to do. Part of me wishes I were still a chef in a big restaurant. Part of me wishes I could just travel all the time. Part of me longs for life in a big city again." She smiled at her older sister. "But you know what? All that pales with the life I'm leading. How about you?"

"Sometimes I just feel the need to get out of my usual routine," Alice said. "Of course there are times I wonder what would have happened if I had married and had children. But that is more a road that never presented itself than a road not taken."

"You do have Mark," Jane pointed out.

"Yes." Alice folded her hands in her lap. "And I'm delighted that we've renewed our friendship after all these years. Sometimes I do just feel the need to do something that is different. Perhaps to start a new hobby."

Jane smiled. "I don't think of you as the hobby type, Alice. Oh, don't give me that wounded look. I didn't mean it as an insult. I meant it as a compliment. You're happiest when you're helping people, either encouraging them or helping them to achieve better health, like in your nursing."

"I do like working with people," Alice said thoughtfully.

"And don't forget your ANGELs," Jane continued. "Where would those middle school girls be without you to teach them and guide them every week? I like cooking and growing things. I love creating something out of nothing and watching buds flower and plants shoot up toward God's great sky. But you, why, you do the same thing with people. You nurture them, Alice. You make them grow. You make *me* grow. Ever since I've moved back to Acorn Hill, I've watched how you interact with people and how you care about them. I want to be more like you."

"Really?" Alice said, stunned. Jane was so vivacious and, well, worldly. Compared to her sister, Alice sometimes felt like a sparrow next to an exotic bird.

Jane nodded. "I wish I had some advice to reassure you.

I'd suggest volunteer work, but you're already busy enough with the inn and nursing."

"I *am* helping Carlene with the historical society," Alice said. "Maybe if she and Irene Watts continue to need my help, that will be an interesting diversion."

"And I'll be helping Craig with his new nursery," Jane said. "Perhaps I can combine my enthusiasm for plants and my desire to help people more."

"And maybe I can help people more and get out of this funk," Alice said.

"There you go!" Jane gave a definitive nod.

Alice pumped a fist into the air. "Hooray for us!"

Chapter Six

Louise led the way to Grace Chapel with Myron Apodaca right alongside her. Studying him covertly, she saw him glance up and watch the sky intently, as though expecting it to rain.

Perhaps he knew something about the weather forecast that she didn't. That might explain the trench coat, which he wore even now in the rays of the summer sun.

He certainly is an odd man.

"Pretty little town you have here," Myron said. "Ray told me he and his family enjoyed staying at your inn."

"Have you and Mr. Roswell known each other a long time?" Louise asked.

Myron chuckled. "We go back all the way to college. We both studied music together. He eventually became a music minister, and I got into organ evaluation and repair."

"Does your business often take you far from home?" Louise asked.

"I stick mostly to the eastern states, but once or twice I've headed out to the West Coast," he said. "Spent a lot of time in Hollywood."

Louise had just touched the knob on the door to the chapel when it swung open and surprised her. "Hello, Louise,"

Rev. Thompson said. "I was opening some windows, and I saw you coming."

"Pastor Thompson, this is Myron Apodaca, who's come to evaluate the organ for us."

"Hello, Myron," Rev. Thompson said, extending a hand. "I'm Kenneth Thompson, pastor of Grace Chapel. We're delighted that you could give us your opinion."

"Hi there, Pastor," Myron said, shaking Rev. Thompson's hand. "I'm glad to help out, if I can. Some of these old organs are pretty far gone. I'll take a look-see and let you know what I think."

They entered the chapel with Rev. Thompson leading the way. Myron removed his hat and held it between his hands, his gaze taking in the chapel with its rich red carpet, warm wooden pews, and intricate stained glass windows. "Beautiful," Louise thought she heard him whisper.

"I'll leave you two to the evaluation," Rev. Thompson said. "It was a pleasure to meet you, Myron. Louise, if you need anything, I'll be downstairs going over some church records."

"Thank you, Pastor," Louise said. "Mr. Apodaca, right this way. The organ . . ." She turned toward Myron, but he had already headed to the organ.

He stared at the old instrument for a few moments, then lifted his right hand as though offering a toast, and out of the side of his mouth, said, "Here's looking at you, kid."

My, this fellow really is a bit strange, thought Louise.

He removed one of the organ pipes, looked down its cylinder as though it were a telescope, then blew into it. "They could use a good cleaning," he said, his voice sounding accusatory.

"Yes," Louise said, but stopped short of saying anything else. She wanted to add that she had mentioned to the board several times that the pipes needed cleaning. Whenever she had, Florence Simpson sighed loudly, and that was the end of that.

Myron moved to the console and to Louise's surprise, removed his trench coat. He folded it neatly in half, then in half again. Louise instinctively held out her arms, and he laid the coat across them, then carefully set the fedora on top. Without another word, he sat on the bench and played a mighty E-flat chord.

The chapel swelled with the music. He manipulated several stops, then ran his fingers over the keys, trilling and thrumming through several scales and arpeggios.

Louise stood amazed, still holding the coat and hat. That Myron Apodaca had talent was undeniable. He played with verve and force until the chapel walls seemed to swell. Unfortunately, not only was the music loud, but the organ moaned and wheezed as though it were drawing its last breath. Anyone sitting in church would no doubt have been forced to cover his ears from the cacophony. Louise wondered that Rev. Thompson didn't bound up from the basement, demanding to know why the organ was playing full throttle.

Suddenly Myron muttered inexplicably, "Play it again, Sam," then broke into "Strike Up the Band." Louise felt as though a circus, or at the very least, a marching band had invaded the chapel. He may have had talent, but she was appalled at Myron's lack of decorum. This was a house of worship, not a circus tent.

"Mr. Apodaca," she said, and when he didn't respond, she repeated herself, raising her voice to a decidedly unladylike pitch. "Mr. Apodaca!"

Startled, he abruptly stopped. Myron took one look at Louise and grinned. "Sorry," he said. "I used to play a Wurlitzer at a movie palace."

Before she could say another word, he soberly launched into Bach's famous Toccata and Fugue in D Minor. At least the music was appropriate for a church, but he didn't lower the volume from his previous musical selection.

Louise would have clamped both hands over her ears,

but her arms were still burdened with his coat and hat. "Mr. Apodaca," she said loudly, then managed to tap him on the shoulder with one encumbered hand.

He snapped his hands back from the keys and whirled to face her. "That's enough of that. Let's have a look at the rest of the old girl. Lead the way to the basement so that I can inspect the leathers and blower, if you please." He bounded up from the bench.

Perplexed, Louise started for the basement stairs, then thought better of it. Tired of being burdened with the responsibility for coat and hat, however, which he had apparently delegated to her for the duration of his inspection, she laid them on the bench. She brushed her hands together, and he grinned, gesturing for her to lead on. Huffing silently, Louise headed for the stairs.

Late that afternoon, Grace Chapel Inn welcomed another guest. Jane and Alice had finished tidying up and had even completed a game of checkers when Theo Dulane showed up at the front door.

Sad-faced with hunched shoulders, Theo was a sixtyish man, whose hair was just beginning to turn gray. His mouth barely turned up at the corners when he greeted Jane and Alice like old friends. "So good to see you, ladies."

The sisters looked at one another. Neither wanted to be impolite enough to inquire about a prior acquaintanceship. Theo sensed their confusion, however, and helped out. "You probably don't remember me without my wife Laverne. We stayed here once before, and she made the arrangements. She's always much more outgoing, so you would probably remember her more than me."

"Ah, Laverne Dulane. I'm sorry I didn't recognize you, Mr. Dulane," Jane said, "but to be honest, you look different than I remember. Where is your wife?"

Theo clasped his hands together and drew a deep breath. "She died six months ago."

"We are so sorry," Alice said.

"Yes," Jane echoed, her expression filled with compassion.

"Thank you," Theo said, nodding at her, then Alice. "People say I do look different—older—since Laverne's passing. I tell them that she made me young. There's that and the fact that I stopped coloring my hair since she left."

Neither Alice nor Jane was quite certain how to respond, so they said nothing. Theo smiled. "I guess my little joke fell flat. I never colored my hair, but it has grayed quite a bit in the last few months."

"I've always heard that a traumatic incident can do that," Jane said, "but I was never sure whether to believe it or not."

"Believe it," he said, then spent a few moments filling out the required forms for registration. When he finished, he passed them to Alice and smiled at Jane. "Do you still make those wonderful breakfasts?"

"They tell me I do," she said cheerfully.

Alice glanced over the forms. "All our rooms are available except for the Sunset Room, Mr. Dulane. We haven't assigned you one yet, so you may have your pick of the others."

"Laverne and I had the Sunset Room on our last trip." He thought for a moment. "Sunset. That was oddly appropriate."

"Would you like the Sunrise Room this time?" Jane asked softly.

Alice looked at Jane. "Or how about the Garden Room? There's something comforting about being among greenery and growing things."

Jane looked at Alice and smiled.

Theo perked up. "Yes, I think I would like that room. Thank you, ladies. I guess I'll head up there now, if one of you would be so kind as to lead the way."

"Alice, would you mind?" Jane asked. "I need to get dinner started. No telling when Louise will be home."

"Right this way, Mr. Dulane," Alice said, gesturing at the stairs.

Theo lifted the one bag he had brought with him, a small black carry-on scarcely larger than a briefcase. Alice eyed it and said casually, "I thought I remembered you had reserved a room for nearly two weeks."

"That's right," he said, nodding, but didn't say anything further.

Alice showed him to the Garden Room. "Let us know if you need anything, Mr. Dulane."

"You can call me Theo," he suggested. He surveyed the room, sighing. "The room will do just fine. Thank you, and if you'll excuse me . . ."

"Certainly." Alice backed out of the room, paused at the closed door for a moment, then deep in thought, retreated down the stairs.

In the kitchen, Jane was busy with dinner preparations. "Did Mr. Dulane like the room?"

"I suppose so," Alice said, leaning against the counter as Jane gathered bowls and plates from cabinets on either side of her sister. "Jane, did you notice anything unusual about Mr. Dulane?"

"Just that he looked extraordinarily unhappy. I'm sure I would be too, if I were a recent widower." Jane looked up from consulting a cookbook. "Why do you ask?"

"He only had one bag, and it was quite small for some-one who's staying nearly two weeks. I know I read a lot of mysteries, but you don't suppose he plans to . . ." She couldn't finish the sentence.

". . . Do away with himself?" Jane uttered the words dramatically.

"Why would someone who was so grief-stricken return to a place he had traveled with his wife?"

"I like a good mystery novel as much as the next person," Jane said, "but I don't think that's the explanation for the small bag."

"Then what?"

Jane shrugged. "Maybe he has another bag in the car."

"Of course," Alice said, smiling with relief. "That must be it. I do believe you're becoming more practical every day. You're starting to think like Louise."

Jane laughed. "I'll take that as a compliment."

Alice wondered what was keeping Louise. Concerned, she decided to head over to the chapel, but then she spotted her sister saying good-bye to Myron Apodaca outside the chapel doors. Alice met her sister at the door to the inn. "Did you invite him to dinner?"

"I did," she said, sighing. "But, thank goodness, he declined. He is one odd man."

They watched him drive off, and they both waved. "I noticed he was wearing a trench coat," Alice said.

"That's only one of his peculiarities," Louise said, leading the way inside the house. A look of relief seemed to wash over her face as she closed the door behind her. "We spent so much time together looking at the organ that he had time to tell me a lot about himself. It seems he is a film buff, and he patterns himself after Humphrey Bogart's detective characters, who favored trench coats and fedoras."

Alice grinned. "How funny."

Alice was thinking of asking Louise about the organ, then decided that it would be easier for Louise to tell the story only once, when all the sisters were together. Jane had prepared chicken cacciatore for dinner. Once the food had been blessed, Alice could stand the suspense no longer. "What did Mr. Apodaca recommend regarding the organ?"

Louise took a bite of chicken, swallowed, and daintily wiped her mouth with her napkin. "He said that we should consider junking it."

"Oh, Louise," Alice said sorrowfully, laying down her fork. "Is it really that bad?"

Louise nodded. "He did give me an estimate of what he thought it would cost to repair the organ, but it's way beyond what Grace Chapel can afford."

"How do we know that for certain?" Jane asked. "I'll bet there are lots of church members who would pay to keep the organ. Other Acorn Hill folk too. It's part of the chapel's heritage."

Louise shook her head. "I don't think so, Jane. When you compare the price of repairing that old pipe organ to that of buying a new, electronic model, there's no room for senti-ment. At least, that's what a lot of people would argue." She drew a deep breath. "And they would probably be right."

Alice laid her hand over her sister's. "I'm so sorry, Louise. Does that mean that you're ready to present your findings to the church board?"

Louise nodded, unable to speak for the lump in her throat.

"I'll suggest another meeting then," Alice said sadly. She lifted her fork to resume eating, but she found that she had lost her appetite.

Chapter Seven

The next afternoon, Jane walked to Acorn Hill to purchase some cut flowers from Wild Things. Theo Dulane had seemed as unhappy at breakfast that morning as he had the previous afternoon. While she knew that men didn't always notice flowers, she hoped it might make his breakfasts in the dining room more pleasant.

Trevor Walker met her at the door, on his way out with a large sack of potting soil. "Hi, Ms. Howard," he said. "Let me toss this in my pickup, and I'll be right with you. Mr. Tracy's out at the nursery. He left me in charge of the store."

While Trevor toted the potting soil, Jane perused the flowers Craig had in his refrigerator. The large glass doors were frosty, as though someone had recently opened them, and she waited for a moment until they cleared.

"*Hmm.* Roses? No. Not quite right for a man," Jane said, thinking of Theo Dulane. "Carnations? Too frilly. Gladiolus?"

The last flower offered a strong possibility, and she was about to reach into the refrigerator to select a few stems, when Trevor reappeared.

"What can I help you with?" he said, straight white teeth flashing in his tanned face as he smiled.

"I'm looking for some flowers to accent our dining room

table. Our lone guest right now is a man, so I need something that won't look too frilly. What do you think of gladiolus?"

Trevor considered for a moment. "Glads would be okay, but I think the bird of paradise would also make a nice arrangement."

He moved away from the refrigerator to a prep area where several tropical flowers were stored. For her inspection, he lifted one long, green-stemmed flower that bent at a near forty-five-degree angle in a ruffled display of orange, yellow and purple. "It's a Hawaiian flower and a good choice for a man."

"I like it," Jane said, examining the flower. "It's very exotic looking."

"If you want an arrangement, it would look good with some anthurium, which is also Hawaiian." He held up a shiny, red, heart-shaped flower.

Jane studied the two flowers side by side. "Very cheery. And believe me, this guest needs some special cheering. Can Craig make me an arrangement?"

"I can make one for you now if you're not in a hurry," Trevor said. "How about three or four of each, and I'll add some protea and eucalyptus to the mix?"

"Sounds great."

Trevor retrieved all the necessary flowers, shears and a deep wicker planter and took them to the back counter. Jane followed, watching as he worked.

"Speaking of cheering people up," Trevor said, "I know you and Mr. Tracy are good friends, so I thought you'd be interested in learning that he could use a little himself."

"What's wrong?"

Trevor snipped the ends of the stems so the flowers would stay fresh longer. "Some of the nursery retailers he had hoped to sell his plants to don't seem interested after all."

"Oh no," Jane said. "That's a shame."

"He hasn't freaked out or anything, but he's sort of down about all the hard work he's put in."

"I'm glad he's had you to help," Jane said.

Trevor shook his head. "I wish I could do more. Even the shop has been slow today." He nodded at the opposite end of the counter. "I've spent most of the time looking at this horticulture magazine."

"Did you learn anything new?"

"Just that there's a big flower-and-plant show at a convention center in Philadelphia the weekend after next. I thought I might talk Mr. Tracy into going."

Jane thought she remembered reading about the annual show. "The Southeastern Pennsylvania show?"

Trevor nodded. "I thought I could go with him to help out and look around, if he'll have me along."

"I'd like that myself . . . if he'll have *me* along." Jane picked up the magazine and thumbed through it until she found the article. "Wait a minute, Trevor, look. It says that the show is not only accepting vendors but applicants for various competitions: best greenhouse flower, best hybrid, and look, best native plant. Oh, I hope it's not too late for Craig to enter."

Trevor stopped working on the arrangement and looked over her shoulder. "No, it's not too late, see? The deadline to enter is this Friday. Mr. Tracy can still make it."

"What a wonderful opportunity to sell some of his plants," Jane said. "Just think. At the very least, he'd draw some attention to his work. I'll bet buyers come from all over to this show. And not just individual buyers like the average suburban gardener, but wholesalers too."

"Ms. Howard, you're a genius."

"Not me. You were the one who mentioned the article."

Trevor showed her the floral arrangement. "All finished with this too."

Jane studied the exotic bouquet in the wicker basket. It was cheery and certainly not too feminine for Theo Dulane. "Wow! That looks even better than I expected," she said. "Total me up, Trevor."

He rang up her purchase and counted back her change.

"Why don't *you* tell Mr. Tracy?" Trevor said. "If I do, he may just think I'm a high school kid with a crazy idea."

"I don't know why." Jane restudied the exotic floral arrangement. "I don't know any high school kids who know as much about horticulture, botany and floral arrangement as you do."

"If you're not doing anything, could you come back around four o'clock? That's when Mr. Tracy's supposed to be back from the nursery. We could both tell him then."

"That's fine," Jane said, then glanced at her watch. "Can I keep this arrangement in a safe place while I do some shopping? I might pop over to the library or Nine Lives while I'm waiting."

"Sure thing." Craig set the basket off to the side, behind the counter.

Jane left Wild Things and walked down Acorn Avenue. She turned right, into Berry Lane, then headed toward Nine Lives Bookstore. She passed Town Hall and met Acorn Hill's mayor, Lloyd Tynan, out front. He flagged her with a cheery wave. "Hello, Jane," he said. "How are you?"

Lloyd was the companion of the sisters' aunt, Ethel Buckley. Because he frequently visited Ethel, and because he loved Jane's cooking, he often popped in at Grace Chapel Inn. But the sisters hadn't seen him much lately. "I'm fine, Lloyd. Where have you been?"

"Here and there, here and there," he said. He ran a finger between his white shirt collar and his neck, tugged at his customary bow tie, then whipped a handkerchief from the pocket of his blue seersucker suit. "Whew! It's a hot one today," he said, wiping his brow and the top of his balding head. "How I'd love to take a trip to the ocean and dip my tootsies in the briny deep."

The temperature was probably only in the mid-seventies, a very pleasant day, but Lloyd looked as though he had been sitting in a sauna. "Sounds like a good idea, Lloyd. Why don't you plan a trip?"

He shook his head. "No time. Too much work involved in being a mayor. Let me tell you, Jane, don't ever decide to become one."

Jane patted him on the arm. "I wouldn't dream of it. No one could ever take your place."

Lloyd pocketed the handkerchief. "Well, I guess it's back to work. If I know my secretary, Bella, she'll be combing the streets for me. The last time I saw her, she had a stack of papers she wanted me to go through. Commendations, recommendations, citations, evaluations . . . My goodness, some days this job never seems to stop."

He looked so flustered that Jane felt concerned. "Why don't you take a break, Lloyd? Go over to the Coffee Shop and have something cold to drink."

"No time," he said, repeating his earlier phrase. "Bella—"

"Well, at least go back to your office and sit under the ceiling fan. And have Bella get you some cold water while you're going through all those papers."

"I'll do that, Jane. Say hello to your Aunt Ethel for me, will you? I haven't been able to see her much lately."

Jane headed toward Nine Lives Bookstore, but turned back after a few paces. Lloyd headed back inside Town Hall, and Jane made a mental note to talk to Aunt Ethel about him.

As she opened the beveled glass door to Nine Lives, Jane heard a familiar bell ring above her head. Several customers glanced up and smiled at her, then went back to their book perusal. Donna Mead, the clerk, looked up from where she knelt before a large bookcase, shelving new books. "Hi, Jane."

"Hi, Donna." Jane glanced around. She didn't see the bookstore's owner, Viola Reed, but she did spy a large orange cat across the aisle she hadn't seen before. Viola loved cats and brought some of them to her bookstore, always naming each one after a literary character.

"That's Frodo," Donna said, noticing the direction of

Jane's gaze. She held out her fingers, rubbing them together, calling the cat with a low whisper. "*Psssssssp.* Here, Frodo. Come meet Jane."

The cat yawned, stretched, then ambled over. Jane knelt and held out her hand, and Frodo rubbed under it, consenting to have his head petted, then his back. "All you cats are just alike," Jane said fondly. "You're just like our Wendell."

"He's a pretty nice one," Donna said. "Viola brought him home from the rescue center."

"I'm surprised she named him Frodo," Jane said. "I didn't think *The Lord of the Rings* would be one of Viola's literary favorites."

"It's not." Donna grinned. "She told me I could name this one. Tolkien's my favorite author."

Jane gave Frodo one final scratch behind the ears. Then he stalked off in regal feline fashion. "I'd better let you get back to work," she said to Donna. "I came in to browse."

"Feel free."

"Thanks, Donna."

Sure enough, in the gardening section, she found several books on gardening with native plants. Between studying the books and talking to Craig, she thought that she should be able to decide which plants would prosper in Grace Chapel Inn's garden.

After paying for the books, Jane saw that she still had some time to kill before she needed to be back at Wild Things. She could return early and talk to Trevor, but she didn't want to bother him when he was working. Instead, she sat on the wrought-iron bench outside Nine Lives and opened one of her new books. She recognized several of the plants from Craig's nursery.

Before she knew it, it was four o'clock, and she found herself hurrying to get back to Wild Things on time. When she got there, Craig was already inside, going over the afternoon's receipts with Trevor.

"There you are," Craig said when she entered. He looked

tired and more than a little weary. "Trevor told me you had something you wanted to talk about."

"Yes." Jane grabbed up the horticulture magazine and flipped through it to the right page. "See this article about the Southeastern Pennsylvania Garden Show?"

Craig nodded.

"Trevor and I think you should go. You can enter some of your plants and flowers in the competition, and you can even sell them. Wholesalers will be there, Craig. It'll be a great way to get the word out about your new business."

"That's not a bad idea," Craig said. "I've been so focused on the physical aspects of starting the nursery that I've forgotten about publicity. I'll really need it now. Some of the retailers who originally seemed interested in buying from me have turned me down."

"That's why this garden show would help you out," Trevor said. "You can show them the product."

"And maybe even give a talk about the advantages of landscaping with natives," Jane added. "You know, water conservation, soil retention . . ."

"You've been doing your homework," Craig said.

Jane held out the gardening books. "I went to Nine Lives. I'd love to go along to be your helper. So what do you say?"

"I say let's do it," Craig said. "What do you say, Trevor, are you coming with us?"

"If you don't mind closing the store. I thought I might bring my girlfriend Kaylie. We could take some of the plants in my pickup if you need us to."

"Thanks, Trevor. That sounds great," Craig said. "I'd better read that article and get on the stick about sending in the application. When I figure out what I'm doing, I'll let you know."

"This is so exciting," Jane said.

"I'm glad to have your help, Jane," Craig said. "You can ride with me in the delivery van. That is, if you don't mind a bumpier ride than usual."

"If you'll help me pick out some native plants for my garden, we'll call it even," she said.

"Deal." He held out his hand, and they shook on it.

❦

Later that afternoon the sisters stood in the dining room, studying the bouquet Trevor had created. Alice loved it, but Louise was a little more skeptical. "Isn't it a little too ... tropical looking for the more formal style of this room?"

"On the contrary," Alice said, taking the bouquet out of Jane's hands to set it on the Queen Anne table. "I think it's a lively complement to the walls and the color in the chair pads."

Jane couldn't help but grin. "I think so, too, Alice. The bright colors of the bouquet complement the pale green and give the old-fashioned look of this room a little pizzazz."

"Well . . ." Louise stood back and studied the arrangement more critically. "I suppose it's all right as a *temporary* addition to the room."

"It does look cheery," Alice added.

"And masculine," Jane said. "I didn't want anything too froufrou for Mr. Dulane."

"Yes, this looks like the type of floral arrangement that people send male patients at the hospital," Alice said. "I think he will like it."

"Yoo-hoo!" Ethel Buckley sashayed into the dining room via the kitchen, having entered the house through the back door. She lived in the carriage house next to Grace Chapel Inn and often popped in on the sisters. "I wondered where you girls were," she said.

"How are you, Aunt Ethel?" Louise said.

"Well"—Ethel glanced at her watch—"hungry, I suppose. Why, it's getting rather late, isn't it?"

"Would you like to stay for dinner?" Jane said, winking at her sisters. Lloyd Tynan wasn't the only person who just happened to drop in at mealtimes.

"Now that you mention it, that would be lovely," Ethel said. "Are you almost ready to eat now?"

"I was about to set the table," Jane said. "Alice has her Wednesday meeting with the ANGELs this evening, so we need to get started."

While they dined on curried coconut chicken, Jane told Ethel about running into Lloyd Tynan that afternoon. "He didn't look very well," she concluded. "Has he been to a doctor lately?"

"Not likely," Aunt Ethel said. "I can hardly get him out of that leather chair at Town Hall. He's turned into a workaholic all of a sudden. If I didn't know better, I'd say he was trying to avoid me." She smiled smugly, patting her red hair. "But I do know better."

"What's gotten into him all of a sudden?" Jane asked. "Is there really that much more mayoral work for him to tend to?"

Ethel shrugged, helping herself to more chicken. "He says there is. Well, I can only do so much. I've told that man he needs to slow down, but he won't listen."

"Perhaps you could talk him into seeing Dr. Bentley for a physical," Alice said.

Ethel chewed rapidly and swallowed. "Does he look that bad, Jane?"

"He did look awfully flustered," she said. "If it were just a one-day occurrence, I wouldn't worry about it. But from what you've said, it's an ongoing thing."

A timid rap sounded on the kitchen door. "Excuse me . . . Oh, I didn't realize you ladies were having dinner."

All four heads turned to see Theo Dulane standing hesitantly in the doorway. He eyed their dinner with a mixture of hunger and loneliness, then looked toward Alice. She held the glance and opened her mouth to speak, but Jane covered her hand with her own to silence her. "What can we help you with, Mr. Dulane?"

"I was . . . I was . . ."—he drew his gaze back from the

chicken—"Oh, it was nothing. I'll leave you ladies to your dinner."

"Would you like to join us, Mr. Dulane?" Alice spoke up. "Jane has made plenty of food."

"Thank you, but no. I'm so sorry to intrude," he said, backing out with a guilty expression.

When he was clearly out of earshot, Jane turned to Alice. "That was nice of you to invite him to dinner. I was debating whether or not to ask him as well. I decided not to, though, because he does seem to be in a sad state, and it didn't seem fair to rush him into a social situation with us. He probably needs a little time to grieve."

"You're probably right," Alice said. "I do feel sorry for him, though."

"As do I," Louise said.

"You also shouldn't encourage your male guests," Ethel said, nodding sagely. "You girls must keep your propriety."

Alice sighed quietly, sharing a glance with Jane. "It's not as though we haven't had male guests before, Auntie," Jane said. "We're not exactly blushing maidens either."

Ethel took extra time to wipe her mouth with the corner of her napkin. "You're three, attractive, unmarried women, and in my day, we were more careful with our reputations."

"I believe younger women's reputations were safe if a widow was present to look after them, correct?" Louise asked.

"Yes, and I would worry more about Alice and Jane if you weren't around, Louise. Thank goodness your presence provides some caution at Grace Chapel Inn."

Jane straightened as if to protest but did not when Louise gave her a small wink. Alice caught the gesture too, hiding a smile by bringing her cup to her lips. Jane turned toward Ethel. "Alice and I are both grateful to Louise in more ways than one," she said in what Alice realized was the sweetest voice she could muster.

Chapter Eight

A lice worked part of the next day and came home to find that Carlene had called in her absence. When Alice returned the call to the *Nutshell* office, her friend answered the phone on the first ring.

Alice could hear the sound of typing. "Is this a bad time to talk, Carlene?" she asked.

"I've got just enough time to share my news. Then I have to finish this story." She continued to tap the keyboard furiously. "Irene Watts phoned me to say she spoke with the state historical commission."

"Are they going to declare the *Nutshell* a historic landmark?"

"Well, it's not that simple," Carlene said. "They—"

The receiver clattered to the floor. Alice heard a muffled exclamation, then Carlene said, "Sorry. I dropped the phone. I really need to get something to balance this receiver on my shoulder so that I can type better while I talk. Where was I?"

"They're not going to declare the *Nutshell* a historic landmark," Alice prompted.

"Oh, right. Unfortunately, the requirements for listing in the state register seem to be too specific for the *Nutshell* building. The policies say that the site should be of statewide rather than just local interest. We could go through the nomination process, but Irene's friends don't think the building is special enough."

"I'm sorry, Carlene. That's disappointing."

"Not really." Carlene stopped typing, and Alice could hear her chair squeak as she leaned back. "One of Irene's friends in historical-museum circles heard about the *Nutshell* and is particularly interested in the old press and typography equipment. He's going to drive to Acorn Hill this evening to look at it." She started typing again.

"He doesn't want to buy it, does he?" Alice said, alarmed. She would hate to see Carlene sell off the old equipment.

"No. Well, that is, I don't think so." Carlene stopped typing again. "At least, I hope not. I mean, the *Nutshell* isn't exactly a gold mine, and I could use the money to finance a few changes for the paper, but . . . no! Surely he doesn't want to . . . Pshaw!"

Alice heard her start typing again, her fingers flying over the computer keys. "I'd better let you get back to work, Carlene. Keep me up to date on the typography equipment."

"Will do." The phone went dead, and Alice was certain that Carlene had thrown herself back into the rush to meet deadline.

After she got off the phone, Alice went to her room to change out of her nurse's uniform, then headed back downstairs. Louise was giving a piano lesson, and Jane was puttering in the kitchen. Alice wandered into the library in search of a devotional for the next ANGELs meeting, but wound up studying the photos on the wall of Daniel Howard. Right after his death she had felt so alone. But eventually Louise and Jane decided not only to stay in Acorn Hill but also to open Grace Chapel Inn with her. She would be forever grateful to God for answering her anguished prayers about her father's death with a renewed relationship with her sisters.

A throat cleared. "I'm sorry. I didn't know anyone was in here. I just popped in to find a book."

Alice turned to find Theo Dulane hesitating at the doorway. "Come in, Mr. Dulane," she said. "I was browsing for a book myself. You're welcome to take a look."

Theo stepped into the room and planted himself in front of the bookcases. He and Alice perused the books for a while until he broke the silence by saying abruptly, "My wife loved to read."

Alice turned. "Did she? What type of books?"

"Anything." Theo smiled sadly. "She read best-selling novels, biographies, political books . . . you name it. I'm afraid I never much shared her passion. I thought perhaps I'd give it a try while I'm here."

Alice paused for a moment before saying softly, "Mr. Dulane, does it make you feel better to be here at Grace Chapel Inn or worse?"

"To be reminded of my wife, you mean?"

Alice nodded.

Theo sank into a chair. "It doesn't matter where I go. Every place reminds me of Laverne."

Alice sat in the chair beside him. "I've never been married, so I can't imagine the pain of losing a spouse. But I remember how unhappy I was when my father died."

Theo perked up. "What helped you get over your grief?"

"Having my sisters move back home," she said. "Of course they can never replace Father. But we can talk about him, and we fixed up this house that was his. Those things help us remember him."

"I don't have any close relatives to visit. Laverne and I never had any children," Theo said. He looked so sad that Alice was afraid he was about to cry. While she was pondering what to say, what words could possibly ease his grief, he leaned toward her. "Miss Howard, I know this is horribly presumptuous, but would you consider having dinner with me this evening? I was going to try Zachary's in town for dinner. Everyone says it's wonderful. But the truth is, I just don't feel like eating alone. I . . . I need someone to talk to."

His eyes pleaded, and Alice felt torn. He only wanted someone to talk to, after all, but somehow it might seem like a date to some for the two of them to dine out together. Zachary's was a nice restaurant. She had been there several times with Mark Graves, and those visits had definitely been dates.

Please, God, what should I do? Theo Dulane is hurting and wants to talk, but I don't feel comfortable. He needs someone with more experience in discussing grief.

Theo must have read the expression on her face. He leaned away and shook his head. "Forgive me, Miss Howard. That was too forward of me. You're a busy woman, and it's not your responsibility to tend your guests' broken hearts."

Alice softened. "The sign on our door says that Grace Chapel Inn is a place of hope and healing. While my sisters and I can't always heal those hearts ourselves, we believe that God can and will." She paused. "I notice you haven't left our inn since you arrived on Tuesday. Have you been outdoors to see the town? The weather's so lovely this summer. Maybe it would cheer you up."

"Perhaps," he said, but his expression said otherwise.

"If you're looking for a good book, you're welcome to our library, but you might also try the Nine Lives Bookstore in town," Alice continued. "Or go to our Town Hall. There's a Visitors Center with information about the town and area, and there's a nice town model that one of our citizens made."

"Maybe I'll walk over there before I have dinner," Theo said. He smiled at Alice, then rose. "You've made me feel better just spending a few minutes chatting with me, Miss Howard. Again, I apologize for being presumptuous."

Not certain what to say, Alice simply smiled and nodded.

Theo Dulane left the room, and she breathed a sigh of relief. *Thank You for answering that prayer so quickly, Lord.*

In the parlor, Louise struggled to finish her piano lesson with Jason Ransom. He was an active ten-year-old who, although he'd never said as much to her, preferred playing baseball to playing the piano. She knew because he dragged a grimy, slightly dented aluminum bat to practice every week and leaned it carefully against one of the Victorian chairs, not out of respect for the chairs, but for the bat.

But once he set his mind on the lesson, he was a thoughtful student, following her instructions diligently. Sometimes he set his tongue between his teeth as he concentrated on transferring the notes on the sheet music to the keys at his fingers.

Normally Louise enjoyed teaching Jason because he was one of her few boy students, but today she found herself worrying about the meeting with the church board that had been arranged for that night. She would have to give them Myron Apodaca's recommendation that they purchase a new organ, a decision that still confused her.

Am I just an old fuddy-duddy for my attachment to that instrument? And just because I am the organist doesn't mean it is my organ. Grace Chapel and its congregation will long survive me, I hope. I must do what is best for the church, no matter how I feel. Still . . .

Wham! Jarred by a tremendous chord that Jason had executed, the aluminum bat tipped over and slammed against the floor. It just missed hitting the porcelain doll collection showcased on the three-tier, burl walnut table.

Louise shot Jason a reproving look, saw his contrite expression, then softened. "It's all right, Jason. Nothing was harmed. In the future, though, perhaps you should leave your bat by the front door. Or even out on the porch."

"Yes, Mrs. Smith," he said. "I'm sorry. My mother tells me to leave the bat in the car, but every week when I'm finished here, I go play ball with my friends. It's easier to bring it with me."

"And that's fine, but the bat should probably stay where it can do the least damage." She glanced at her watch and smiled. "I believe it's time for you to go find your friends. Our lesson is over."

Jason whooped, caught Louise's eye, then sobered. "Thank you, Mrs. Smith."

"Have a good week, Jason," she said, her eyes twinkling. "Go enjoy the summer day."

"Yes ma'am," he said and bolted for the door.

"Don't forget to practice your daily drills," she called after him, but the front door had already slammed shut. Louise shook her head and stacked, squared and patted the sheet music. Realizing that Jason was her last student for the day, she smiled again.

She wandered to the kitchen to see what Jane was preparing for dinner. To her surprise, Jane was seated at the kitchen table studying one of several books spread out before her. No cooking was in progress, even though it was late afternoon.

"Jane?" Louise said, slightly concerned. It was unlike her sister to be so absorbed in reading.

"What? Oh, Louise. How was your lesson? I thought I heard a strange noise in the parlor."

"Jason's bat fell over." Louise slid into a chair next to Jane. "Thank goodness it didn't damage anything, but I advised him to leave it on the porch or in the front hall next time."

Jane seemed barely to hear, as her eyes wandered back to the open book before Louise had finished speaking. Louise craned her neck in an attempt to glimpse the page. "What are you reading?"

Without pausing, Jane held up a book so that Louise could see the cover. "Gardening. I'm learning so much. And, oh, Louise"—Jane snapped the book shut and laid it aside— "Craig Tracy is going to enter the Southeastern Pennsylvania Garden Show the weekend after next, and I promised to go along to help him. They have a category for native plants, but he might enter in other categories too. That should help his new wholesale business."

"That's wonderful. I do still worry that he might plan to get out of the florist business all together, and then where would Acorn Hill be?"

Jane shook her head. "That's not likely. He loves Wild Things. This is just something new for him to do, and I must admit that I'm getting swept up in his enthusiasm for gardening and growing plants."

Louise shook her head. "You never cease to amaze me, Jane. You're not happy unless you are doing something with your hands—cooking, gardening, painting, working as a florist's assistant."

"I do like to keep busy," Jane said. "What's that proverb about idle hands being the devil's tools?" She winked.

"Good point." Louise rose and poured herself a glass of lemonade, then gestured at the empty stovetop with the glass pitcher. "By the way, where is dinner?"

"Oh, dinner." Jane looked sheepish. "I meant to start it a while ago, but I got so involved in these books that I didn't even realize what time it was until you came in."

"Everybody needs a rest," Louise said. "Why don't we three eat out? Alice and I will still have time to meet with the church board this evening about the organ."

Jane looked into space, drumming her fingers on the table.

Louise knew that look. Jane liked eating out on occasion, but Louise knew that her sister secretly preferred her own cooking to anyone else's. She was obviously weighing the advantages of eating out against those that came from preparing something at home.

"How about a simple green salad?" Louise said. "I can help you chop vegetables and whatnot. It's so warm, and I don't want a heavy meal all the time anyway."

"I could make a good chef's salad. There's some leftover ham, and I could boil eggs . . ." Jane said, already lost in thoughts of food preparation.

"What are we waiting for? Let's get to work," Louise said.

Once Jane investigated the contents of the refrigerator, the chef salad turned into a Greek salad. To romaine lettuce, she added green and red bell peppers, tomatoes, cucumbers and red onion—all from her garden. She stirred in feta cheese, then topped it all off with a homemade dressing of olive oil, lemon juice and oregano.

While they ate, Alice told them about Theo Dulane's inviting her to dinner. "I'm so glad that I didn't have to turn him down outright," she finished. "He seems so heartbroken that I just want to be a companionable listener. But I think he needs better guidance than I can offer."

"You're probably right," Louise said. "It's not always enough simply to listen to a person's problems."

"Perhaps he needs professional advice," Jane suggested.

"But there must be something we can do," Alice said. "I hate to think that he will have just passed through our inn without our helping, in some way."

"Maybe our inn is only meant to be a place of reflection for him," Louise said. "After all, God doesn't always specifically work through us. Or even the inn itself."

"That's true." She glanced at her watch. "If we're going to get to the board meeting on time, Louise, we'd better help Jane clean up now."

"Ordinarily I'd wave you off and take care of it," Jane said, "but as I was telling Louise earlier, I'm nearly hypnotized by these gardening books I bought at Viola's. I want to learn all that I can. Craig promised to help me put in native plants around the inn, as well, so I want to be well-informed when we have a chance to talk."

"I wish I were more informed to talk with the board tonight," Louise said. "I feel as though reporting Myron Apodaca's recommendations is tantamount to announcing a death sentence."

Alice squeezed her hand in sympathy.

Chapter Nine

Alice and Louise walked together to Grace Chapel. The lights already glowed from the Assembly Room in the basement. Louise didn't often find herself nervous or intimidated, but the thought of walking into this board meeting was daunting for her.

"It will be fine," Alice assured her as she reached for the chapel doorknob.

Louise stopped short of entering. "Will it?"

Alice nodded. "God is in charge, Louise. All we have to do is trust in Him."

Louise took a deep breath and nodded at the timely reminder. *It is only an organ. It's not the chapel itself nor the members of the congregation that are at stake.*

"Hello, Louise, Alice." Rev. Thompson met them inside the door. "I think nearly everyone is here."

"Hello, Pastor Ken," Louise and Alice returned his greeting.

The pastor led them down the stairway to the Assembly Room, where the board members were gathered. Despite the fact that she was nervous, Louise was delighted to see everyone. If all couldn't be considered close friends, they were friends nonetheless, and members not only of Acorn Hill but also of Grace Chapel.

After greetings had been exchanged, Rev. Thompson, an interested observer, opened with a prayer. Then Fred Humbert, as chairman, took over the meeting. Fred's wife Vera was a close friend of Alice's. He conducted some short, unrelated business, then got to the matter at hand.

"We trust that you—"

Florence Simpson leaned forward. "What did your expert recommend for Grace Chapel's organ? Should we give it the heave-ho?"

Louise swallowed, then passed out papers. "I typed up his evaluation so that you could each have it for study and for prayer. I know it may not seem an earthshaking matter, but I believe in God's guidance in any change the church contemplates."

Florence scanned the paper. "Look," she said, nearly crowing. "The price for repairs is way beyond what we can afford."

"We don't know that for sure," Fred said. "We haven't set an actual dollar amount toward the organ."

"Maybe not," Florence continued, tapping the paper, "but I can clearly see from these other figures that a new, electronic organ would be less expensive."

"But do we really want to go electronic?" Cyril Overstreet said, worry edging his voice. "We've always had a pipe organ here."

"Maybe it's time we break with tradition," Sylvia Songer said. "So many churches are getting rid of their old organs." She looked around the group. "Personally, I like the electronic sound. It sounds more modern somehow. And don't we want to reach out to the young people in the Acorn Hill area? We might even get younger folks from other towns to attend Grace Chapel."

"I've always felt that it was the Holy Spirit who called hearts," Alice said gently, "not the music in a worship service."

"And by Sylvia's logic, an electronic organ might drive older members away," Lloyd pointed out.

Sylvia's face flushed.

"What's the difference in sound, Louise?" Fred asked.

Everyone turned, and the room grew quiet. "Electronic organs can only simulate the sound that's made with wind-blown pipes," she said. "Individually, the notes may sound like a pipe organ, but when the notes are played together, it sounds noticeably different from what each note would sound like coming from its own pipe. It lacks a certain fullness. I'm told that even untrained listeners can spot the difference."

June Carter, the Coffee Shop's owner, laughed. "Honey, most of us in the congregation are untrained listeners, but I honestly wonder how much of a difference it would make in our worship experience."

Louise opened her mouth, then caught Alice's gaze. Alice shook her head slightly, and Louise kept quiet.

"What about buying a new pipe organ?" Cyril asked, studying Louise's handout. "This Apodaca fellow say anything about that?"

"A n-new pipe organ!" Pastor Henry Ley said, his eyes shining. "That would be a good c-compromise, wouldn't it?"

Louise stubbornly felt that it would not, but she refrained from saying so. "Myron estimated that it would be slightly more expensive than an electronic organ."

"There. You see?" Florence said. "More money we don't have."

"M-may I make a suggestion?" Pastor Henry Ley spoke up.

Everyone stopped talking and looked at him. Fred smiled in his direction. "Please do."

"We are a l-large, diverse b-board, and we have so much other ch-church business. Let's f-form a smaller committee, s-say of three or four members, to study this issue and report back."

"A splendid idea," Fred said. "Henry, since you're on the

arts and music committee, you would be perfect to head this up. Are you willing?"

Pastor Ley nodded.

"Louise has gotten things rolling with Mr. Apodaca's recommendations," Fred said, "and Henry's right. We could bat this issue back and forth until dawn. We need a smaller group to assess the funds we have available, find out the costs of different options, and perhaps even take a poll of the congregation. Henry will make a good, impartial chairman. All in favor?"

"Aye," they said, though some, like Sylvia Songer and Florence Simpson, looked disappointed.

"Wonderful," Fred said. "Henry, who will you choose for your committee?"

"Louise, of c-course," he said. "Even though she isn't a board member, I don't think we c-could make a decision without her input."

"Agreed," Fred said.

She nodded her thanks.

"Florence?"

"You have my pledge," Florence said, setting her mouth in a straight line.

Henry looked around the group. "Lloyd?"

He glanced at his watch. "I hate not to help, but I'm pretty swamped down at Town Hall. Would someone like to take my place?"

"I will, Lloyd," Ethel said. She glanced at him with a worried expression. "You need to get your rest."

"That's three, plus Henry to oversee things," Fred said. "I know the committee will choose wisely for Grace Chapel's future."

Louise nodded, but seeing the smug expression on Florence's face, she wasn't so certain that the committee would.

After some more board business, the group began to disband. A few members huddled to chitchat, but eventually all drifted toward the door.

Ethel pulled Alice and Louise aside. "Girls, are you ready? I thought we could walk home together."

"Go ahead, Louise," Alice said. "I'll help Pastor Ken straighten up here first."

"Thank you, Alice," Rev. Thompson said, then turned to Louise. "I'll make sure she gets home safely."

"Thank you," she said. Alice thought she looked like she wanted to say more, but Ethel grabbed her arm, gabbing a mile a minute, and they headed out the door.

Alice began to put up the folding chairs that the committee had used, while Rev. Thompson said good night to everyone else. When the room was empty, he helped her stack the chairs against the wall. "Is this organ situation troubling you, Alice?" he said, after a while.

"I hate to see Louise distressed. And I fear we may be in for some strife on the board."

"I've worried about that too," he said. "I know that Louise will never stand in the way of what's best for Grace Chapel, but I also know how attached she is to the organ. And I understand how integral it is to Grace Chapel's history."

Rev. Thompson watched as Alice continued to tidy up the already clean room. "It's late, Alice. Are you afraid to face Louise's disappointment at home?"

She sighed, straightening. "It's more like I'm afraid to face one of our guests." Rev. Thompson's face clouded with concern. "Oh, he isn't unpleasant," she said hurriedly in response. "He's a recent widower and he's lonely. He wants someone to talk to, and for some reason he's chosen me."

"That's not surprising," Rev. Thompson said. "You're a good listener, Alice."

"I enjoy listening to people, but . . ." she paused.

"You don't feel comfortable talking one-on-one with a man about such a sensitive issue?"

"Exactly," she said, relieved that he had put it so easily into words. "He asked me to dinner, and while I know he didn't mean it as a date, the whole idea just made me uncomfortable. I was prepared to turn down his offer, but he fortunately withdrew it before I had to."

"You were wise to be cautious," Rev. Thompson said. "You have such a counselor's heart, but I would hate to see it trampled on by a possible misunderstanding."

"That's what Ethel said. She advised us to be careful of becoming too familiar with our guests, particularly the single male ones, though we don't have them as guests as often as we do couples or single women."

"That's good advice. Though I know you and your sisters are wise enough to know that already."

Rev. Thompson looked about the Assembly Room. "There. All neat and tidy. Thank you, Alice. Are you ready to go home?"

She nodded.

He turned off the lights and shut the church for the night. As they crossed over to Grace Chapel Inn, the pastor asked, "Would you and your sisters mind if I dropped by Sunday?"

"Why, of course not, Pastor," Alice said, confused. "You never need an invitation with us."

"I thought I might stop by and meet your guest . . . what was his name?"

"Theo Dulane."

"Well, I have a feeling that Theo Dulane and I might have some common ground regarding grief. Perhaps he wouldn't mind joining me somewhere so that we could talk."

Alice felt relieved. Why hadn't she thought of going to Rev. Thompson or Pastor Ley? She should have known that they would be interested in talking to Theo. Moreover, Rev. Thompson wouldn't just be a sympathetic ear; he would be counseling as someone with firsthand experience, inasmuch as his own wife had died several years before.

"Please come for Sunday dinner," she said. "I have a feeling he'll jump at the chance to talk with you."

Rev. Thompson walked with her up the porch steps to the inn. "Thank you for walking me home," she said. "We'll look for you Sunday then."

He smiled, said good night, then headed back down the stairs. Alice watched him go as she took in a deep breath. The summer night was so beautiful. The air had a gentle breeze, the temperature felt balmy, and crickets chirped pleasantly to each other. She treasured nights like this and, unwilling to end it, she sank into the porch swing.

"There you are." Louise drifted onto the porch a few minutes later and sat beside her. She let out a sigh.

"Are you pleased with the idea of a committee to study the organ situation?" Alice asked.

"Yes," Louise said, then added, "and no. Part of me was hoping to get the issue resolved tonight. Part of me has hope that it can be salvaged. I wanted to bargain with God to make the committee see things my way, but I have told Him that I will accept whatever the committee may say."

"I wanted to volunteer for the committee," Alice said, "but I felt it would be a conflict of interest. Selfishly, I also didn't want to reach a decision that might be painful for you."

Louise patted her hand, smiling. "Thank you, Alice. One thing I do know is that I would rather things were right between us than that Grace Chapel keeps the organ."

Alice set the porch swing into gentle motion, and the sisters sat side by side, silent. At last Alice broke the stillness of the night. "I wonder what Father would have done, if he were still pastor of Grace Chapel."

"Exactly what was done tonight. He would have established a committee to look into the situation," Louise said. "I've been wondering what he would want me to do."

"Exactly what you're doing. Giving it over to God," Alice said, without hesitation.

The sisters looked at each other and smiled. "It's so simple, and yet I often forget," Louise said.

Alice nodded. "Me too. I've been worrying about Theo Dulane and his loneliness. I told Pastor Ken about it while we were fixing up the Assembly Room, and he volunteered to talk to Theo."

"That makes good sense," Louise said. "He is first and foremost a pastor, but he can also identify with Theo's grief."

"He said he would stop by Sunday to introduce himself to Theo. My goodness, tomorrow is Friday, and the Havertys will return. I'll check in the morning to make sure their room is ready."

"I hope they had a good visit with their son."

The screen door opened, and Jane stepped out onto the porch. "You two have the right idea. It's absolutely beautiful out tonight."

"Would you like to join us?" Alice asked. "I think we can squeeze another sister onto the swing."

Jane shook her head. "You might be able to squeeze me in there, but we also might not have a swing anymore. It's not that any of us is overweight, but I still don't want to take chances. I'll just pull up a chair."

She pulled a chair next to Louise, then leaned back, hands behind her head. "Weather this beautiful just shouldn't be legal. I'll bet Craig's plants are loving it."

"How is Craig?" Louise asked.

"We're going to get together tomorrow to talk about the plant show. He faxed the application, and he was accepted. Now he's just awaiting word on whether they want him to give a speech."

"That would surely help his business," Alice observed.

"He really has a lot of information to share," Jane said, then stretched out her arms and legs. "This weather has an odd effect on me. It makes me tired."

"More likely you're weary from running in so many different directions," Louise said.

"Well, at least I'm not bored," Jane said cheerfully.

"No one can ever accuse you of that, dear," Louise responded. "You said you like to learn and do new things."

Jane thought for a moment. "Yes, that's exactly how I feel. Helping Craig has given me a new outlet. It must be how you feel when you help people, Alice. Each person, each situation, is a new opportunity for learning."

"It's better to give than to receive," she said, smiling at what some considered to be just a cliché.

"All I know is that I'm very excited about this garden show and Craig's new nursery business. I think it's given him a new lease on life."

Alice glanced at Louise surreptitiously. If the new committee voted to do away with Grace Chapel's organ, would Louise need a new lease on life too?

Chapter Ten

The next morning, Friday, Jane checked with Louise and Alice to make sure that everything was ready for the Havertys' return. She didn't want to leave her sisters with any last-minute details, so once she was assured that everything was set, she headed out to Wild Things.

Craig was working in the store when she entered. "Hi, Jane. I was just going to call you."

"What's up?"

"I got a phone call from the garden show this morning. They had a last-minute cancellation, and they want me to host a workshop on native plants."

"That's great," she said.

"I've been thinking all morning about what I want to talk about," he said, "and I thought it would be helpful to have samples of the plants as visual aids while I speak."

"I can help you organize them and hold them up while you talk," Jane said, "if that would be helpful."

Craig thought for a moment. "The program chairman said that there would be roughly a hundred people in attendance at the workshop. What if I provided each of them with a sample cutting?"

"I think that's a great idea. You could put a sticker on the side that gives the name of the plant—"

"—As well as the name, address and Web site of my business," Craig finished for her.

"It's a great marketing tool," Jane said, beaming. "Do you have a Web site already?"

"I contacted Hank Young, Acorn Hill's own computer geek," Craig said.

Jane laughed. Hank was a recent college graduate and Acorn Hill native. He had returned to his hometown after a few years in Ohio. He laughingly claimed that he missed his mother's cooking, but everyone in Acorn Hill realized that he was one of the rare young twenties singles who missed the small-town atmosphere. They were delighted to have him back.

Now he worked out of an old house he had bought near town, fixing Acorn Hill's computer woes and designing the occasional Web site. Most businesses in town did not need Web sites, since they dealt in strictly local commerce, but others who wanted a more visible presence on the World Wide Web often enlisted Hank's help.

"We designed our own Web site for Grace Chapel Inn," Jane said, "but Hank was kind enough to offer us some free pointers on improving the overall look. He found a cheaper Web-hosting service for me too. I know he'll fix you up right."

"He already has," Craig said, gesturing toward the computer behind the counter. "Want to take a look?"

He typed in the address, and up popped a photo of Craig's nursery and surrounding land. Natural looking greens and blues dominated the page, with large, helpful buttons to the left where a customer could click for more information.

A photo of Craig leaning against the side of a weathered post, dressed in blue jeans and work shirt, was also positioned on the page. "You look like the quintessential gardener," Jane said. "Hank did a lot of work quickly. And it looks great."

"He's been working on it for a few weeks," Craig said, "but I did ask him to rush things yesterday when I found out

I would be attending the garden show. Check this out too. It's my motto."

He scrolled to the bottom of the page, where Jane read "Wild Things Were Meant to Be Grown."

"Do you like it?" he asked.

"It's great! It incorporates the name of your business and says how you feel about native plants. It will build an effective 'brand,' I believe marketers call it."

"Exactly. I plan to get Carlene to help me make up some brochures and press releases to take to the garden show, announcing my native plant venture. The brochures will be for anyone, but I'm hoping the press releases will generate some extra interest with the media. Carlene told me that she would write an article, of course, but to gain business outside the Acorn Hill area, I have to cast a wider net to gain attention."

Jane laughed. "I think that net is going to gain you *lots* of attention."

Louise agreed to wait for the Havertys, and Alice headed to the *Nutshell*. She wanted to hear how Carlene's visit from the man interested in the typesetting equipment had gone. Remembering how the telephone receiver kept slipping from Carlene's shoulder during their last conversation, Alice decided it would be better to see Carlene in person.

The newspaper editor wasn't at her accustomed spot at the front of the office. Rather, she was standing at the back of the room with a short, bald stranger in a tweed suit and bow tie. "Hi, Alice," Carlene said, waving. "Come back here."

The stranger bobbed at the waist and extended his hand. "How do you do? You must be Alice Howard. I'm David Nix. Miss Moss tells me that you were instrumental in gaining my attention."

"I beg your pardon?" Alice said, bewildered.

"He's the friend of Irene Watts who's interested in the typesetting equipment," Carlene said. "He came out yesterday and asked if he could look around again today."

"Beautiful old equipment," David said, turning. "You don't often see printing history like this anymore. You see, Miss Howard, early printed books were made using wooden blocks with text carved on them. These were turned into a plate for printing. Then Johannes Gutenberg . . . I'm sure you've heard of him?"

"Yes. Something about a Bible, I believe," Alice said, smiling.

"Exactly. He invented movable type in the fifteenth century, which allowed Bibles, and other books, to be produced and shared with the masses. It was quite popular."

"I can imagine," Alice said dryly.

"Anyway," David went on, really wound up now, his hands gesturing with animation, "movable type is also called hot type because each piece with the raised image of a letter was cast from molten metal. Strung together, these letters were inked for printing and were called the face. That's where we get the term *typeface*."

Alice knew that Carlene gave a similar lecture when she hosted school field trips. She exchanged a glance with Carlene, and they each smiled covertly. "That's interesting," she said to be polite. "Please go on, Mr. Nix."

"Do you know those shadow boxes that a lot of people use to display little knickknacks?" he asked.

Alice nodded.

"The cubbyholes in the box were originally used by printers to keep individual letters and numbers separate," he said. "Compositors lined up the letters they needed on a composing stick, then put spaces between the words till they filled up the line. They would set up the newspaper that way, line by line. The type was backward, though, because it would face the correct way when it was inked and paper pressed directly on the type. When the newspaper had been printed, the type was taken apart, cleaned and put back in the box until it was needed again."

"Your father had one of those boxes, didn't he, Carlene?" Alice asked.

"Right here. I got it out when Mr. Nix arrived." Carlene retrieved a wooden box from behind the typesetting equipment. The box was still filled with various letters and numbers, faint traces of ink still staining them. "He inherited it from his father," she said proudly.

"Obviously this wasn't an efficient method of disseminating news," David said. "Although I understand that some of the old-timers were quite speedy at setting the type. Their fingers quickly learned the locations of the individual letters, and the best setters could accomplish their work without even looking."

"I wonder how many people could do that today," Alice said, feeling a bit nostalgic.

"Good question," David said. "It's a lost trade. Just like operating a Linotype, this beautiful old machine here. Compositors set lines of type using a keyboard, which transferred the assembled text to a mold-making device. Metal was forced into the mold, which hardened to make bars with raised letters.

"A teletypewriter was added to this Linotype around 1913. It controlled composition with a perforated tape, which was punched on a separate keyboard. A tape-reader translated the punched code into electrical signals that could be sent by wire to tape-punching units in many cities simultaneously. The duplicate tapes were used to operate linecasting machines like the Linotype."

Carlene and Alice exchanged another tolerant glance. It was clear that David Nix knew and loved his subject. He was wound up like a child's top as he shared his knowledge.

He moved to another machine, this one more sleek and

modern looking. "After the Linotype, printing evolved to photo-mechanical composition that involved disks of films, drums with typefaces that rotated at high speed in front of lenses, and light that projected a character onto film."

"Today of course we have desktop publishing and laser technology," Carlene said. She shook her head somewhat sadly. "My father would have been amazed."

"What a blessing it was for Gutenberg to have invented movable type in his day," Alice said, "and the advances of the last one hundred years have been extraordinary as well."

"It boggles the mind to think about how far we will no doubt go in the future," David said. "At any rate, Miss Moss, you have quite a piece of history in your office here."

"Thank you. I'm quite proud of it," Carlene said.

"Would you consider selling? I'm a dealer of antiques, particularly of printing-related items. I know a gentleman who would be very interested in these machines."

"I'm afraid I wouldn't be interested," Carlene said. "This equipment has always been with the *Nutshell*."

"Forgive me," he said, smiling apologetically. "I should have made you an offer." He named a large sum.

Carlene's jaw dropped. She closed it and swallowed hard. "You're joking, right?"

David shook his head.

"So much?" Carlene said. She glanced at Alice as if to ask if she could believe it either.

"I assure you that the buyer would take excellent care of the equipment. It wouldn't be allowed to deteriorate."

Carlene snorted. "For that price, I would hope not. What does he want it for?"

"That, I'm not at liberty to divulge. He likes to keep his privacy." He withdrew a silver case from inside his jacket, then took out a card from it. "I can see you'll want some time to think about it. Let me give you my card. I'll be in Potterston until next Friday." He scribbled on the back of the card. "Here's where I can be contacted. I hope you can reach a positive decision by then."

Carlene accepted the card, her fingers trembling as though he were already handing her hard cash for the purchase. "Thank you, Mr. Nix."

He shook her hand, then covered it with his other. "You will think about it, won't you? Please don't dismiss the offer out of hand."

Carlene laughed. "Oh, I'll think about it all right. I don't know anyone who couldn't use that kind of money, let alone a single woman trying to keep the small-town newspaper afloat."

"Good. It was nice to talk with you. And nice to meet you, Miss Howard. Thank you for setting all this in motion."

"Nice to meet you too," Alice returned. Did he have to remind her and Carlene that she had been the one to instigate this situation?

When he had gone, Carlene collapsed into her desk chair. "Well! Did you *hear* how much he offered me, Alice?"

"It was quite a lot."

"*A lot?* I could move to a condo in Philly. I could upgrade the *Nutshell*. I could purchase new equipment and update my printing and production methods."

"You wouldn't leave Acorn Hill, would you?" Alice said, alarmed.

"I'd have to think long and hard about it," Carlene said, grinning, then when she saw Alice's shocked expression, she said, "Oh, I'm just teasing, Alice. This is my home."

"Yes, but the money . . ." Alice said faintly.

"It *is* something to think about," Carlene said, resting her elbows on the desk, chin in her hands.

Alice had a feeling that that was *all* Carlene would think about for the next week.

∽

Late that afternoon, Louise finished her last piano lesson for the day. She noticed afterward that her fingers felt a little stiff, or maybe they were simply itching to run free across the keys instead of restricting themselves to showing Bobby Pfiffer how to execute scales and arpeggios.

She sat at the baby grand and played a few warm-up scales and arpeggios of her own. Then she let her fingers slip automatically into Beethoven's "Moonlight Sonata." It wasn't a particularly difficult piece for her, but its haunting melody seemed to fit her mood lately.

When she had played all three movements, she sat back, flushed. To her surprise, she heard applause.

Walter and Kathleen Haverty rose from the Victorian chairs against the wall. "Beautiful," Kathleen said, smiling.

Walter nodded. "I hope you don't mind, but we heard you playing and snuck in. We didn't want to interrupt your Beethoven. You played the piece beautifully."

"And we also enjoyed the free concert," Kathleen added with a wink.

Louise smiled. "I'm sorry I didn't hear you come in. We have been expecting you, of course."

"We don't doubt that," Walter said. "You ladies are always the best hostesses of any we encounter in our travels."

"Grace Chapel Inn feels like our home away from home now," Kathleen said. "I think even if we didn't drive this way to visit our son, we would want to come here."

"Thank you," Louise said. "That's quite a compliment. I'm sure you two travel quite a bit with your musical group, Walter."

"Oh, we do, and let me tell you, this place is A-OK. I was thinking about bringing the entire band up here to visit sometime. We love our home state of Texas, but we love good company, good digs and good food as well. We might just have to find us a place to play around these parts so that we could combine business with pleasure. Know anybody who needs to hire a band for a special occasion?"

Louise laughed. "I'm afraid I don't. You might have more luck in Philadelphia, though."

Walter tugged thoughtfully on his goatee. "I used to spend a lot of time in the East years and years ago. I might ought to look into drumming up some business here again. Everybody likes good country-western music."

Louise couldn't in good conscience agree, but she held her tongue. That Walter, a musician with such popular tastes, appreciated classical music was something of a mystery to her. Well, everyone was familiar with the "Moonlight Sonata." That probably explained his enthusiasm and his familiarity with Beethoven.

"Let me show you to your room," she said, heading for the door.

"No bother," Walter boomed cheerfully. "We're not like calves balking at a new gate around here. We'll find our own way."

"We put you in the Sunset Room again," Louise said. "We thought that you would like that."

"Wonderful," Walter boomed. "It reminds us of the West, doesn't it, Kathleen?"

"It does," she said, nodding.

"Jane thought you might like to have a reminder of Texas, so she plans to make something called Alamo waffles tomorrow for breakfast," Louise said.

Walter Haverty looked at his wife and called out in glee, "Oh boy!"

Chapter Eleven

Saturday morning, the next day, Alice laced up her walking shoes and headed downstairs, full of enthusiasm. She didn't have to work, and she felt like a kid enjoying a summer break from school. She often thought it would be wonderful if all working people got two-month summer vacations.

She voiced the same belief to her good friend Vera Humbert as they started out on their walk together. Vera was a fifth-grade teacher at Acorn Hill's elementary school, and she and Alice had been close friends for a long time.

"Having summers off is one of my favorite perks of being a teacher," Vera said. "It just wouldn't be the same if we got, say, *winter* months off. We'd have to spend a lot of that time indoors, but summer allows you to kick off your shoes and run barefoot through the grass. That's what I remember about being a schoolgirl on summer break."

"Even though I don't get summers off from nursing since I switched to part-time work, I often experience the same freedom," Alice confessed. "For some reason, summertime always reminds me of checking out a stack of books from the library. Not books that I had to read for school, but books from a series like the Bobbsey Twins or the Cherry Ames nurse books."

"I was a Nancy Drew fan myself," Vera said. She nudged Alice in the side with an elbow and nodded across the street in the direction of the library. "Why don't we go inside and check out a few fun children's books? I love to do that during the summer."

Alice smiled. "Oh, Vera, I really don't have the time to—"

"What? You don't have time to have fun? Come on, let's go in. Besides, it'll be nice to see Nia. I don't see her as much as I'd like."

"Well, I suppose you're right," Alice said, allowing herself to be persuaded. She *could* use something fun to read.

Inside the library Nia was sorting books that had recently been checked in. She looked up from her work and smiled when she saw Vera and Alice. "Hello, ladies. Out for a stroll?"

"Yes, and we decided we wanted to check out some fun literature," Vera said.

"I just received some new mysteries and women's fiction," Nia said, gesturing toward the new-book section. "Then there's—"

Vera shook her head. "We're interested in children's literature."

"Getting a head start on school this fall?"

Vera laughed. "No, Alice and I are regressing, I think. We were talking about how much we enjoyed reading during the summer when we were girls, and we decided to stop in and find some kids' books to read."

"I think that's a great idea," Nia said. "Do you need any help? Any recommendations?"

"Thank you, but I'd just like to browse," Alice said.

"Me too," Vera chimed in.

They headed straight for the children's section. When they had passed the plastic play tables and beanbag chairs by the front window, they nearly tripped over Lloyd, seated on the floor.

"Why, Lloyd Tynan," Vera said, laying a hand over her heart. "You nearly frightened the daylights out of me. What on earth are you doing down there?"

"Oh, I didn't hear you ladies." He glanced up from a stack of books piled beside him. He had discarded several volumes that lay strewn about.

Alice smiled. "You have the same idea we did, Lloyd. Vera and I decided to look for children's books to read this summer."

"I wish these were for me," he said. "I'm trying to select some books for Acorn Hill's children's summer reading list." He seemed to sway a bit and reached out toward a shelf to steady himself.

"Why, Lloyd, I could have helped you with that," Vera said. "Nia could have suggested books too."

Lloyd snapped a handkerchief from his pocket and wiped his forehead. Alice noticed with concern that he was sweating and that his breathing seemed labored. "I feel like it's my responsibility, Vera, though I appreciate the—Oh my."

Alice took one look at his face, then pressed on his back to encourage him to lean over. "Put your head between your knees."

"*Whaaa?*" he said. He sounded confused, but he complied. "I just feel a little dizzy," he mumbled.

"Exactly," Alice said. "Let the blood rush to your head for a moment." She signaled to Vera that she should get Nia.

"Where's she going?" Lloyd managed to ask.

Alice leaned over and noticed that his face looked as white as the pages of the books on the floor. "You need to go home, Lloyd. You look exhausted."

Lloyd started to rise. "Why, there's no need—"

"*Shh.*" Alice pressed his shoulders back down so that he remained slumped over. "You don't want to faint. I think you should get checked out by a doctor."

He started to protest again, then abruptly his face softened. "I've been feeling tired lately."

Nia knelt beside the mayor. "What's wrong? Are you all right, Lloyd?"

"I'm fine. Just a little tired." Lloyd groaned. "If word gets out that I'm not well, no one may want me to be mayor anymore."

"Acorn Hill will always want you to be mayor," Alice said soothingly. "Is that why you've been working so hard?"

Lloyd looked sheepish.

Alice felt a wave of sorrow for him. However he had got it into his head that he had to work so hard, he was needlessly paying a price now. "Is there anyone here who can drive Lloyd home, Nia? I can always go get my car, but that will take time, and I think Dr. Bentley needs to see Lloyd as soon as possible. He should be in bed, resting."

Nia nodded. "Gerald Morton is here. Let me see if he can drive Lloyd." She rose and headed away from the children's section. Vera took his hand. "We'll wait right here with you, Lloyd," she said. Nia returned with Gerald Morton close behind her. A burly man with strong muscles, Gerald worked construction projects in Potterston but lived on the edges of Acorn Hill. He took one look at Lloyd and grinned. "You look like you need a good rest."

Lloyd groaned. "That's what these alarmist women keep telling me."

"Now, Lloyd," Alice cautioned. "You told me yourself that you've been feeling tired lately. Let Gerald drive you home, and I'll send Dr. Bentley out to look at you, all right?"

Lloyd looked like he wanted to protest, but he smiled weakly, giving in. "All right," he said in a small voice.

While Gerald helped Lloyd to his feet, Alice turned to Nia. "Thank you, you've been very kind," she said.

"Is there anything else we can do?" the librarian asked, her dark eyes showing her concern.

"I think we should pray," Vera said. She closed her eyes and offered a short petition for Lloyd's health. Everyone joined her, including Lloyd, who seemed to be resting easier when she finished. Alice noticed that a little color had returned to his face too.

Before long they had assisted Lloyd into the backseat of Gerald Morton's large, old Buick.

"I'll tell Dr. Bentley to come over as soon as possible," Alice promised. Lloyd saluted weakly before Gerald drove away.

"I need to call Fred," Vera said. "And we should tell Ethel, don't you think?"

"Yes, as gently as possible. And my sisters will want to know. Do you mind if we stop by my house? You could call Fred from there."

When they reached Grace Chapel Inn, Alice found Louise entertaining the Havertys in the parlor.

"Is everything all right?" Louise asked, noticing the distress on her sister's face.

"I need to call Dr. Bentley," Alice said. "Lloyd nearly passed out at the library."

"*What?*"

Jane popped in from the kitchen, floured rolling pin in hand. "What did I hear about Lloyd?"

"Does anyone know if Aunt Ethel's home?" Alice asked. "I need to let her know."

"About what?" Jane demanded. "What's this about Lloyd?"

"We were at the library," Vera said, "and we found Lloyd there, looking through a big stack of children's books. He was working on some summer reading project."

"He looked ready to faint," Alice said. "Gerald Morton has taken him home. I want Dr. Bentley to have a look at him as soon as possible."

"Oh my goodness," Louise said.

"Is there anything we can do to help?" Walter Haverty asked.

"Oh no, but thank you," Alice said. "I'm sorry to interrupt your time with Louise, but this matter requires our attention."

"Of course it does," Kathleen Haverty said. "Do whatever you need to."

Alice ducked out of the room, heading for the phone.

"We need to tell Aunt Ethel," Louise said. "Would someone please . . . now where did Jane go?"

"Why, she was just right here," Vera said.

"Here I am," Jane said, bustling back into the room, half dragging Ethel by the elbow. "I didn't wait to hear what was wrong, I just went to get Aunt Ethel."

Ethel looked bewildered, her hair wrapped in a large shower cap and a towel draped across her shoulders. "What's going on?"

Louise wrapped an arm around her aunt and explained gently, "Lloyd nearly fainted at the library, Auntie. Gerald Morton's taken him home, and Alice is calling Dr. Bentley to come look at him."

"Oh no! Oh, my poor Lloyd! Will someone please take me to him?" She glanced from one niece to the other. "I'm such a wreck."

She reached up and touched the shower cap. "My hair! I just finished washing it when Jane rushed in. Now what am I going to do? I have to get to Lloyd."

"Just blow dry it as usual, Aunt Ethel. You'll have time to get yourself together, and I'll drive you," Jane said.

Alice stepped back into the room. "Dr. Bentley said he would head right over to Lloyd's house. I'd like to hear what he says."

"Me too," Vera said.

"Thank goodness we can still count on a doctor to make house calls here in Acorn Hill." Jane clasped her hands in a gesture of gratitude.

"I'll stay here and take care of the inn," Louise said.

"Vera, why don't you call Fred while Aunt Ethel is drying her hair?"

"I'll turn off the oven and store the cookie batter in the

refrigerator for later," Jane said. "Come on, ladies. Let's meet back here in ten minutes."

Jane drove with Vera sitting in the front seat. In the back, Ethel leaned against Alice's shoulder, sobbing. "I told that man he was working too hard. And now something bad's happened to him, and . . ."

She sobbed once again, then blew her nose loudly into a handkerchief. "There there, Aunt Ethel," Alice said, drawing her aunt closer. "I'm sure he's fine. We would have called for an ambulance, otherwise."

"Yes, I'm sure it's just fatigue," Jane said. "Hang on, Auntie."

At Lloyd's house, they rushed inside. Dr. Bentley's car was already parked out front, alongside Gerald Morton's Buick. The construction worker was waiting in Lloyd's living room. "The doc just got here," he said, helping himself to a magazine from Lloyd's coffee table as though he were in a hospital waiting room.

Jane looked bemused. "We might as well all have a seat," she said, picking up a *Politics for Local Governments* magazine from the table.

Alice wondered if she should go back to help Dr. Bentley; she anxiously watched the hallway for signs of him.

At last he appeared, and he strode out to meet them. "Why, hello, everybody," he said, looking surprised to see such a large group.

"Hello, Dr. Bentley," Alice said. "We're all concerned about Lloyd."

"Hello, Ethel," Dr. Bentley said, shaking her hand. "Lloyd mentioned you several times during my examination. He's concerned about you."

"About *me*?" Ethel said, sniffling. "Oh, that crazy man. *He's* the one who's sick."

"I should have phrased that better. He was concerned how you would take the news about him."

"I won't do well until I know he's going to be better," she said, dabbing at her eyes with the corner of the handkerchief.

"How is he, Doctor?" Jane asked.

"I don't think he needs any major tests, but I did recommend that he get some routine blood work done when he's feeling a little rested. I don't expect to find anything wrong. I think with lots of rest and less work for a while, he'll be feeling as good as new."

"That's a relief," Alice said, and the others indicated their agreement. "Thank you, Dr. Bentley."

Ethel frowned. "I warned that man over and over not to work so hard. If anything happens to him, why, I'll strangle him with my own two hands."

Jane grinned. "That's the spirit."

"Oh, I don't know what I'm saying. Thank the good Lord it wasn't anything more serious."

"Amen to that," Jane said.

"I want him to rest," Dr. Bentley said. "I've given him strict orders to cut back on his workload."

"Thank you, Doctor," Alice said. "We appreciate all you've done."

Dr. Bentley smiled at everyone, patted Ethel's shoulder, and left the house. Gerald Morton left, too, with the women expressing their gratitude for his help.

"I'm so glad it wasn't anything more serious," Vera said to the others.

"It's still serious enough that he needs to change his lifestyle," Alice said. "Stress *can* lead to all kinds of health problems."

"What can we do to help Lloyd?" Jane asked. "He's been working so hard lately. Is there any way we can help him relax?"

"Oh, he'll learn to relax," Ethel said, setting her face and grinding her fists together as though entering a prizefight, "or rest assured he'll answer to *me*."

Chapter Twelve

Once Louise got the good news about Lloyd, she was able to relax with the Havertys. They had chatted about music, and she was surprised that Walter knew quite a bit about the classics. She would have thought that a "fiddle" player would be concerned exclusively with country-western, hoedown, square dance—or whatever they called it—music.

When Walter spoke of his favorite classical music, his folksy demeanor did not change, his country accent did not fade, and his sense of humor did not diminish. After years of living with Eliot, she was accustomed to academic discussions about music. Walter Haverty held his own there but also infused his conversation with a love for the music that she had spent much of her life studying and performing.

"Yes ma'am, I dearly love the classics. I keep telling the boys in my band that they need to study the old masters if they really want to learn how to play," he said. "But I'm afraid if the composer's name isn't Hank Williams, Bob Wills or Porter Wagoner, they aren't a bit interested."

Louise felt bewildered. "I'm sorry . . . who?"

Kathleen smiled. Walter roared in laughter, slapping his knee. "You're a funny one, Louise. I can see who has all the humor in your family."

Louise smiled faintly, not certain whether to be flattered or flabbergasted.

"Hoo, that was a good one," Walter said, wiping his eyes.

Kathleen glanced at her husband then back at Louise. "How is the organ at your church?" she asked, gently redirecting the conversation. "Before we left you mentioned that it was in need of repair."

Louise sighed. "I'm afraid that we are in no better shape than we were during your last visit. In fact, things appear to be worse." She briefly detailed what had happened in the past few days with Myron Apodaca's evaluation, the church board's forming an organ committee, and the members' division about what should be done.

"So now we will check our available funds and estimate what we think we can spend. That will determine whether restoration or replacement is in order."

Walter tugged gently at his goatee, contemplating. "Sounds like you also might want another evaluation," he said, sufficiently recovered from his chuckling. "A second opinion, so to speak."

"It would be a shame if the committee recommended replacement without getting a second evaluation," Kathleen said. She shook her head. "It's such a beautiful old organ."

"It is," Louise said, "but anything we undertake will depend on whatever we can come up with financially. Grace Chapel doesn't have an organ fund. Yet, anyway. Perhaps the committee will recommend we begin one. We are meeting tomorrow night to discuss the situation."

"Well, let's just hope and pray that you're able to save the old girl," Walter said.

"You just can't replace a beautiful old instrument like that," Kathleen added. "I wish we could stay and hear you play tomorrow, but we have to leave soon to get on the road."

"Would you do us the honor of favoring us with a tune on the piano?" Walter asked.

"Why . . . certainly," Louise said, surprised that he would ask, but more than willing to oblige. "Is there anything in particular that you would like to hear?"

Walter thought for a moment. "How about something you learned at the conservatory?"

"That was so many years ago," Louise said, laughing lightly, "but I think I recall one that I learned when I was still in school."

She positioned herself at the piano, her fingers hovering over the keys a moment before they moved into action. She chose something short, "Of Foreign Lands and People" by Robert Schumann, because she didn't want to bore the Havertys.

While she played, she thought about Eliot. He had used this particular song when he instructed her in music theory, and it always reminded her of him. The music had taken a bittersweet place in her heart since his death.

When she finished, she paused for a moment, letting the last tones of the final note ring from the piano. Then she raised her hands from the keyboard. Walter Haverty was smiling, but he also wiped his eyes. "That was just beautiful," he said. "It reminds me of my early musician days."

"It was lovely," Kathleen agreed.

"You must miss your husband very much," Walter said.

"Why . . . yes," Louise said. "But why do you say that?"

"Oh, no reason," he said. "Your face took on kind of a pensive look, and I thought maybe you were thinking of him." He rose abruptly, clearing his throat. "Kathleen, we had better get a move on if we're going get going before noon."

Before heading to Grace Chapel for services the next morning, the sisters invited Theo Dulane to attend with them. He politely declined but did accept their invitation to dinner.

The sisters exchanged a knowing glance, hoping that Rev. Thompson would still be able to join them. It would be good for Theo to meet with him.

After the service, Rev. Thompson greeted Alice and Jane. "Hello, ladies."

"Hello, Pastor Ken. We're so glad you'll be joining us for dinner today," Jane said.

"Yes," Alice said. "Our guest, Theo Dulane has already agreed to dine with us."

"I'm delighted," he said, smiling.

They hurried back to Grace Chapel Inn and finished setting the places at the dining room table. Louise followed them after she had tidied up the organ area and put her music away.

"I thought the organ sounded better today," Alice said to Louise as they set out the silverware.

"Thank you, Alice, but if I didn't know better, I would say that you're just trying to spare my feelings," Louise said.

"You caught me," Alice said, smiling.

"Am I late?" Theo said, clearing his throat.

"Not at all, Mr. Dulane," Alice said, ushering him into the room. "Please have a seat. Jane will be serving lunch soon. We've invited our pastor for dinner, as well."

"You . . . ?" Theo had started to sit, but stood up. "Maybe this wouldn't be a good—"

"Nonsense," Louise said, smiling and putting a hand on his shoulder. "Please have a seat. Pastor Ken is an old friend."

"And since he doesn't have a wife, we often invite him to Sunday dinner," Alice said.

"Oh," Theo said. "Well, I guess it will be all right."

The doorbell rang, and Louise smiled. "That must be Pastor Ken now."

Theo looked worriedly at Alice. "You didn't invite him to dinner so that he could chastise me for inviting you to dinner the other night, did you?"

"No," Alice said, a little too hurriedly. "That is . . ."

"I understand how it is," Theo said, looking miserable. "Well, I suppose it's the medicine I must take for being so forward."

"It's not like that, Mr. Dulane," Alice said. "I understood that you were lonely and wanted someone to talk to."

Theo didn't answer, but stared down at his empty plate.

"Here's Pastor Ken," Louise said cheerfully, leading the way into the parlor. "This is Theo Dulane. Mr. Dulane, this is the pastor of Grace Chapel and our dear friend, Pastor Kenneth Thompson."

"How do you do, Pastor?" Theo said halfheartedly, extending a hand. He scarcely looked up.

"I'm fine, Mr. Dulane." Rev. Thompson shook his hand. "It's a pleasure to meet you."

Jane entered the dining room from the kitchen, bearing a platter of pork chops and a plate of spiced baked apples. "Dinner is ready, if everyone will have a seat."

Louise arranged it so that Rev. Thompson sat next to Theo Dulane. Alice sat across from Theo, wondering if this arranged introduction had been a good idea after all. Theo kept his head down during the meal as if waiting for the Sword of Damocles to fall on him. He barely said anything beyond "Please pass the apples" or "Thank you." Alice felt uneasy to think that they might have caused more grief for one of their guests.

Meanwhile, Rev. Thompson kept the conversation moving with humorous stories and light talk. He spoke lovingly of Acorn Hill and its inhabitants, but not in a way that excluded Theo. He tried to draw Theo into the conversation, but he was not to be engaged.

When the meal was over, Alice helped Jane to clear the table. In the kitchen, Jane whispered, "That didn't go over very well, did it?"

"I'm afraid not," Alice said. "I think we did more harm than good to poor Mr. Dulane. He confided to me that he thinks we invited Pastor Ken to chastise him for inviting me to dinner."

"Oh no," Jane said. "The poor man. No wonder he looks so miserable. Hopefully, Pastor Ken has put him at ease by now."

"I hope so," Alice said doubtfully, then lifted several plates of coconut cake to serve.

Back in the dining room, she was surprised to find that Rev. Thompson had somehow managed to engage Theo in a conversation. He was actually looking up from his plate, and he smiled at something Rev. Thompson said when Alice set a plate of cake in front of the guest. "Why, thank you," he said to her, as though surprised to be served dessert.

"You're welcome," Alice said, sitting down again. "I didn't mean to interrupt your conversation," she said to the men. "Please continue."

"We were discussing fishing," Rev. Thompson said. "I was recalling the summers I spent as a child fishing on my grandfather's boat. It turns out that Mr. Dulane is an avid fisherman."

"Please call me Theo, Pastor," he said. "Yes, I do love fishing, Miss Howard. It was the one interest that I shared apart from my dear Laverne. My wife passed away recently, Pastor." His face fell into a glum expression again.

"I understand," Pastor said gently. "I'm a widower myself."

Theo glanced up, blinking with surprise. Rev. Thompson wiped his mouth and laid his napkin to the side. "I was thinking about hitting a wonderful fishing spot that I know of not far from here. Would you like to join me . . . Theo? I have extra gear."

Theo appeared to waver for a moment. Alice held her

breath, a forkful of coconut cake suspended in midair. Theo's expression softened, and he smiled at Rev. Thompson. "I'd love to. When can we leave?"

"Let me change into more suitable fishing clothes, and I'll meet you back here in fifteen minutes," Rev. Thompson said.

Theo nodded his head in agreement. The two men excused themselves from the women, gave their compliments to Jane for the wonderful meal, then all but bolted from the dining room.

"What is it about fishing with some men?" Jane said, finishing her cake.

"It's wonderful that they have found something in common," Louise said.

"Yes," Alice agreed. "I was afraid that Theo was going to be angry at us for certain."

"Well *I'm* angry all right," Jane said.

"Why?" Louise and Alice glanced up, shocked.

Grinning, Jane gestured at Theo and Rev. Thompson's half-full dessert plates. "They didn't finish my cake."

Alice helped Jane to clean up the dishes, and afterward decided to head over to Carlene's. She knew that Carlene occasionally had to work on Sunday, but thought that perhaps she was free today. She wondered if her friend had given any more thought to David Nix's offer to buy the *Nutshell*'s old typesetting equipment.

Carlene lived one street over from Vera and Fred Humbert in a quiet, tree-shaded residential area. Alice rang the doorbell and waited.

No answer.

Alice rang again, just to be certain, but she knew that Carlene was probably at the *Nutshell* office after all. When she was home on Sundays, Carlene usually sat in the front room after lunch, reading the newspaper.

Again, no answer.

"Oh well," Alice said. She decided against bothering Carlene at the *Nutshell*. She probably did not need a visitor while she was trying to work. Alice realized that she could always return home, call and leave a message on Carlene's machine; but she decided that as long as she was at her friend's home, she would scribble a quick note to let Carlene know she had stopped by.

"Sorry I missed you," Alice said out loud as she wrote on a piece of scrap paper from her purse. "Let me know what you've decided about the equipment. Alice." She carefully folded the paper and tucked it between the screen door and the jamb.

The walk back to Grace Chapel Inn was delightful. A hint of summer breeze played through her hair, and the sun warmed her face. Several young children rolled past on skateboards, skates and scooters, whooping with delight. Once again, the memories of summer youth stirred in Alice, and she recalled that she had never checked out any juvenile books from the library.

Then she remembered that Aunt Ethel had planned to spend the day with Lloyd, who was home recuperating. Jane had volunteered to make Lloyd a meal, and Alice had promised to deliver it with her. It was probably just as well that Carlene hadn't been at home.

As she headed up Chapel Road and toward home, she saw a shiny, two-seater, silver convertible zip past. David Nix sat behind the wheel, driving a bit faster than the posted speed limit, and Carlene sat in the passenger's seat. Carlene laughed at something David had said and leaned her head back to feel the wind.

"Carlene!" Alice called, hoping to catch the attention of

her friend, but the breeze took her words and carried them out of hearing distance.

David and Carlene zoomed out of town, and Alice stood at the corner, just outside Fred Humbert's hardware store, staring after them. *Well, I'll be. Could there be a little romance in the air?*

She smiled and headed for home.

Jane stirred the vegetable soup one last time, then turned off the burner and dished the hot broth into a glass container. In her opinion, soup did not transport well nor taste good in plastic.

With the container topped with a lid and ready to be fer-ried to Lloyd's, she drew homemade French bread out of the oven to cool. Soup and bread could cure any illness, she believed, particularly Lloyd's fatigue. He needed pampering and coddling, and she would do her best to put him on the road to recovery with some of her best homemade comfort food.

Alice entered through the back door. "Oh good," Jane said. "I'm almost ready to head over to Lloyd's, and I was hoping you could drive me. I don't want the soup container to tip over on the way. You do feel like going, don't you?" she asked, peering into Alice's bemused face. "What's up?"

"I'd be glad to go," Alice said, then smiled. "As for 'what's up' . . ."

"Out with it," Jane said. Alice bit her lip, as if trying to suppress another smile. "It's probably nothing, Jane. It's just that that David Nix offered Carlene a lot of money to sell the typesetting equipment."

Jane nodded. "Go on."

"I went to Carlene's house to see if she had decided about the matter, and she wasn't home. Later, while I was walking up Chapel Road, I saw her in David Nix's car."

"So?" Jane shrugged.

"It was a really nice car, Jane, an expensive convertible. Carlene almost looked like a girl again, riding with him."

Jane smiled. "Sounds like she was having a good time. That's good. She works too hard."

"Yes," Alice said, then paused. "You don't think it's something like a conflict of interest since he wants to buy the printing equipment, do you?"

"No. I think a woman is entitled to a little fun, that's all. She'll reach the decision that's best for her *and* the *Nutshell*, I'm sure. Now if you'll wait just a moment, I want to wrap this bread while it's warm. Then I'll be ready to leave for Lloyd's. How about you?"

"I'm ready," Alice said, letting Jane's words dispel her concerns about Carlene and David Nix.

Chapter ⛪ Thirteen

Jane got into the front passenger seat of Alice's car, and Alice handed her the container of soup. She held it carefully, as though it were a small child, and Alice set the loaf of French bread between the front seats.

"Careful," Jane said, overprotective of the bread too. "We don't want it to break."

Alice smiled as she slid behind the wheel. "I'll drive as slowly as possible and change gears only when necessary."

"Good," Jane said, reluctant to catch on to any humor when it involved her cooking. "I don't want your gear shift to hurt the bread."

They drove to Lloyd's house, which was a former Quaker meeting place. Ethel opened the door for them, looking more chipper than when they had seen her the day before.

"Come in, girls, come in," she said cheerfully, ushering them inside. "Lloyd will be so delighted that you stopped by."

"I brought him some of my vegetable soup and French bread," Jane said. "The soup is full of nutrients and vitamins— everything he needs to get back on his feet."

"And it tastes good too, I know," Ethel said. "Right this way, and let's set it in the kitchen. I'll heat it up for dinner tonight."

"Great," Jane said, as Alice placed the container on a

counter next to Lloyd's old-fashioned stove. "You might want to simmer it. It could still stand a little cooking down."

"Oh, the bread is still warm," Ethel said, taking the loaf out of Jane's hands. "It looks delicious. Lloyd will appreciate this so much."

"Tell him that I'll cook him something for tomorrow too," Jane said.

"You can tell him yourself," Ethel said.

"We don't want to bother him if he's resting," Alice said.

"I'm not allowing him to see just anybody," Ethel said. "Besides"—she winked—"you're some of his favorite people."

"We won't stay long," Alice assured her.

"Right this way," Ethel said, leading her nieces through the house as though she were its owner.

Alice glanced at Jane, her eyes twinkling. Jane coughed to cover a smile. Ethel had apparently taken charge of Lloyd, his health *and* his home. If it were anyone else, it would be irritating, but because it was Ethel and they knew how much she cared for Lloyd, it was endearing.

Lloyd, propped up in bed by what looked to be ten fluffy pillows, was reading the Sunday Philadelphia paper. He wore maroon silk pajamas and seemed much more relaxed than either of the sisters could remember seeing him in a long time.

When he saw them, he laid the newspaper aside. "Hello, ladies."

"Hi Lloyd," Jane said, leaning over to kiss him on the forehead.

"It's good to see you looking better," Alice said, taking his hand. "Vera and I were worried when we came across you at the library."

"Yes, and I have *you* to thank for acting so promptly," Lloyd said. "I would have gone on pushing myself and trying to do everything—"

"—And probably would have flat-out collapsed," Ethel finished for him.

Lloyd looked embarrassed. "Your aunt is right," he said. "I tried to do too much by myself."

"But why?" Alice asked.

"Because he's an insecure old coot," Ethel said. "And don't you glare at me, Lloyd Tynan. You know it's true. You confessed as much to me."

Lloyd turned to Alice and Jane. "She's right, though perhaps I wouldn't have phrased it quite like that." He shot Ethel a glance. "I attended a national mayors' conference in Boston two months ago. Listening to all those other hotshot mayors talk about the programs they organize in their towns, the committees they organize to study problems ... I just felt like I wasn't doing enough for Acorn Hill and needed to put forth more of an effort."

"But Lloyd, Acorn Hill is a small town," Alice said. "We don't need all the programs that larger cities need."

"And besides," Jane put in, "you weren't asking anyone to assist you. You were trying to do it all by yourself."

"And that was my mistake," Lloyd said, hanging his head. "I was too puffed up with pride."

"But that's going to change, isn't it?" Ethel said, prodding him gently on the shoulder.

"Yes, it is," he said. "When I go back to work . . . which won't be for a few days yet," he said, catching a heated look from Ethel, "I'll go through my To Do list and pare it down or delegate responsibilities."

"As it should be," Ethel said, nodding her head once, sagely.

Lloyd gave her a sidelong, indulging glance. "Meanwhile," he turned to the sisters, "what is new in your worlds?"

"Louise is preparing for the organ committee meeting tonight. You'll be there, Aunt Ethel, won't you?" Alice asked.

"Yes. I've already arranged for Wilhelm Wood to sit with Lloyd while I'm gone."

"*Sit?* I don't need fussing over every minute," Lloyd grumbled.

"Nevertheless," Ethel proceeded, "someone should be here in case you need anything."

"Confound it, woman," Lloyd began, then grew meek under her steady gaze. "Oh, very well."

Ethel crossed her arms, triumphant.

"Anyway," Jane continued, hoping to redirect the conversation. "Did you hear about Craig Tracy attending the garden show in Philadelphia next weekend?"

"I did hear something about his new, native plant venture," Lloyd said. "Tell me more."

Jane cheerfully obliged, making Lloyd fully informed. "And so I volunteered to go with Craig to Philadelphia, along with—"

"No," Ethel said.

"No?" Jane said, her expression puzzled.

"No. It's simply not done, Jane Howard."

"What's not, Auntie?" Alice asked.

Ethel turned her gaze on her. "I should think *you'd* understand, Alice, after our discussion about your Grace Chapel Inn guest. It's just not proper for a single woman like Jane to accompany a single man, unchaperoned."

Jane stared for a moment, confused, then burst out laughing. "You can't be serious!"

Ethel looked hurt, then her expression hardened. "Of course I'm serious. Dead serious. You have a reputation to protect."

"But Auntie, this is the twenty-first century, not the nineteenth."

"Nevertheless, convention remains convention," Ethel said. "You'll be staying overnight in Philadelphia?"

"Well, yes, but . . . Oh, Aunt Ethel, this is absurd. Craig's high school worker, Trevor Walker, and his girlfriend are going, too, if that makes you feel any better."

"It does not," she said. "Who's going to watch *those* two?"

"Now, Aunt Ethel, Jane will share a hotel room with Trevor's girlfriend, and Craig with Trevor. It's perfectly fine," Alice said.

"Maybe for you, but not for me. I won't have my niece trotting around unsupervised."

Jane shook her head. *What has gotten into Aunt Ethel? Bossing Lloyd back to good health, now overseeing my "reputation." Imagine!*

"However, being the fast-thinking and magnanimous person that I am, I have a solution," Ethel said.

"Well, please, do tell," Jane said.

Alice gave her a glance that clearly asked her to hear their aunt out without condemnation.

"Lloyd needs a rest. I was going to propose a trip to Ocean City or somewhere else on the shore."

"Unchaperoned?" Jane, feeling wicked, couldn't help but ask.

Alice touched her shoulder, and Jane sighed. "I'm sorry, Aunt Ethel, please continue."

"I was going to propose that since he needs a vacation of sorts, we should accompany you, Craig, Trevor and his girl-friend to this garden show. It would lend respectability to your travels."

Jane wondered about the wisdom of bunking an elderly woman, herself and a high school girl together—not to mention keeping Ethel and Lloyd up to pace with what would no doubt be a hectic weekend. She also wondered how much of Ethel's concern was motivated by "propriety" and how much by a desire to join the trip to Philadelphia.

"It seems like a generous offer," Alice said, always the peacemaker. "But how about you, Lloyd? Do you feel like making a trip to Philadelphia next weekend?"

"I would love to go," he said. "I always enjoy a trip there."

"But maybe the beach would be more restful," Jane said hopefully.

Lloyd shook his head. "I can think of nothing more relaxing

than attending a garden show. *And* cheering on Acorn Hill's florist in his new endeavors."

"Then it's settled," Ethel said, sounding as if she had suppressed the desire to crow. "I'll contact Craig Tracy and the parents of Trevor Walker and his girlfriend to make the necessary arrangements."

Jane sighed, resigned. *Oh well. How much trouble can two extra people in the entourage be anyway?*

That evening Louise prepared for the meeting with Grace Chapel's organ committee. As she brushed her hair and studied her outfit, she thought about Walter and Kathleen Haverty. She had hated to say good-bye to them the day before.

They had spoken with such interest about the organ and seemed so concerned about its future. Louise wondered if perhaps she had been too hasty in dismissing Walter Haverty's musical skills as simply those of a commercial musician. When she asked him where he had learned so much about classical music, he waved away her question. "Aw, Miz Louise, that information's private, I'm afraid. It's difficult for me to talk about."

She had thought his answer odd, but she certainly respected his decision. At any rate, she had said good-bye to the Havertys with a new appreciation and hoped that they would be visiting again.

The organ committee met in Grace Chapel's Assembly Room. Pastor Ley, the head of the committee, greeted her warmly, as he did Florence. Ethel came bustling in last of all.

"Wilhelm Wood was late coming to sit with Lloyd," she said. "I didn't want to leave the poor man alone for one minute."

All were delighted to hear about Lloyd's recovery, and they discussed that for a while. Louise hoped that talking about the improved health of one of the church board members would put the somewhat divided committee in a pleasant mood, but once Henry Ley gently steered the conversation to the issue for the evening, good will declined.

"Henry and I have gone over the church finances," Florence said, "and there simply isn't any money to be spent on that organ."

"Now, Florence, that's n-not quite true," Henry said. "We have *some* money available."

"Yes," she said, smiling smugly. "See for yourselves." She passed around a printed sheet showing the available money from Grace Chapel. "We have nearly enough for an electronic organ, but not enough for a new pipe organ and certainly not enough to fund repairs for the dinosaur we have now."

Louise felt her face warm, but she said nothing.

"That's a shame," Ethel said sadly, studying the figures. "I was really hoping we'd have enough money to keep the old one."

Louise murmured her agreement. "It's part of this church," she said.

"Stuff and nonsense," Florence said. "It's high time we moved into the twenty-first century. When will you sentimentalists learn that we respect the history and tradition of Grace Chapel, but we must also be prepared to move forward?"

"What if the old organ didn't make such a r-racket?"

All eyes turned to Pastor Ley. He looked embarrassed by the attention, but he swallowed hard and bravely proceeded. "What if we c-could *raise* the money to get the organ fixed?"

"I think that's a wonderful idea," Ethel said. "I printed out the costs of repairs and of various organs. Let's look at those figures again."

She passed the sheet around, and everyone consulted the costs that were listed. An electronic organ would be the least expensive, followed by a new pipe organ, which cost slightly more. Repairs to the existing organ cost the most. Louise winced at seeing the figures again. She had forgotten how high they were.

"We have to raise money for an electronic organ anyway,"

Ethel said. "Why not set it as our goal to raise money for repairs, instead? I think we can make it."

"We could have a fund-raiser," Louise said, warming with hope.

"Like when the high school kids have car washes and sell candy?" Florence asked, skeptical.

"I was thinking of something more ambitious," Louise said. "Perhaps an auction or a sale of some sort. At any rate, I'm sure we could get the town to help."

"Maybe even folks in Potterston," Ethel said.

"Let's p-put it to a vote," Henry Ley said. "All in favor of commencing with fund-raising for either a new organ or repairs to the existing one, say 'aye.'"

"Aye!" Each member raised a hand. Florence Simpson raised hers reluctantly, knowing that she was outnumbered. It was clear that she would press for an electronic organ to the end, but even that would require more money than the church had available.

"I'd be delighted to head the fund-raising efforts," Ethel said, "seeing as how I'm director of committees at the church anyway."

"I'll be glad to help you, Aunt Ethel," Louise said.

"W-wonderful, ladies," Henry said. "What sort of time frame do you have in mind?"

Ethel thought for a moment. "We need to do this as quickly as possible. No offense, Louise, but it does sound like that organ won't last much longer. I'll be in Philadelphia next weekend, but how about the weekend after that? We could have some kind of special fund-raiser for that Saturday and Sunday?"

Everyone nodded in agreement. Ethel beamed. "Good. Put on your thinking caps as to how you can contribute. Most importantly, spread the word to everyone in Acorn Hill and beyond. One way or another, we are going to have new music sounding from Grace Chapel as soon as possible."

Chapter Fourteen

News of Grace Chapel's efforts to raise money for its organ spread. Soon Acorn Hill itself became divided on whether the church should replace or repair the existing organ. Some people said they would only donate money if it went for repairs, and others stipulated that they would only donate for a new organ.

Louise took Alice aside on the Wednesday after the committee meeting and said, "I do wish people would stop squabbling about this. Do you suppose there's any way we can get across to the town that they either donate money and abide by the committee's final recommendation or not donate money at all? I know that no one on the committee wants to be forced to keep track of a separate fund for repairs and a separate fund for a new organ."

"Perhaps I could get Carlene to put a small article in the *Nutshell*," Alice said. "I am going to visit her anyway."

"Thank you," Louise said, heaving a sigh. "First the division was within the church and now it's spread to all of Acorn Hill. It's not worth all this fuss."

"I agree," Alice said. "I would love to see the old organ repaired, but not at the expense of alienating people."

"Especially people who don't go to Grace Chapel," Louise added. "What impression will that give them of our church?"

When Alice got to the *Nutshell*'s building, she found Carlene slaving away at her desk, as usual. Unusual, however, were the dozen pink roses sitting on her desk in full view of the front window.

But if the roses looked lovely, Carlene, frankly, did not. Her gray-streaked brown hair, normally pulled back in a tiny ponytail, hung loose in frizzy strands. She had bags under her eyes and she had chewed off most of her lipstick.

Alice stood in front of Carlene's desk, hoping to gain her attention. Carlene, however, never acknowledged her. "The roses are beautiful," Alice finally said, gesturing at the flowers when Carlene finally looked up from her work.

"Thanks," Carlene said, then immediately went back to typing. "If there's something you want, Alice, make it fast. The *Nutshell* was supposed to come out today, and I'll be lucky if it comes out tomorrow. If at all."

"The *Nutshell* is going to be late this week?" Alice was stunned. The newspaper always came out on Wednesday and had never been late. Not after the great blizzard during Alice's youth, nor during Carlene's father's declining years, nor during the early years when Carlene took over the publishing.

Carlene whacked her hands next to the keyboard and glared at Alice. "Yes, it's going to be late, all right? What did you want, anyway?"

Alice backed away. She had never seen Carlene like this. "It can wait," she said, reaching for the doorknob.

Instantly, Carlene's expression changed. "I'm sorry, Alice. Wait!"

Alice had already fled the building, but Carlene followed her out the door. "Alice, wait!"

Halfway down the block and blinking back tears, Alice wanted to keep moving, but she stopped. Daniel Howard had always told her not to pass up the opportunity to mend a wounded friendship.

Carlene caught up with her, clutching a hand over her heart. Alice softened and touched her friend's shoulder. "Catch your breath, Carlene."

"I'm . . . so . . . sorry," she said, her eyes pleading. "I don't know what got into me. I shouldn't have snapped at you like that. Can you forgive me?"

"Of course I can," Alice said. "What happened?"

Carlene hung her head. "David Nix has been entertaining me quite a bit lately, and I'm afraid I'm way behind in my work."

Alice bit her lip. Should she say anything? Voice her feelings? She drew a deep breath. "Where is Mr. Nix today?"

"He said he had business in Potterston. Some sort of transaction for the mysterious gentleman he represents," Carlene said.

"The one who wants to buy your printing equipment?"

Carlene nodded. "And now I'm trying to catch up on the work I should have been doing the past few days. I've never been late with the *Nutshell*, Alice. Never." She looked as though she was going to burst into tears.

Alice hated to see her friend so distressed. Carlene was so devoted to her work, rarely taking time for herself. It was no wonder that David Nix had apparently managed to turn her head.

"Is there anything I can do to help?" Alice asked, handing Carlene a handkerchief, and shelving any request for an article about the organ situation.

Carlene dabbed at her eyes, sniffling. "No, but I suppose I should get back to work. I'm hoping to e-mail the layout to the Potterston printers before they close. They should be able to print off the newspapers by tomorrow, and I'll have them delivered." She sniffled again. "A day late."

Alice drew her into a hug. "It's not the end of the world, Carlene. I hate to see you so upset."

"But it's my fault. My father would *never* have let anything like this happen. I'm so confused about what to do with that old equipment. It's all I can think about, what with David talking about it all the time."

"What advice do you think your father would give you, if he could?" Alice said, knowing that Carlene's father had been both understanding and wise, as her own father had been.

"About the state of the *Nutshell*? He would probably tell me to forgive myself and move on. And not to let it happen again."

Alice gave her one final hug, then patted her on the back before releasing her. "Then that's what you should do."

"Okay," Carlene said, sniffling one final time. "I can try. But I still don't know whether to sell that old equipment or not." She sighed. "Thanks, Alice. I don't deserve your kindness—or your handkerchief. I'll return it after I wash it."

"That's fine, Carlene," Alice said. "Just finish the *Nutshell* first." She started to leave, then turned back. "After you get this issue out, why don't we have lunch together? When I have to make a difficult decision, it sometimes helps me to sound out the issues with a friend."

"That'd be great, Alice. Thanks. I'm sure I could use a friendly listener."

As she watched her friend scurry back to the *Nutshell* office, Alice said a silent prayer that she could always be that friendly listener for Carlene.

That afternoon, Jane headed over to Wild Things, where she found Trevor Walker alone in the store, bustling between the workroom and the front counter.

"Craig's gotten lots of orders since he agreed to do the garden show," Trevor said, when he had a moment in between loads of floral Styrofoam and vases that he was hauling to the front. He had stocked the area behind the counter with a variety of floral supplies, with barely enough room to walk between the counter and the workroom.

"Good grief," Jane said, eyeing the supplies. "Who's doing all the ordering?"

"People from Potterston mostly," Trevor said. "Craig did a radio show there, and the orders just started pouring in. He talked about native plants, and then the radio host played a game called Name That Floral Arrangement."

Jane stared at him quizzically.

"It was a phone-in show, and he encouraged listeners to phone in their most difficult people to buy flowers for. They'd give a brief description like 'nosy grandmother,' and Craig would come up with a simple, yet distinctive bouquet."

"But that doesn't sound too difficult," she said. "He could recommend carnations or roses for most folks and they'd be pleased."

Trevor shook his head. "He didn't pick just your average floral arrangements. He came up with native plants that could be used in floral arrangements—sometimes on their own or sometimes combined with hothouse flowers. Listeners were completely charmed."

"Well," Jane said, "anything that increases Craig's business is all right with me."

Trevor laughed. "It keeps me busy too. I've been making up displays and scheduling deliveries like crazy. My girlfriend Kaylie complains that she never gets to see me."

"Speaking of which, did your mother and Kaylie's mother get a call from my aunt, Ethel Buckley?" Jane asked.

Trevor grinned, lifting a large box of silk flowers onto the counter. "Yep. It got me in trouble with my mom, who got off the phone convinced that Kaylie and I should not be going to Philadelphia this weekend. I tried to tell her that it was on the up-and-up from the beginning, but she still chewed me out. I thought I wasn't going to be able to go at all, but she finally said that seeing as how that nice Ethel Buckley and the mayor were going to be our chaperones, it would be all right."

Jane resisted the urge to roll her eyes, only out of deference to her elderly aunt. "Would you believe that my aunt said the same thing about Craig and me? She apparently doesn't think we can be trusted on an out-of-town trip together."

"You're kidding." Trevor saw that her expression didn't change, and he burst out laughing. "That's crazy, Ms. Howard. Why you must be older than . . ." He broke off, realizing that he was moving into dangerous water when speculating about a woman's age. He grinned sheepishly.

"It's all right, Trevor." Jane smiled. "It doesn't offend me. And by the way, I'm fifty. If you think that's old, that's fine. I was your age once."

"Sorry, Ms. H," he said.

The front door opened, and Craig backed into the room holding a large box with both hands. "Hey! It's Jane," Craig said. "I hear your Aunt Ethel and Lloyd Tynan have signed on to the garden show trip." Craig had lifted the box onto the counter, alongside the one Trevor had already put there.

"Yeah. Sorry about that," Jane said. "It all started because—"

He held up a hand. "Don't worry, Jane. I think it's sweet that your aunt worries about you and your reputation. I also think it's nice that Lloyd's going to get some rest. I think a garden show will be a great way for him to relax."

"Kaylie's stoked about it too," Trevor said. "She's looking forward to meeting you guys and having the mayor go with us. She thinks that's pretty cool."

"And it doesn't hurt that her mother knows she'll be well watched out for either, does it?" Craig said, smiling.

"Well, no," Trevor admitted.

"Hey, Craig," Jane said, "I hear you were a celebrity on a Potterston radio show."

Craig laughed. "That was pretty fun. Mr. Williams, the manager at WCLI, wants me to host a weekly garden show."

"That's great, Craig. I hear you're a natural."

"Carlene's talked about having me write a garden column for the *Nutshell* as well," he said.

"You're going to be busy, Mr. Tracy," Trevor said.

"That's the truth." Craig sighed.

"I guess I'd better let you gentlemen get back to work then," Jane said.

"Oh, Jane, one more thing," Craig said. "Your aunt told me about Grace Chapel's organ fund-raising efforts. She was so enthusiastic about it that I pledged all the profits from my plant sales at the garden show to go toward that fund."

"Really, Craig?" She smiled. "I hope Aunt Ethel didn't strong-arm you into making that promise. You're not even a member of Grace Chapel."

He shrugged. "I know. But I've heard the organ at Christmas concerts, and I know how much it means to Louise and other members of the congregation. Besides, I'd like to give something back to Acorn Hill for all the help they've given me since I've been here, especially in my latest endeavor."

Jane touched his sleeve, warmed by his kindness. "I'll tell Louise what you said. She'll be delighted."

Ethel began her fund-raising efforts in earnest, sitting down that afternoon with Louise in the kitchen at Grace Chapel Inn. "I think we should have a silent auction," she said to Louise.

"What is a silent auction?" Louise asked.

"People donate items to auction. We put each one on display, then potential buyers write their bids and put them in envelopes, without seeing the others' bids. The person who pledges the highest amount wins the item."

"It sounds far less complicated than a standard auction," Louise said. "No one has to oversee the bidding, and the bidders don't have to compete with each other on the spot."

Ethel nodded. "Exactly what I was thinking. You know, we can hold the fund-raiser on the Grace Chapel grounds and promote it as a special event for Acorn Hill. That will draw people in."

"What if it rains?" Louise asked.

Ethel waved her hand in a dismissive gesture. "The weather will be beautiful, and if it isn't, we'll just move it indoors."

Drawing on her aunt's enthusiasm, Louise found herself pulled into the plans. "Maybe we could raffle off a few things too. Do you think a silent auction *and* a raffle would be too much?"

"Not at all," Ethel said, then winked slyly. "Some items will fetch a pretty penny at a silent auction, but some would do better as raffle items. People would be glad to pay a dollar or two for a chance to win theater tickets, for example, but wouldn't bid nearly close enough to their true dollar amount if they were in a silent auction."

"Oh," Louise said, not certain that she would know the difference, but trusting that Ethel did.

"Here's a list of people for you to contact," Ethel said, "and here's a list for me."

Louise scanned the lengthy list of names on the page. "It looks like over twenty names here."

"Yes, and I have just as many on my list," she said proudly. "If I know Acorn Hill, everyone in town will want to help out, and those we contact will help spread the word."

"But not everyone will have something to donate for a silent auction or a raffle," Louise pointed out. "Most people probably just have old items they want to get rid of. Garage sale junk."

"Garage sale! That's it, Louise," Ethel said. "We can have

a garage sale, too, for everything not good enough for auction or raffle."

Louise felt her skepticism reappear; after all, the fund-raiser was scheduled in little more than a week. "Aunt Ethel, are you sure this is not getting out of hand?" She was beginning to picture the event as a giant flea market. And on the grounds of Grace Chapel, no less.

"The more action, the better." Ethel said. She fixed her sternest gaze on Louise. "You *do* want to raise money for the organ, do you not?"

"Of course I do. But the event is starting to seem a little, well, involved." *Garage sale junk, after all!*

"We just need a good title," Ethel said. "Something to attract people, but to let them know it's for a good cause. *Hmm.* What can we call it?"

Louise wished that Jane were available. She always came up with good names and titles for things. "How about the Grace Chapel Organ Festival?"

"Oh dear, no," Ethel said. "It sounds as though we're celebrating a kidney or a liver. I think we should leave the word *organ* out of the title altogether. It could be a distraction if it's misread, don't you think?"

"Perhaps you're right," Louise murmured.

"Let's see," Ethel said, tapping a finger against the side of her head. "What could we call it? It will have to be something distinctive and interesting, to spark interest. It has to have pizzazz."

"I think we should mention Grace Chapel in the title, so that people will know right away who's sponsoring it."

"Yes, and who will benefit from the proceeds," Ethel said. "And perhaps we should have the term *fund-raiser* in the title so that it will be clear that this is to raise money and not strictly a social event."

"So how about the Grace Chapel Fund-Raiser?" Louise

asked. "We will probably want to make up flyers about the event to post around town, correct?"

Ethel nodded.

"Then we can add a paragraph describing the objective of the fund-raiser: to replace or repair the church organ."

"I like it," Ethel said. "It's to the point. Although . . ." She cupped her hand around her chin, deep in thought.

"Although what?" Louise asked, wondering if they were going to spend hours over something as simple as a name for the event. She hoped that they could come up with a title as soon as possible, so that they could get on with their plans.

"The name alone doesn't sound terribly inviting," Ethel said. "We need to add a little something to make the event more appealing. Something like the Grace Chapel Harmony Fund-Raiser. How about that?"

"I like it," Louise said, sighing with relief. "It does make the event sound more appealing. The word *harmony* gives a clue as to what the fund-raiser is all about. We are also more likely to draw attendance from people who are not there strictly to help us raise money for the organ. And *harmony* doesn't have to relate strictly to music."

"My thoughts exactly," Ethel said, rising from her chair. "Well, we'd better get to work contacting the people on this list if we want to have anything at all to sell at this fund-raiser."

Chapter Fifteen

Finished with piano lessons for the day and with Alice back at the inn to answer the phone, Louise started at the beginning of her list. It was such a beautiful day that she had decided to walk to town. She hoped that if she asked people in person, they would feel more inclined to contribute to the fund-raiser.

Fred Humbert was busy selling a customer a new outdoor light fixture at his hardware store, so she lingered in the paint aisle, studying the cans of various colors. She felt an involuntary shudder, remembering all the decorating decisions she and her sisters had had to make when they first decided to open their home as a bed and breakfast.

When he was finished with the customer, Fred sauntered up the paint aisle toward her. "Hi, Louise. Thinking about redecorating the old homestead?"

"No, thank you," she said. "I'm here to ask if there's anything you would like to contribute for the Harmony Fund-Raiser."

"Oh yes. For the organ," he said. "I'm so glad you and Ethel are heading that up. Of course I'd be delighted to help. As a matter of fact, I have a new electric lawn mower that I'd be glad to donate for the silent auction. It's good for the environment and runs on a battery, so it only has to be recharged."

"Splendid." Louise said, writing in the small notebook that she had brought with her for recording donations. "Thank you, Fred. That's very generous of you."

"Anything to help," he said, then bustled off to help another customer.

Louise moved down Hill Street to the Coffee Shop. Inside, Hope Collins was behind the counter. The place seemed busy, so Louise didn't plan to linger, but June Carter, the owner, spied her from the kitchen and bustled out to the dining area.

"Louise Smith," she said, wiping her hands on her apron. "Are you here to see what we can contribute to the organ fund?"

"We are calling it the Grace Chapel Harmony Fund-Raiser," Louise said, deciding that she might as well become accustomed to calling it by its name. "And yes, I would love to have you contribute something to the raffle or silent auction."

June thought for a moment. "I'd be delighted to raffle off a twenty-dollar lunch for two. Would that help?"

"It certainly would," Louise said, writing in the notebook. "Thank you, June."

On the street again Louise breathed a sigh of relief that things were going well so far. "At least two of the church board members have agreed to participate," she said to herself.

The next stop, Acorn Hill Antiques, was run by Joseph and Rachel Holzmann. Louise always felt that she should be silent inside their store since it was filled with lovely old furniture, paintings, decorations and glass cases of jewelry. Classical music wafted through the store, and she felt herself relaxing in the coolness of the air-conditioning.

"Hello, Louise," Joseph said, coming from around a glass counter. He adjusted his gold, wire-rimmed glasses to see her better. "What can I do for you?"

Louise explained about the fund-raising festival and asked if he and Rachel had anything that they would like to donate. Joseph stroked his beard while he thought, then snapped his fingers. "We have the very thing. Rachel inherited a cloisonné vase from one of her distant relatives. It doesn't fit the décor in our German Inglenook bungalow, so we were just going to sell it."

"Are you sure you want to donate a family heirloom?"

He nodded. "It's not very old, Louise, and that relative really was distant. Besides, we would rather see Grace Chapel benefit from its sale, especially if it's for the organ. We're quite fond of that instrument."

Louise felt a wave of gratitude. Like Craig Tracy, Joseph and Rachel were not even members of Grace Chapel. "That's very kind of you."

"Speaking of the organ, I recently met a man who is an organ appraiser. If you need someone else to evaluate it, let me know. Or at the very least, before you do away with it, will you let him have a look at it? He might want to take it off your hands. That would add some extra money to a fund for a new one . . . if you do decide to buy a new one, that is."

"Thank you, Joseph," Louise said. "I hadn't even thought that we might make some money from the old organ. But between you and me, I hope that we don't have to resort to replacing it."

"I understand. So does Rachel. We treasure old things. The craftsmanship is usually so much better than contemporary versions."

Louise nodded her agreement. She was glad that someone else understood.

She went to several other shops and ran into interested individuals on the street, most of whom pledged to donate items for the raffle and auction. Everyone else volunteered at least to bring something for the garage sale.

Louise decided to make one more stop before calling it a day. The last person in the area who was on her list was Sylvia Songer. She had been in favor of replacing the pipe organ with an electronic one, but no doubt she would want to help with the fund-raiser. Sylvia, who enjoyed a warm relationship with all three sisters, could always be counted on to lend her assistance when needed.

Inside her seamstress shop, Sylvia's Buttons, Sylvia was cutting a huge bolt of white material with a pair of large scissors. Without glancing up, she said, distractedly, "Hang on just one second. This satin is tricky stuff." She fearlessly cut through the delicate fabric, then finished with a triumphant *snip* of the shears. "There! Oh hi, Louise."

Louise smiled at the sight of Sylvia at work. She was quite a talented seamstress. "Hello, Sylvia. I've come to see if you would like to donate something from your shop for the fund-raiser."

"I would love to," she said. "I want to help with the fund as much as anyone else."

Louise bit her tongue, thinking of Florence Simpson, who might not be as obliging. Even Sylvia had questioned Louise's position regarding the organ.

"Look, Louise," Sylvia said, as though reading her mind. "I know we have different ideas about what's best music-wise for Grace Chapel, but I don't want it to affect our friendship."

Louise smiled. "Nor do I, Sylvia. Perhaps I'm far more attached to the old pipe organ than I should be. But after so many years, it seems like a dear friend."

"I understand." She set down her scissors and moved to a cupboard. She drew out a quilt and laid it on the counter between the friends. "I made this quilt several years ago, completely by hand. I was saving it for a special present, and I think this is just such an occasion. No matter what the organ committee decides, I hope this helps bring in some much-needed money."

Louise stroked the quilt, appreciative of how fine a donation it was. It was composed of matching, brightly colored squares in what felt like expensive material. Every stitch was small and nearly identical, obviously the result of painstaking work. That Sylvia would donate this for the fund showed how highly she regarded the organ issue.

"Thank you, Sylvia," Louise said. "It's beautiful, and you are very dear and very generous. We will put it in the silent auction. I'm sure it will command a high price."

The next morning Alice was called into work for half a day. As she walked out of Potterston Hospital, she reflected on the fact that there were two times during the year when she felt particularly sorry for patients in the hospital: holidays and summertime. She could hear the trill of nearby mockingbirds, feel the gentle breeze, and relish the manicured green lawns and blooming marigolds on the hospital grounds.

Alice had just put her key in the lock of the car door when she heard her name called. She turned, thinking it was one of the hospital employees. Instead of a co-worker, it was Rev. Thompson.

"I was hoping to find you here, just to say hello," he said, catching up with her. "I was at the hospital to see George Nathan, who had minor surgery."

"I stopped by his room earlier today," Alice said, referring to the fellow Grace Chapel member. "I'm glad to see he's doing well. How are *you*?" she asked. "How was your fishing trip with Theo Dulane on Sunday?"

"I caught a bass, and Theo caught a catfish."

Alice pushed her sunglasses down the bridge of her nose, smiling. "That's not exactly what I meant."

He laughed. "Sorry, Alice. Actually, we had a good chat. Theo needed someone to talk to about the grief process he's going through, and you ladies were kind enough to direct him to me. Thank you for that."

"As I understand from the training I've taken as a nurse, grief is not a process with a start and finish," Alice said.

Rev. Thompson nodded. "It's more like a circle with different stops along the way. People often move from point to point, then back again. Sometimes it seems like progress, sometimes a regression."

"I remember how horrible I felt when Father died," Alice said. "Gradually I felt better, yet some days the pain feels fresh all over again."

"But not so difficult, I imagine," Rev. Thompson said, "because you know that when you have a down day, you will one day feel better. That's what Theo needs to know right now. Actually, that was the second reason I was hoping to bump into you . . . besides saying hello, of course."

"What's that?" Alice asked.

"For several weeks I've been leading an ecumenical grief counseling session in Potterston with several other religious leaders. I've asked Theo Dulane to attend, and I thought you might be interested, as well."

"Me?"

"Strictly from your nursing standpoint," he said. "I thought it might help with some of the crisis counseling you handle as a nurse."

Alice thought for a moment. It *was* difficult to help someone at the hospital whose loved one had just died. She never had the right words to say, usually resorting to a simple "I'm so sorry" and a hug. Although those actions usually seemed exactly what was called for, she would appreciate having more insight into handling grief.

"We're meeting tomorrow here in one of the hospital education rooms," Rev. Thompson said. "I'd be glad to drive you."

"Thank you. And yes, I'd like to attend. I'm sure I could benefit from such a meeting."

"Wonderful." Rev. Thompson smiled.

Alice sighed. "If only getting over grief were as easy as catching a bass."

Rev. Thompson smiled, giving her a little salute as he headed toward his car. "That shows how little you know about fishing, Alice."

∞

Around noon Jane fixed a picnic basket with lunch for four and carried it to Wild Things. Craig had called a meeting of those going to the garden show. He did not include Ethel and Lloyd since they wouldn't be helping but only going along for the ride. When she got to Wild Things, Trevor Walker and Kaylie McKissack, along with Craig, were already waiting for Jane.

Craig flipped the store sign to CLOSED and ushered everyone to the workroom in back, where he moved a stack of new clay pots and clear vases for them to have a space to eat.

"Thanks for bringing lunch, Jane," he said, as she opened the basket.

"You're welcome. I brought sandwiches—my special tuna fish as well as chicken salad."

"And chips," Trevor said, pouncing on the store-bought bag she had purchased especially for the teens.

Craig smiled at Jane with an indulgent what-do-teenagers-know-about-real-food look. Jane smiled back and produced plastic plates, and Craig distributed napkins from Jane's basket.

"Anyway," he said, once everyone had taken a sandwich and some chips, "I wanted to consult with you all about the final arrangements for this weekend. I've talked to your parents, Trevor and Kaylie, and they're fine with our arrangements."

Kaylie set down her sandwich. "My parents wouldn't have let me go at all if the mayor and Mrs. Buckley weren't going. Mrs. Buckley had a long phone call with my mom."

"I'll bet it was long. Well, I'm glad they're tagging along," Jane said, "because I know you were excited about coming."

"And we can definitely use the help," Craig said.

"Just tell us what to do, Mr. T," Trevor said, reaching for his second sandwich.

"The biggest thing you and Kaylie can help with is carrying some of the plants in the back of your pickup. I'll be taking the delivery van, of course, but it would help if you could carry some too."

"You're talking about the plants you'll use to hand out as samples?" Jane asked.

Craig nodded. "Since my target consumers are wholesalers, I have certain plants, better plants, that I want to give them. I have smaller plants to give out to individuals. I want to encourage them to grow native plants, but I don't really expect them to patronize Wild Things."

"How will you know the difference between the people at the convention?" Jane asked. She didn't want to give the wrong plant to the wrong customer.

"Everyone at the garden show will have a badge. Wholesalers are one color, individual shop owners another, and guests—those not in the business—will have still another."

"What can I do to help?" Jane asked.

"I was hoping you would ask," Craig smiled. "Besides helping me set up for my speech and passing out plants there, I'm hoping that you'll help me in the booth by passing out literature and plants."

"I'd be delighted," she said. It would be fun to talk about the plants and get to meet people at the convention.

"Kaylie and I can help at the booth too," Trevor said. "We weren't thinking of just cutting loose after we set up at the show. We plan to stick around the whole time."

"Good," Craig said. "I was also hoping you'd stay close so that I can introduce you to any botanists or horticulturists that might be around. It'd be good for you to meet them, especially if that's what you want to study in college. Think of it as a preadmission interview in a relaxed environment."

Trevor beamed. "That'd be great, Mr. Tracy. I appreciate your looking out for me that way."

Kaylie squeezed Trevor's arm, smiling at him. She clearly adored him and was pleased by anything that made him happy.

"Now . . . back to Ethel and Lloyd," Craig said.

Jane set down her sandwich. "What about them, Craig?"

"I'm glad they're going, because, as I said before, that means that Kaylie can go with us. But I also want this to be a stress-free time for Lloyd. This is supposed to be a relaxing trip for him, and I don't want him to encounter any tense situations." He looked at each one of them individually. "So I want everyone to be on his or her best behavior. Is that understood?"

"Yes sir," Trevor and Kaylie said solemnly, nodding their heads in agreement.

Why did Jane feel as though he might be talking to her as well as to the teenagers? Perhaps it was her concerns about Ethel and Lloyd's going along. She would just have to maintain an even disposition toward them. It was only for a weekend. Surely she could last that long. They might get in the way, but it could be that those senior citizens might want to tool around Philadelphia by themselves instead, leaving the rest of them to take care of the garden show business.

"Yes," Jane said, "I understand too."

Chapter Sixteen

When Alice got home from the hospital, she checked the mail that Louise had left on the business desk. The postman had apparently brought only bills and a cooking magazine for Jane.

"One-and-two-and-keep-your-wrists-even."

Alice could hear Louise giving a piano lesson in the parlor. She had forgotten to shut the door again.

Alice was just about to head upstairs to change out of her nursing uniform when she saw a note on the desk from Louise directing Alice to call Carlene.

Carlene had managed to get the *Nutshell* out only one day late. The sisters had already received it, but neither Louise nor Jane had commented on its being late. Perhaps few other people in Acorn Hill would notice either. For Carlene's sake Alice hoped that that was the case.

She dialed the number for the *Nutshell*'s office, and Carlene picked up on the first ring. "Hi," Alice said. "Louise left me a message that you called."

There was a pause at Carlene's end of the line. "I thought this might be a good day to take you up on that lunch . . . ?" Carlene ended her sentence with a questioning tone, as though she was afraid that Alice would decline.

"Of course," Alice said. "Would you like to meet at the Coffee Shop?"

"I'd rather meet at Good Apple Bakery."

"All right," Alice said, puzzled. "I'll be there in about thirty minutes."

She hung up the phone. Why would Carlene want to meet at the Good Apple? Although it had several wrought-iron chairs and tables, they were not intended, nor comfortable enough, for leisurely dining.

Nevertheless, Alice was at the Good Apple, as promised, within thirty minutes. Carlene was already waiting for her, standing in the line at the counter. "Clarissa is going to fix up a little lunch just for us," Carlene whispered, apparently not wanting the other waiting patrons to learn of the Good Apple owner's special service.

"Oh," Alice said, feeling as though she were in the middle of a spy novel.

Clarissa stepped up to the counter, passing a white bakery box over the counter, along with two lemonades. "Here you go," she said, winking at Carlene.

"Thank you," Carlene said, counting out some bills. "I won't need any change, Clarissa."

The elderly woman smiled, her face wrinkling beneath the hair net she wore for work. "Thanks."

"Shall we eat here?" Carlene asked.

Alice eyed the uncomfortable chairs and crowded bakery. "It's only a few blocks to the park. How about eating there?"

Carlene checked the weather outside the bakery: warm sun, bright sky and fluffy clouds. "Yes, I think that would be a marvelous idea. Just what I need."

They walked the two blocks to Acorn Hill Park, sipping from their lemonades and chatting about the *Nutshell*. Carlene related some of the difficulties she had had with the layout, the Potterston printers and even delivery. Fortunately, in the end she had made it all work.

"I'm glad you were able to get it out today," Alice said. "I know that meant a lot to you."

"It did. And to the people of Acorn Hill too. I've already had a few people mention about its being late, but not too many."

"That's good. I know you've been under a lot of stress lately," Alice said.

Carlene didn't say anything.

When they got to the park, they found an empty picnic table where they set down their lemonades and opened the box Clarissa had prepared. Carlene took out two wax paper-wrapped sandwiches, chicken salad on fresh croissants.

"These look delicious, don't they?" she asked, setting one in front of Alice.

"They do, but I still wonder why you didn't want to eat at the Coffee Shop," Alice said.

Carlene took a bite of her sandwich, then set it down. She chewed thoughtfully, swallowed, then said, "I was afraid David Nix would be looking for me there. He knows I eat there a lot."

"Are you avoiding him for some reason?"

Carlene took another bite of her sandwich, delaying an answer to the question. "I think he's been trying to romance me, Alice."

"Really?" Alice didn't know what to say. She thought of seeing Carlene riding in David Nix's convertible, but she had looked happy. "Is that a bad thing?" she asked.

"I think so," Carlene said, hanging her head. "I thought he was being nice because he really liked my company, but now I suspect that he just wants to get me to agree to sell the printing equipment."

"What makes you think that?" Alice asked.

"At first he hardly talked about it at all. He talked about everything else under the sun—books, films, politics. Lately, however, he's been talking more and more about the equipment that I own."

"Maybe he's just trying to make conversation," Alice said.

"I thought the same thing at first too," Carlene said, "but he's been pressing me more, asking me whatever in the world I'm going to do with that 'old junk,' and why I don't let him take it off my hands . . . stuff like that."

"If you're not interested in selling, perhaps you should just be up-front and tell him so," Alice said.

"But I don't know that for certain." She sighed. "As I said, I could really use the money. Not just to make my lifestyle easier, but also to pay the bills. The *Nutshell* doesn't generate that much revenue, Alice."

A squirrel crept up to their picnic area, then sat on his hind legs. Carlene smiled, then pinched off a bit of the croissant and tossed it to him. He caught it in the air and scurried off to a safe distance, where he held it between his paws and nibbled.

"Don't tell Clarissa I did that, okay?" Carlene said. "She might think I don't appreciate her baking skills." She tried to smile wider, but her mouth shook a little, as though she were on the verge of tears.

Alice covered Carlene's hand with her own. "I didn't realize that the *Nutshell* wasn't doing well. I can understand why selling or keeping the equipment would be such a difficult decision."

"Yes," Carlene said, swiping at her eyes. "And every time I resolve to sell it, I keep seeing my father working there, or the other old typesetters who used to create the *Nutshell* on it, long ago. Oh, Alice, if you were me, what would you do?"

Alice said a silent prayer for wisdom, then spoke slowly. "I know that I wouldn't let anyone else pressure me into deciding in his favor."

Carlene nodded. "I've been trying to do that by staying away from David. As I said, that's why I didn't want to go to the Coffee Shop."

"That's a good first step," Alice said. "Take the time you need to make up your mind."

"But what do I do next?" Carlene asked. "How do I decide?"

"How about making a list where you write the pros of selling the equipment on one side, and the cons on the other?"

Carlene considered for a moment. "I could try that."

"Sometimes it helps to see your choices laid out on paper," Alice said. "One side is usually stronger than the other, and it's easier to see what you really want."

"Thank you, Alice. That's a good idea."

"There's something else I do before I make a big decision," Alice said.

"What's that?"

Alice smiled gently. "Pray. Even more important than making a list, it allows me to give the decision to God. I often have to acknowledge to Him and to myself that He is in control anyway. Frankly, just reminding myself of that often makes my decision so much easier."

"How so?" Carlene looked puzzled.

"Because it reminds me that no matter what decision I make, He can always use it for good. Then the decision doesn't look as threatening, and I don't worry about making the wrong choice."

Carlene smiled. "Thank you, Alice. I feel so much better after talking to you. I need to decide by Saturday, when David goes back to Philadelphia. You've armed me with a lot of new thoughts . . . and prayer, of course."

She finished the last of her sandwich, then crumpled the wax paper with purpose. She took careful aim at a nearby trash container, then tossed it in a perfect arc into its center. Glancing around the park with new enthusiasm, she smiled at a trio of boys playing tag, a young mother keeping watch over a toddler in the sandbox, and two girls taking turns at the slide. Carlene sighed. "It *is* a beautiful day, isn't it?"

Alice smiled at the obvious improvement in her friend's outlook. "Yes, it is, Carlene. Yes, it is."

The next morning, Jane, Craig, Trevor and Kaylie headed out to the nursery to pack Trevor's pickup and Craig's van with plants for the trip to Philadelphia. Jane and Craig wore their oldest shorts and short-sleeved shirts, but Trevor and Kaylie were even more casually dressed, in cut-offs and T-shirts. Trevor also wore a straw cowboy hat.

Craig directed them to load edible plants, such as wild strawberries, pennycress and wild ginger, for wholesalers and shop owners. His main presentation, open only to them and excluding mere garden enthusiasts, concerned selling and marketing native plants "for show and plate." For individual gardeners who might stop by the Wild Things booth, he had an assortment of smaller plants to hand out. No matter what type of plant, though, each pot had a sticker bearing the logo, address, phone number and Web address of Wild Things.

"Pack them like this in the cardboard trays," Craig said, demonstrating by arranging the small plastic pots together. "This way they won't crush each other during transport. Group the ones for wholesalers and shop owners together, so that I can get to them easily during the presentation. Group the plants for individual gardeners together on separate flats."

"Gotcha, boss," Trevor said, packing plants into trays.

Kaylie helped him while he worked, smiling at him the way teenagers often do. At one point she tipped the brim of his straw hat over his eyes in a playful gesture. He smiled, pushed it back up and chucked her under the chin.

Jane smiled to herself. *Ah, young love.*

"What's going on here?"

Jane groaned to herself. That voice was as distinctive as

the red hair on its owner's head. She turned. "Hi, Aunt Ethel. What are you doing here?" *Couldn't they have a moment's peace to plan for the trip?*

Accompanied by Lloyd, Ethel stood at the edge of the greenhouse, hands on her hips. She marched forward, Lloyd walking meekly in her wake. "What am *I* doing here? What are *you* people doing here?"

Jane squeezed a plastic pot tightly between her fingers. She recognized that tone in her aunt's voice. It signaled her desire to take charge, and Jane didn't like it. Ethel had no right being here. This was Craig's business and his concern *only*. The two oldsters weren't even going to help with the plants. "Aunt Ethel, you need to—"

"I'm delighted that you and Lloyd are here to see my nursery," Craig cut in. "Is there something wrong?"

Jane tapped her foot. Craig hadn't known Ethel as long as she had. He was being nice, entirely *too* nice. Give Ethel an inch, and she would take a yard. Give her a plant, and she would take over the entire nursery.

"Yes, there's something wrong," Ethel said. "I stop by your shop to finalize plans for our trip today, and I find a note that says you're closed for the day and out at your nursery. I had to ask around town to find out exactly where it was located. Why wasn't I told you were coming out here?"

Jane tapped her foot faster.

Craig smiled winningly. "I'm sorry, Ethel. We're loading up the van and Trevor's truck with all these samples I plan to hand out. I didn't stop to think that you and Lloyd might be interested in helping us lift and load all these plants."

Jane stopped tapping, a smile crinkling the corners of her mouth.

"*Hmmph*," Ethel said, surveying the heavy flats. "If that's all you're doing—"

"We didn't mean to disturb you," Lloyd said, with an apologetic expression. He tugged at Ethel's elbow. "Maybe we'd better leave them to their work. They don't need a couple of old fogies here to get in their way."

"Nonsense," Jane said, feeling a tad malicious. She took Ethel's other arm. "We don't want you to feel left out."

Ethel shook off the hands of both escorts. "Jane Howard. You know how I feel about women doing heavy lifting. It's not flattering or becoming to a woman's more gentle nature. Besides, it builds"—she shuddered—"muscles."

Jane frowned, opening her mouth for a retort.

"Now now," Craig said, stepping between the women and effectively diffusing the situation. "You're right, Ethel, I should have let you known where we were so that you wouldn't worry. But there's no need for you and Lloyd to do any work dealing with the plants on this trip. We're delighted just to have your company."

"Well . . ." Ethel's face softened. "I guess we were a bit hasty about rushing out here. We were worried that you might leave early. Without us."

Lloyd patted her on the shoulder. "Now, Ethel. We know they wouldn't do that. They wouldn't invite us to go with them and then just ditch us."

"Of course not, Mrs. B.," Trevor said, then lifted his hat in Lloyd's direction. "Mayor T. There's no way we would leave without you."

"We planned to leave at one P.M., as scheduled," Craig said. "With *everyone*. As far as I'm concerned, we're a team."

Jane felt the last of her irritation dissolve. Why was she so often quick to get angry with her aunt, when a kind word or two might settle a situation without hurting anyone's feelings? Besides, Craig had admonished each of them to treat Ethel and Lloyd with the utmost respect. It was funny how he had addressed his words to the teenagers, yet even then she had secretly known that he was addressing her.

"I have to go back and throw some clothes in a suitcase myself," she said, humbler now. "If it's all right, I can get

Lloyd to take Aunt Ethel and me back into town to finish up. How about if he then brings us back here at the nursery by one o'clock, Craig? That will save you from having to pick us up."

"That would work for me," Lloyd said. "I was planning to drive my SUV in case Ethel and I wanted to do some extra sightseeing while you're all at the garden show. I can easily fit Jane's things into my vehicle, then transfer them to your van once we get back to the nursery."

"Trevor and I packed our suitcases this morning and put them in the backseat of his pickup," Kaylie said. "I can ride with him to Philadelphia. That is, if it's all right with everyone."

Ethel put an arm around her shoulder. "Of course it is, dear. Especially since we'll all be caravanning our vehicles, anyway. We'll be able to keep a close eye on you and your young man."

Jane opened her mouth to ask why Ethel and Lloyd had carte blanche to sightsee alone around Philadelphia, but Trevor and Kaylie couldn't ride in a pickup without getting out of view. Then she remembered Craig's admonition and that Ethel only had the teenagers' interests at heart. Ethel meant well.

Still, a little teasing couldn't hurt. She gently elbowed Ethel. "Who's going to chaperone you and Lloyd? You two are young enough at heart that we should keep an eye on you."

"Yeah, Mrs. B.," Trevor said.

Kaylie nodded. Craig smiled.

Ethel blushed, waving her hand, obviously flattered. "Oh, get on. You've got lots of work to do."

Chapter Seventeen

Jane had told Louise and Alice not to wait for her for lunch, since she would be helping Craig pack up for the trip to Philadelphia. She had, however, left them a bowl of tuna salad, which Louise made into sandwiches for their lunch.

Alice opened the refrigerator to find something for them to drink.

"Would you like some buttermilk, Louise?" she asked.

"Ha ha," Louise said as a mock chuckle.

"I'm not teasing," Alice said. "There's still some in here."

Louise looked up from where she was trimming the crusts from the sandwiches. "I suppose you just want to tease me through our entire lunch."

"No," Alice said, holding out the carton. "I was serious when I said I've decided to bury the hatchet where the buttermilk kidding is concerned. It seems to me like Jane and I have given you enough grief about it over the years. You're a grown woman, and if you like buttermilk, you should be free to drink it without fear of criticism."

Louise set down the knife. "Well, thank you, Alice Howard. In that case, pour me some."

Alice nodded. She opened the spout and filled a tall glass tumbler for her sister. She set the carton on the countertop, then began to pour herself a tall glass of whole milk. Before her glass was half full, however, she set down the carton. "This one's empty." She reached way back into the refrigerator for a new carton, then struggled to unfasten its spout.

While Alice had her back turned, Louise turned the other way and quickly poured the remaining contents of the buttermilk carton into the empty milk one. Alice might be understanding of Louise's imbibing, but Jane wouldn't be. When Alice turned back to top off her milk glass, Louise stashed the carton at the back of the refrigerator where Jane would be less likely to find it, and secreted the empty container in the trash basket..

"There." Alice set down her glass of milk. "All ready to eat." Louise placed their sandwiches on the table, and after a short prayer, they began to eat.

Louise chewed thoughtfully, swallowed, then said, "Nobody makes tuna salad like Jane."

Alice nodded. "I guess you and I are on our own for eating this weekend while she's in Philadelphia."

"Oh dear. I hope I can remember how to cook. I've gotten so spoiled."

Alice grinned. "Maybe we could eat at the Coffee Shop and the Good Apple all weekend."

"Don't forget Zachary's."

"Or Dairyland," Alice said, referring to Acorn Hill's convenience store.

"There's always a trip to Potterston restaurants too," Louise said, getting into the spirit of speculation.

"Goodness! There won't be time enough to sample so much," Alice said.

The sisters laughed, rapidly finishing the last of their sandwiches. Both of them knew that they could never be satisfied with any cooking other than Jane's. She truly *had* spoiled their culinary palates.

"I won't have much time to eat anyway," Louise said. "I'm still trying to round up donations for the fund-raiser next weekend."

"How's that going?"

"Very well. The organ committee has started storing items in the church basement. We have quite a collection now."

"I wish I had something to contribute to the silent auction or raffle," Alice said, "but I can't think of anything."

"You can certainly help with the auction or the raffle. You can also feel free to spend your money on any of the items." Louise smiled. "We need plenty of buyers too."

"Do you think you'll raise enough money?"

Louise drank the last of the buttermilk and wiped her mouth with her napkin. "I believe that we'll raise quite a bit of money, but I'm not sure if we'll raise enough to repair the organ. To buy an electronic one, probably. To buy a new pipe organ, maybe. But repairs?" She shrugged.

The back door burst open, and Jane rushed inside.

"What's wrong?" Louise asked.

"I have to get my bag. In a hurry," Jane said, glancing around the kitchen to see if she needed to take anything from there. "Lloyd dropped me and Aunt Ethel here to grab our suitcases. Then he'll take us back to Craig's nursery. We'll leave for Philadelphia from there."

She disappeared in the direction of the staircase. Louise and Alice started to clean up their lunch dishes, and while they were stacking the plates in the dishwasher, Jane returned, clutching the handle of her red, soft-sided suitcase on wheels. "Well, I'm off," she said. "You two gals stay out of trouble while I'm gone."

Louise hugged her. "I hope it goes well."

"Yes, particularly with Craig's presentations and sales," Alice said. "We'll be praying."

"Thank you," Jane said, hugging each of her sisters in turn. "Please do pray. A lot is riding on this for his new business. And please pray that I don't slug Aunt Ethel before this weekend is over. She's already driving me crazy."

Alice smiled. "Auntie means well."

"I know, but she has a habit of irritating me. Like a pebble in your shoe. Or sand in your bathing suit. Or—"

Honk!

"Hurry up there, Jane Howard," Ethel called from Lloyd's car in the driveway. "We're going to be late."

Jane groaned. "Remember what I said about praying for me."

"We will," Louise said, not doubting for a minute that Jane would at least manage to restrain herself enough not to murder their aunt. Beyond that, she wasn't quite certain.

"Have a wonderful time," Alice said.

Honk!

"Coming!" Jane yelled, then scurried out the back door, pulling the suitcase on wheels behind her. "Take care!" she called over her shoulder.

Then she was gone. Louise and Alice looked at each other, each feeling a little bereft at their sister's departure. It no longer seemed the same when one of the sisters was gone from the house for more than a day.

"Well," Louise said, "at least I have my fund-raising activities to keep me busy."

"And I have my grief meeting with Theo Dulane and Pastor Ken," Alice said.

"Are you riding to Potterston with Mr. Dulane?"

"No, Pastor Ken is taking me. Apparently Theo was planning to spend the day in Potterston." She paused. "I'm glad Pastor Ken offered to drive because I wouldn't feel comfortable riding alone with Theo."

Louise's brow wrinkled. "Has he upset you in some way?"

"Oh no," Alice said hastily. "But I don't know him well, and he, well . . . oh, it sounds so egotistical to say it—"

"—But he was interested enough in you to ask you to

dinner," Louise said, smiling. She fingered the strand of pale pearls around her neck. "Alice Howard, you seem to have trouble realizing that you're a wonderful woman. Why is it so difficult to believe that a man might be interested in you?"

Alice smiled. "Now you sound like Jane."

"For once I agree with her," Louise said, returning the smile. "There's nothing wrong with some male companionship in a woman's life. Even an older woman's. But I agree with *you* as well, that you don't want to cultivate a relationship with a man whom you scarcely know without more time. Especially with one of our guests."

"Then you see why I'm glad that Pastor Ken is driving me."

"Yes," Louise said. "And not to change the subject, but I'm also glad you are going to this meeting."

"Because it's about grief support?"

Louise nodded. "Not only do I think that you'll benefit as a nurse, but you'll benefit as a daughter who has lost her father. And I'm hoping that you'll share any tips you receive with me."

Alice paused thoughtfully. "You never really do get over the loss of a loved one, whether it's a father as for you and me, or a spouse, as for you and Theo."

"No, you never really do," Louise said softly. Then she smiled. "But the days do become better, and the world looks brighter again. This is what I pray for Theo to find. I also pray that he finds the love of others, as I did, to help him through his grief."

Feeling renewed, Alice gave Louise a hug. They held each other for a moment, then released, smiling, without a word, to go their separate ways for the afternoon.

Since Ethel had left town for the weekend to go to Philadelphia, Louise was in full charge of getting the fund-raiser organized for the following weekend. Fred Humbert had volunteered lumber and nails from his hardware store to create booths. His wife Vera quietly promised Louise and Ethel that she would add a woman's touch to the booths with decorative signs and bunting. Louise's understanding was that the Humberts were recruiting others to help them with their labors.

Meanwhile, Henry Ley had planned the best placement for the fund-raiser around the chapel grounds, and he and others were busy marking off spots for individual booths to hold garage sale items, game areas for children, and special areas for the silent auction and raffle. Louise saw the associate pastor, his wife and several other members from the church pacing off areas on the ground. Patsy Ley even laid strips of string as they walked, presumably to mark the various locations.

Louise waved hello, then headed for the chapel basement to check the supplies for the fund-raiser. She and Ethel had designated one area for silent auction items and one area for raffle items. In the silent auction area, they already had Fred's electric mower, Sylvia's beautiful handmade quilt, a first-edition, autographed book donated by Viola Reed from her bookstore and the cloisonné vase donated by Joseph and Rachel Holzmann.

In the raffle area, they had secured gift certificates from various Acorn Hill businesses, including the Coffee Shop, the dry cleaner and the Good Apple Bakery. They had also obtained a gift basket of various teas from Wilhelm Wood's Time for Tea and the promise of a special, private dinner courtesy of Zachary's.

Louise studied the list of people who hadn't donated items but had pledged to volunteer their time helping with the auction or raffle, or to bring garage sale items to set up in individual booths. As usual, Acorn Hill rallied for a good cause. All she and Ethel had had to do was ask, and the town members responded.

Thinking of Ethel, Louise wondered about the trip to Philadelphia. It had never crossed her mind to ask if she could tag along, even though she had lived in that city after she had married Eliot not long after graduating from college. That had been so many years ago. Yet even though she had spent so much of her life in Philadelphia, since her return to Acorn Hill and her sisters, she didn't feel the need to visit the city on a regular basis. Sometimes she did think fondly of the nineteenth-century, Greek revival house that she and Eliot had restored, but it had new owners now carving out a new history, as was she, with her home in Acorn Hill.

She smiled, double-checked her list and headed out to make sure that the flyers for the Grace Chapel Harmony Fund-Raiser had been duly posted around town.

Rev. Thompson and Alice arrived at Potterston for the grief support meeting. The hospital parking lot seemed less crowded on a Friday afternoon, and after parking in a designated clergy spot, the pastor led Alice toward the education room where the meeting was to be held.

"How long have you been participating in this group?" Alice asked as they walked along.

"Just during the summer. The group rotates different leaders every couple of months, so that none of us becomes burned out with the task. I'll be finished soon. Then someone else will take my place."

"I think it's a wonderful idea," Alice said. "Is it mostly clergy who participate?"

The pastor shook his head. "We've had hospice and home health-care workers, along with other professionals. We don't always talk about death or even impending death, such as with terminal cases. Grief can involve even those with every reasonable expectation of living, but with altered lifestyles, such as amputees or people with chronic, incurable illnesses."

"Do you have separate classes for people with different situations then?"

Rev. Thompson nodded. "For example, we have specialized classes for cancer survivors, family members of suicide deaths, and parents of stillborns. Today will be strictly grief recovery after death, no matter what the process. We're expecting quite a few participants besides you and Theo."

He led the way inside the education building and opened a classroom door. The sterile environment had been made more inviting by the arrangement of desks into a circle. A coffeepot hummed on a back counter where several people quietly mingled. Someone had written on the dry-erase board up front, "You are special. You are loved."

A man whom Alice recognized as a rabbi from a Potterston synagogue approached, all smiles. "Hi, Kenneth."

"Hello, Ben," Rev. Thompson said, shaking the man's hand. "I'd like you to meet Alice Howard, who's a nurse here at the hospital. She's going to sit in on our session. Alice, this is Rabbi Ben Cohen."

"Yes, Alice," Ben said, turning his smile her way. "We've met several times here, if I'm not mistaken."

"You're not," she said, shaking his proffered hand, "but unfortunately, it's usually under tragic circumstances involving a patient."

Ben nodded soberly, holding onto her hand. "That's true. We should have tea together in the cafeteria sometime. Kenneth has told me about the bed-and-breakfast that you and your sisters fixed up. I would love to hear more about it. My wife and I are interested in restoring an old home here in Potterston."

"I'd like that. Perhaps I can provide a few tips to make your plans go smoothly." Alice smiled.

"Then tea it shall be and, with your permission, maybe I'll take notes."

Despite the somberness of the meeting's purpose, Alice

continued to smile. Rabbi Cohen had always seemed to have a realistic but humorous outlook on life, and she imagined that he brought many smiles to the grief-stricken who appeared in this classroom or in the hospital corridors.

"Alice, this is Father Albert Modano," Rev. Thompson said, introducing a tall, blond man wearing a clerical collar.

"Hello, Father," she said.

"Hello, Alice. We've never met, but I've learned from several of my parishioners about you and your splendid care here at the hospital."

"That's good to hear," she said, though her cheeks warmed a little at the compliment.

Rev. Thompson introduced her to other leaders, including a female hospice chaplain, a female nonsectarian grief counselor and a male psychologist. Other men and women sat or spoke quietly, hovering around the coffeepot or in quiet groups elsewhere in the room.

She hadn't seen Theo Dulane yet, but just as she was beginning to wonder if he was going to make it, she saw him rush into the room as Rev. Thompson was encouraging everyone to take a seat.

"Sorry," he said, panting slightly. "I lost track of time at a sporting goods store at the mall."

Rev. Thompson lifted an eyebrow. "Was it this season's new fishing gear?"

Theo hung his head, the corners of his mouth lifting up. "You pegged me, Pastor."

Rev. Thompson smiled. "Have a seat, Theo. As you can see, Alice has decided to join us today."

"It's good to see you," Theo said, nodding in her direction. "Can I get you a cup of coffee before we start?"

"No, thank you, I don't drink coffee," she said. "But I'll save you a desk beside me if you want to get one."

Theo beamed, the first real smile she had seen from him

since he had been staying at Grace Chapel Inn. "Thanks, Alice. I think I'll do that."

Rev. Thompson winked at Alice, and she felt as though she had been let in on an inside joke. This Theo Dulane seemed different from the one who had been skulking around the inn. Could only one outing with Rev. Thompson have made such a difference?

Chapter Eighteen

While Jane rode with Craig to Philadelphia, she managed to keep a civil tongue about Ethel as long as possible. She said not a word when Ethel and Lloyd produced walkie-talkies so that they could all communicate with one another in their separate cars. Jane also didn't say a word when Ethel used the walkie-talkie at least every five minutes to announce some new requirement, such as when to stop for a bathroom break or when to fill up her thermos with cold water at a roadside stop.

But Jane finally exploded after they had stopped for the third side trip, this one for a second bathroom visit. "Honestly, Craig," she huffed, as they watched Ethel and Lloyd pile back into the mayor's SUV, "doesn't she know we're in a hurry to get to the garden show and set up? Can't she go one hour from Acorn Hill to Philadelphia without these delays?"

Craig put his van into gear and headed back onto the highway. "I think she enjoys road trips, and to some people part of the enjoyment is stopping occasionally."

"But every twenty miles?" Jane tapped the side of her head. "Is it old people in general, or is it just my aunt?"

Craig smiled, keeping a careful eye on the thickening highway traffic. An eighteen-wheeler whizzed past them in the left lane, followed by a two-seater sports car. "I like to hope that people will indulge my eccentricities when I'm older."

"Ouch!" Jane said, covering her heart with her hand. "That hurt, Craig. That sounded like chastisement, plain and simple, to me."

He waved out his side window at Trevor in his pickup, who followed the example of the red sports car by passing Craig. They could see the stacks of plants waving in the wind in the back of the truck. Kaylie picked up the walkie-talkie as she went past and said, "Last one to Philadelphia has to unload all the plants."

Craig laughed. They heard static over the transmitter, then Ethel, who was one car behind Craig in Lloyd's sport utility vehicle. "You two slow down up there. Life's a journey, not a destination."

Jane flipped off the walkie-talkie's switch. "And the last hour has seen the longest journey I've ever undertaken," she muttered.

"It's all right," Craig said. "We have plenty of time and—"
Bang!

"Craig, look out!" Jane yelled, pushing her feet against the floorboard, as though slamming on the brakes.

The eighteen-wheeler, several cars ahead in the left lane, had suddenly blown a tire. The driver wrestled the truck to the grassy median on the left at a point where there was no guardrail. Boxed in by traffic on the right, the sports car, however, deftly slipped between the rear of the truck and a minivan in the right lane. The driver sped ahead without looking back. The minivan slammed on its brakes and swerved to the right shoulder, forcing a Volkswagen Beetle, then Craig, to do the same to avoid a rear-end collision.

Jane closed her eyes, fearing a pileup, but when she felt Craig's van come to rest without any impact, she cautiously opened her eyes. Breathing a sigh of relief, she turned to Craig. "Whew! We were lucky."

"Trevor and Kaylie weren't," he said grimly, setting the brake.

"Why, what—?"

"When that sports car cut between the eighteen-wheeler and our lane, Trevor had to swerve to avoid both of the vehicles. I think he rolled his pickup." Craig checked traffic, then opened his door.

"Oh no!" Jane opened her door too, able to exit faster since she wasn't on the traffic side. Several cars had already stopped at the side of the highway, their occupants rushing to help. When traffic was clear, Jane and Craig crossed the highway.

Trevor's pickup had landed against a guardrail with the front, driver's side wheel caught on the metal railing. Trevor and Kaylie, however, seemed to be all right as they slowly exited Kaylie's passenger-side door.

The hood of Trevor's cab was crushed, and the bed of the truck was crumpled. Craig's plastic-potted plants were strewn up and down the highway, some crushed under passing automobile wheels and some smashed along the median.

Trevor and Kaylie leaned against the side of the truck. Kaylie sobbed uncontrollably, and Trevor took her in his arms. Both had bruises on their faces and arms, and blood trickled from a cut on Kaylie's forehead. Trevor whipped out a bandana and stanched the bleeding.

Craig and Jane rushed up. "Are you two all right?"

"I think so," Trevor said, still cradling Kaylie. "Are you, Kaylie?"

She nodded, unable to speak. She touched the wound on her forehead, and when she saw the blood on her fingers, she shuddered.

"It's okay," Trevor said soothingly. "It's not deep. It'll stop bleeding. Here, put this bandana against it until help comes."

Jane's mind raced. *Help. We need to call someone. Where, oh where, can we reach Alice? She's a nurse. She would know what to do in a situation like this.*

"I've got a cell phone here," Craig said, reaching into his pocket.

"No need," a voice behind them said. They turned to find Lloyd and Ethel standing behind them. Lloyd held up his cell phone. "I've already called 911 and the highway patrol. Someone will be here soon. Why don't you two sit in my car? I'm going to check on that truck driver. He may need help too. The passersby can help out if they're needed."

"Come on, dear," Ethel said soothingly to Kaylie, gently easing her from Trevor's arms. "You need to sit down. Let me get you some ice water for your forehead and a clean hankie."

"Th-thank you," Kaylie said, letting Ethel enfold her in an embrace. The older woman led the teenager to Lloyd's SUV.

Trevor's gaze followed them, but he seemed to accept that Kaylie was in capable hands. "Are you sure you're all right as well?" Craig asked.

"I'm okay," Trevor insisted. "Kaylie took the worst of the wreck." He shook his head. "Man, that was the freakiest thing. One minute we're cruising along. The next thing I know, I'm looking at the ceiling of my cab flipping over. I'm just glad we landed right side up again."

"I'm grateful you were wearing seat belts," Jane said.

Craig held out his phone. "Would you like to call your parents?"

"Yeah, that's probably a good idea," Trevor said. He turned an apologetic gaze to Craig. "I'm sorry about your plants, Mr. Tracy. I'd be glad to stay and see what we can salvage."

Craig shook his head. "Forget it. Most of them are okay, and you two are much more important. I'm so glad you're safe. Besides, you need to take care of Kaylie."

"Yeah," Trevor said, glancing at Lloyd's SUV. "If it were

just me, I'd forge on, but I'd better make sure she gets home safely. I promised her parents I'd take care of her."

"That's exactly what I want you to do," Craig said, patting Trevor's back. "Call your parents and Kaylie's parents. If they need me to take you home, I can."

"No sir, I don't want to delay you," Trevor said. "I'll ask my dad to come get us."

"Then we'll wait here until he does," Craig said.

Trevor moved off to make the phone call. Jane turned back to the SUV and saw that Ethel was ably tending to Kaylie, pressing a damp hankie to her forehead and giving her sips of ice water to drink. She spoke soothingly to the girl, rubbing her hands and keeping her from fingering her bruised face and forehead and thus getting more upset.

Jane's thoughts went back many years to when she had skinned her knees roller skating at Aunt Ethel and Uncle Bob's farm. They had warned her that the gravel road to their house wasn't a good place to skate, but she had blithely thrown off their words and insisted on having her way. When she had crawled, sobbing, to the front door, both knees deeply skinned, Aunt Ethel had hurried out the front door, wiped her hands on her apron and led Jane into the house. Inside, she had calmly cleaned the wounds, bandaged her up, wiped and kissed both tear-stained cheeks and later made her a batch of ginger cookies. Not once had she said, "I told you so" or admonished Jane for disobedience.

Funny how I had forgotten that. Auntie really knows how to help people when they're hurting. Now I know where Alice gets her nursing skills. As well as her compassion.

Trevor walked toward them, handing back the phone to Craig. "My dad will be here as soon as he can."

Sirens wailed. A highway patrol car followed by an ambulance pulled up, both vehicles' lights flashing. Paramedics jumped out and, directed by Trevor, moved toward Lloyd's vehicle carrying medical kits and other apparatus. While they worked, the patrol officers took statements from witnesses. Jane described what little she had seen, wishing now that she hadn't been such a baby in keeping her eyes closed.

The paramedics cleaned Kaylie's wound and covered it with fresh gauze and tape. As they stored their gear back in the ambulance, Craig introduced himself as Trevor's employer and asked about their condition. A young, male paramedic stopped working to relay the information. "The girl will be all right, but I told her to check with her doctor tomorrow if she has a bad headache or feels sleepy."

"How about Trevor?" Craig asked. "Did you check him out?"

The paramedic nodded. "He's all right. They both just got banged up a bit. They'll probably have multicolored bruises tomorrow where their seat belts snapped against them during the impact, but thank God they were wearing them. They would be in much worse shape if they hadn't. Lots of kids their age don't think traffic accidents can happen to them, but they do."

"What about the truck driver?" Jane asked.

The paramedic smiled. "He's fine. He feels bad that the blowout was the cause of the accident."

"I think a sports car caused the problem," Craig said. "It would have been nice if he'd stuck around to see what kind of trouble he caused by zipping in between the eighteen-wheeler and the rest of us."

The paramedic frowned. "I hope that the cops will catch up with him."

"Thank you for your help," Craig said.

The paramedic nodded, then went back to work, quickly restoring the ambulance to its original condition before driving off to the next crisis.

Several patrol officers had been policing the stretch of highway where the accident had occurred, directing rubber-neckers past the scene. Others had been clearing the roadway, making it safe for travel again. The truck driver had gotten help with his blown-out tire.

Trevor went to sit with Kaylie, who had stopped sobbing. She even smiled at something funny that he'd said, then leaned against him in the SUV for support.

Jane shaded her eyes against the sun. She was about to suggest to Craig that they call the garden show to let them know that they would be later than expected, when she saw Lloyd and Ethel collecting cardboard trays from the median.

She nudged Craig. "What are they doing?"

"I think they're trying to clean up the mess," he said. Striding toward them, he called, "Come on, you two. You don't have to do that. The highway crew will clean that up."

Lloyd straightened from where he bent over a plastic pot. He held it out for Craig's approval. "What clean up? We can save a lot of these plants. You've worked hard to raise them, Craig. Not to mention getting them to this show. Ethel and I can save as many as possible and put them in the back of my SUV to take to Philadelphia."

"But Lloyd," Jane protested. "You need your rest. The doctor said so."

"Phooey!" he said, waving a hand. "I'm not straining myself. This is good exercise."

"I think there's some plants over here too," Ethel said, climbing over the guardrail to reach the other side of the median. She bent down and picked up one, holding it proudly. "These things really flew."

"Let's see," Jane said, studying the plant in Ethel's hand.

Sure enough, the plant had loosened from its mooring in the plastic pot, but it could easily be pushed back in and the soil tamped down. The plant itself didn't seem any worse for wear.

Jane smiled. *One thing you can sure say about these native plants—they're a hardy lot.*

"What do you say, Jane?" Ethel asked. "Want to help?"

Her aunt's face beamed with such optimism that Jane had to smile. "Isn't this improper work for a woman?" she couldn't resist adding as an affectionate tease.

Ethel shook her head, her red hair catching the glints of summer sun. "Helping someone in need is never improper for a woman."

Jane touched her aunt's shoulder. She would have given the older woman a hug right there, but the guardrail blocked the space between them. "Then let's get to work," she said instead.

The grief support meeting kept Alice enthralled. Though she had already dealt with her father's death and thought that she had hurdled all the stages, she realized anew that sometimes the stages reappeared: denial, anger, bargaining and more. As time passed, however, they receded more quickly into the background, and the support class was designed to ease the bereaved step by step into healthier stages so that they could get on with their lives.

As she listened to Rev. Thompson speak, Alice realized that that was what he had done with Theo Dulane. He had found a special interest, fishing, that they had in common and connected with the hurting man that way. Theo did seem more cheerful today, and he had admitted to shopping at a sporting goods store. He had rarely left Grace Chapel Inn before that, but now he seemed willing to move back into society. Fishing, or anything else, would never replace his beloved Laverne, of course, but it was a step in the right direction.

Rabbi Cohen used humor to reach those in the class. Alice watched the faces of the audience. Before the rabbi started speaking, they were all somber. Some looked on the verge of tears. He met them where they were hurting, however, and did not shy from gentle jokes about the grieving process.

"Grief is like an elephant in the living room," he said.

"It's taking up all the space, but no one wants to talk about it, so we all tippy-toe around it with the weakest phrases you've ever heard. 'I'm so sorry for your loss.' 'I'm here for you.' 'It was God's will.' Please"—the rabbi pushed his hands against the air—"just once, could someone acknowledge the elephant?" He cupped his hands around his mouth like a megaphone. "'Hey! What can I do to help get this pachyderm out of your way?'"

The audience laughed. Some immediately looked embarrassed, covering their mouths with their hands. Rabbi Cohen pointed at a young woman accusingly. "You don't think you're allowed to have fun? It's wrong you should laugh?"

She glanced nervously at her young husband, then her eyes welled with tears. "We lost our baby two months ago to Sudden Infant Death Syndrome. She wasn't even three months old."

The rabbi's face softened. "This I understand. One of the reasons I help with this class is to help myself. Why, you ask? Because ten years ago my wife and I expected the birth of our first child. Nearly halfway through the pregnancy, we were informed that our child had severe heart and brain damage that wouldn't allow him to live past birth. In fact, we were told he could die any time in the womb.

"The doctors all said that we should have an abortion and save ourselves the grief later. Some of my dearest friends said that it was even God's will. But my sweet, wise Gail wouldn't hear of it. 'Who are we to shorten the life span that's been given this child?' she said. 'No, Ben. I will carry this baby until the time he's been given is over. Not one moment sooner. If he lives only ten minutes, *that* is God's will.'"

Alice felt a lump in her throat. The young woman leaned forward, tears glistening on her face. "What happened?"

The rabbi smiled. "Our Caleb lived thirteen minutes. Long enough for us to give thanks for his brief but precious life, which taught us so much about God's will."

The young woman wiped the tears from her face with the back of her hand. Smiling gently, Rabbi Cohen handed her a tissue. "My brother always wanted to work in paper products because he figured that life's sorrows are God's way of keeping tissue manufacturers in business." He shrugged. "Who knew?"

The woman smiled, then laughed.

Rabbi Cohen pointed. "You see? We've talked about the elephant in my living room and in yours. Some days it's hideous looking, with big tusks. But I say this to you, if you'll acknowledge that elephant—and laughing is part of that acknowledgment—one day he'll be so small that you can capture him in a glass no larger than a jelly jar. He'll never permanently leave your house—you'll always know he's there—but one day he won't have the size or the means to threaten you as much. Start corralling him by at least talking about his presence."

The woman nodded. "I think I see what you mean, Rabbi. Thank you."

After further discussions, Alice noticed that Theo was quietly blowing his nose into a handkerchief. His expression had changed as he listened to one professional after another address the issue of grief, his face showed a new peacefulness. Judging from the expressions of everyone else in the room, they all appeared to share the same condition.

When at last the meeting broke up, she hugged a few participants who had shared their tragedies and shook the hands of the professionals who had shared their time and expertise. She chatted briefly with the hospital chaplain, with whom she was well acquainted, then shook the hand of Father Modano.

"Thank you for the discussion about steps in the grief process," she said. "It's always a good reminder to hear that it's not a journey from point A to point B, but a circle."

"That's a comfort to some people and discouraging to

others," he said. "Some people want to hear that there will be a day when their grief is completely gone. I think that it's better for them to hear the truth."

"I agree," Alice said, moving on to thank the grief counselor.

When she got to Rabbi Cohen, she smiled. "Thank you for being so open," she said. "I wish I had known you when I first lost my father."

He patted her hand, smiling. "Thank you, Alice. And you can expect a call from my wife about redecorating. She really needs some help, my Gail."

Alice squeezed his hand as he gave her a farewell handshake. "I imagine that Gail will do just fine."

Chapter Nineteen

When Trevor's father arrived, he bundled Kaylie into the backseat, with Trevor beside her for moral support. She had stopped crying but was still shaken up. "I'm so sorry this happened," she had said several times to Craig. "I didn't mean to spoil the garden show for you."

"*Shh*," Trevor said, holding her close. "They'll still be able to make it."

"And we'll call and check in on you," Jane assured her. "Go home and rest up."

"You too, Trevor," Craig said. "There will always be plenty of work for you at Wild Things. Take the time you need to recuperate."

"Will do," Trevor said.

Craig phoned the garden show to let them know he was running late; but fortunately, his speech was not scheduled until the next day. Jane was doubly delighted because that also meant they would have more time to salvage as many of the wrecked plants as possible. She and Craig took over retrieving the scattered plants and plastic pots from the median and the edge of the highway. Lloyd and Ethel sat in the shade of Lloyd's SUV trying to repot as many as possible.

Ethel shook her head as she gently pushed the roots of a

strawberry plant back into the pot. "Poor Kaylie. Poor Trevor. They were looking forward to this trip."

"They helped a lot just getting us this far," Craig said, "so any good that comes from the garden show is largely due to their help. I'll have to figure out some way to make it up to them when we get back."

At last they had rescued as many plants as possible, scattering the rejects onto the grassy median. Lloyd drove his SUV behind Craig's van the rest of the way to Philadelphia, and this time, Ethel did not request any stops. She did not even bother to turn on the walkie-talkie.

It was a much more somber group checking into the hotel than the one that had started out in Acorn Hill. Ethel and Jane carried their baggage up to their room, and Craig and Lloyd did the same, two floors below. By the time they had hastily cleaned up and driven to the garden show at the Pennsylvania Convention Center, however, they were feeling somewhat better, though none of them could forget about Kaylie.

Since Craig wasn't lecturing that day, they all sat in the booth that he had leased to promote his plants. Jane helped him arrange the eye-catching signs and stand-up cardboard cutouts detailing the good points of growing native plants. Ethel set out the plants themselves and, when she had finished, started hawking them.

Jane was mortified, until she saw that if for no other reason than to gawk at an energetic, elderly woman with bottle-dyed red hair, people were stopping at Craig's booth. Jane quietly handed out sample plants, referring questions to Craig. Ethel, however, had stationed herself at the plants for sale and did business like an expert.

"Look at this beauty," she said, holding up an orange plant. "The tag says its botanical name is"—she checked the bottom—"*asclepias tuberosa*. But between you and me, it's known as butterflyweed. Why they call it a weed I don't know because it's lovely."

She kept up the patter, impressively drawing people to the booth. Jane noticed that Ethel made sure to keep the plant in full view, following the marketing maxim of product placement.

"And this one is *echinacea purpurea*. Purple coneflower. Pretty, isn't it? I bet that the echinacea supplement comes from this plant, and I know just who could enlighten us. Craig, where are you? Oh, Craig!"

Craig turned at the sound of the trill in her voice and ably took over the discussion. Ethel wisely kept silent while he spoke, holding up an identical plant for all in the crowd to see when he briefly held up each plant for discussion.

Unneeded for the moment, Jane shifted to the side of the booth, alongside Lloyd Tynan. "She's amazing," Jane said, shaking her head.

"She certainly is," Lloyd said, beaming fondly.

"I'll bet she could sell ice in Antarctica."

Lloyd turned, "She's not quite ready for the Shopping Network. Ethel Buckley can only throw herself into something she truly believes in, Jane, like the interests of you and your sisters. Whatever concerns you concerns her. Remember that Craig promised all the proceeds from the sale of these plants to Louise's organ committee fund."

A flush of shame crept across the back of her neck. She knew that she would do well to remember Lloyd's words in the future, particularly the next time she felt inclined to be annoyed with Ethel.

"I'm glad you picked these flowers to show the folks," Craig said to Ethel, so that the audience could hear. "Ladies and gentlemen, these are Pennsylvania native perennials that you can plant in the sun. Aren't they pretty? Now for planting in the shade, you might want to try a cardinal flower here."

"*Lobelia cardinalis*," Ethel said, deliberately scrunching up her face as she read the Latin, causing the audience to laugh. Several people lined up, money in hand, to purchase the plants that Craig discussed. Ethel served as cashier, expertly handling the transactions.

Lloyd smiled, nudging Jane with his elbow. "Looks like we need to set out some more plants for sale. And there's a couple of customers who would like a free sample."

Jane straightened, feeling much more cheerful than she had since the accident earlier in the day. "Time to get to work then."

The next morning when Alice woke up, she took a few extra minutes to stretch in bed before rising. She loved her career as a nurse, but it was nice to have a free day ahead of her. *Ah, no work today. A day off.*

After she dressed and made up the bed, carefully adjusting the pastel patchwork quilt, she headed downstairs. Just as she passed the phone near the staircase, it rang.

"Grace Chapel Inn," she answered.

"Alice?"

"Carlene," Alice said, smiling. "How are you?"

"Well, I could use someone to talk to, but I can't leave the office."

"I'd love to have a chat. I'll be right over."

She hung up the phone. Louise had heard the phone and come from the kitchen. "Trouble?"

"I'm not sure. Carlene just said she needed to talk to someone."

"Perhaps she has reached a decision about the typography equipment," Louise said. "I believe Mr. Nix was leaving today, correct?"

"That's right," Alice said. "I hope you don't mind if I go to see Carlene. I suppose one of us should stay here in case Theo Dulane needs anything. And we do have a guest or two checking in today, I believe."

"I'm fine," Louise said. "Now you better have tea and a muffin before you go to see what Carlene wants."

After her snack, Alice headed toward the *Nutshell*. She assumed that Carlene would naturally be hard at work, but the office was eerily silent. The shades were drawn, throwing the room into near darkness.

"Carlene?" she called tentatively.

"I'm back here."

Alice peered into the darkness. "Where?"

"Here. Behind the equipment."

Alice felt her way carefully past the desk and to the back of the room. By the time she bumped against the old Linotype, her eyes had adjusted to the dark. Carlene was sitting dejectedly on a parson's bench located along the back wall. She glanced up and tried to smile. "Thanks for coming," she said, then teared up.

Alice sat on the bench beside her, wrapping an arm around her friend's shoulder. "What's the matter?"

Carlene sniffled a bit, then pulled a handkerchief from her skirt pocket and blew her nose. "I'm sorry, Alice. I just needed a friend. I made my decision today, and it was difficult."

"A decision about the equipment?"

Carlene nodded. "David . . . Mr. Nix had to go home today, and he needed to know one way or another." She drew a deep breath.

"And?" Alice prompted.

"And I told him that I wasn't selling."

Despite her previous intention to accept whatever Carlene said, Alice felt a wave of relief. "I'm glad," she said.

Carlene sniffled. "Really?"

Alice nodded. "Even if the equipment and the *Nutshell* don't have historic designations, they are still important to those of us who live in Acorn Hill. They are tied to our past. A lot of our history has been printed on the *Nutshell*'s pages, and we have you, your father and others in the press to thank for that. I would hate to see all those memories lost to someone we don't even know."

Carlene nodded. "That was what helped me make my decision. David would never tell me whom he represented. I don't know if it was a museum or an eccentric rich man who just wanted to buy up historic toys." She twisted the handkerchief in her hands. "But oh, Alice, the money. The *Nutshell* could have used it." She gestured around the aging office, with its dust, chipped bricks and gouged wood floor.

Alice hugged her. "I know, Carlene. I think it was a bold decision you made. And one you won't regret. I believe your father would be proud. Now the school kids can still enjoy their field trips here every year."

"The opening of school won't be long in coming," Carlene said, her face cheering. "I like having the kids come to see the equipment."

Alice had an idea. "Why don't you see if someone would like to train on it? Maybe someone from high school who plans to major in journalism would like to get extra credit for learning the old typography ways. It would help you keep the equipment in good shape and make sure that the craft doesn't die out."

Carlene smiled for the first time since Alice had arrived. "That's a wonderful idea, Alice. Perhaps I could even get the intern to help me with the newspaper itself. I couldn't afford to pay anything, of course."

"But that's the point of an internship," Alice reminded her. "For an apprentice to gain experience. That's why I thought a high school student would be a good choice."

"You're right." Carlene nodded. Then her face fell again.

"Now what's wrong, dear?" Alice prodded gently.

"I guess David Nix was just 'romancing' me so that I would sell the equipment. For a while I believed differently. I felt like a high school kid, Alice. I felt ... *wanted*. I really did.

But when I told him no sale today, he practically fled out the door."

Alice thought for a moment, choosing her words carefully. It was true that Carlene hadn't had much dating experience. Neither had Alice over the years, but she had always found contentment in her worship, family and work. Carlene was not a churchgoer, nor did she have any family.

"You always have me, Jane and Louise," Alice said softly. "And everyone else in Acorn Hill. You're important to us all. You're so busy all the time with the newspaper . . . perhaps an intern would help free up some of your time, too, so that you can get out more." She drew a deep breath. "We'd love to have you worship with us at Grace Chapel, for instance."

Carlene blinked. "I know. Church just isn't for me. Not being married . . . I feel so alone there."

Alice squeezed her hand. "I know how you feel. I'm not married either. I often feel left out when I think that Louise and Jane both had husbands."

Suddenly she remembered the grief support group and her resolve to pay more attention to others' suffering, spoken or unspoken. "But there are plenty of us who are unmarried."

"Yeah," Carlene said, a trace of bitterness in her voice. "But you have Mark Graves."

"Mark is a good friend," Alice said, "but we do not have any type of permanent relationship. Why, he doesn't even live in Acorn Hill. I enjoy his company, but when he's not here, I have plenty of things to keep me busy. And friends like you to share time with."

Carlene considered for a moment. "Maybe you're right, Alice. Maybe I've spent too much time typing on the keyboard and not enough allowing myself to have fun."

"There are plenty of things to do in Acorn Hill," Alice said gently, "and if you look around, there are plenty of people to enjoy them with. You can always start with me."

Carlene gave her a hug. "I know. That's why I called you. I knew you'd understand."

"Of course I do," Alice said, returning the hug. "And in celebration of your decision, and my day off from work, let's go to the Coffee Shop for lunch."

Carlene wiped her nose one last time and her smile said it all. "Done."

After manning the booth at the convention center on Friday, the Acorn Hill foursome found that the garden show was a much livelier place the next day. Word of mouth about the plants must have been considerable because there were twice as many people at the booth on Saturday. With Jane's help, Craig gave several minilectures in addition to his speech, while Ethel and Lloyd stayed at the booth to handle plant sales and answer what questions they could. Fortunately, Craig had printed a brochure with native-plant information, and with the Wild Things Web address and store information.

"Look at all the business cards we collected while you were gone," Ethel said, showing Craig and Jane a fishbowl nearly half full. Craig planned to draw a name for a grand prizewinner of a lovely maidenhair fern. He would also use all the contact information from the business cards to establish a computer database, which he would use for future e-mail and standard newsletters.

"How did your speech go?" Lloyd asked, interested, since oration was one of his many tasks as mayor of Acorn Hill.

"It went very well," Jane said before Craig could respond. "He dazzled them with helpful information about native plants."

"And it certainly didn't hurt that Jane assisted by holding up examples. Seeing the real thing, rather than slides, made it much more effective," Craig said.

"I'm afraid I still don't have Aunt Ethel's salesmanship," Jane said, smiling at the older woman.

Ethel returned the smile. "I'd be glad to give you a few pointers if you want, Jane. Though I think you do pretty well on your own."

"I don't know what I would have done without you two," Craig said, nodding toward Lloyd and Ethel. "I can't tell you how much I appreciate the fact that you pitched in to replace Trevor and Kaylie."

"Has anyone called to see how they're doing?" Jane asked.

Lloyd nodded. "I called during your speech. Kaylie's mother said she was resting and doing well. Trevor's dad said the same."

"I'm so glad," Jane said.

"Are you two sure you don't want to do some Philadelphia sightseeing on your own?" Craig asked Lloyd and Ethel.

Ethel shook her head. "We're having much more fun doing this. We can tour Philadelphia anytime."

A stylish, middle-aged brunette in an expensive business suit stepped up to the booth. "Excuse me. Which one of you is Craig Tracy?"

"I'm Craig."

The woman smiled, extending her hand. "I'm Dora Lundt from *Home and Garden World*."

"Wow," Jane whispered to Ethel. "That's a national magazine."

"It's a pleasure to meet you, Ms. Lundt," Craig said. "How can I help you?"

"I'd like to interview you, if I may, for a future issue of our publication. I think our readers would be interested in hearing about your work with native plants. There's a thriving organic, back-to-nature movement in gardening, and native plants fit right into that subject."

"But I only specialize in native plants of Pennsylvania."

Jane stifled a groan. Craig's candor was going to cost him valuable publicity.

Fortunately, Dora smiled, waving a manicured hand that looked as though it had never touched a pot full of soil. "It will be a wonderful angle in general, and in particular for our Pennsylvania readers." She paused. "I also understand that you had some difficulties getting to the garden show."

Craig nodded soberly. "My high school worker and his girlfriend were involved in a traffic accident on the way here. Fortunately, they're all right. The rest of my team pitched in to salvage the plants and get us set up here."

Dora turned to Ethel. "And I hear that *this* delightful woman has been instrumental in drawing attention to your booth."

Ethel flushed. "I believe in Craig and what he's doing with native plants. I've also had lots of help from Lloyd and Jane here."

Dora smiled. "I might want to talk to you three, as well. But first, Craig, do you mind if I take a few minutes of your time to get some questions answered? I thought we could go to the press room. It's quiet there, and it's just around the corner. I promise not to keep you long. I know you're busy."

"I don't mind at all," Craig said.

Dora said her good-byes to everyone else, then led the way toward the press room. Craig followed, winking behind her back at Jane as if to say he understood what a great chance he had to get some free publicity for Wild Things.

Jane sighed with relief.

The interview went well, as did the rest of the garden show. When they packed up Sunday afternoon, exhausted from a long, busy weekend, not a single plant remained. All the samples had been given away, and all the other plants had been sold. Everyone regarded the venture to be a success.

"It was a great weekend and a great start for my new business," Craig said to Jane on the trip back to Acorn Hill. "And I owe it all to you and Trevor for coming up with the idea."

"You had some help in Ethel, Lloyd and Kaylie too."

"Don't think I haven't forgotten. I plan to keep an eye on Trevor once he starts college. He's the kind of enthusiastic, knowledgeable person I'd like to have working for me during the summers and perhaps even after he graduates. He already has a lot of valuable knowledge and experience."

Jane sighed, stretching her arms as best she could in the limited space of the van. Because of the last-minute plant repotting, lifting and demonstrating all weekend, she had muscles aching that she hadn't felt for years. It was worth it, though. She had had a great time, and all the effort had helped Craig. "I bet your business will be booming soon."

Craig grinned. "I hope so. Though if orders grow quickly, I may need a full-time helper. Any chance you'd be interested?

Jane shook her head. "I've enjoyed learning about the plant business, but I'm content with things at Grace Chapel Inn. This was a lark."

"Your lark has been my business growth," he said. "And I'm still going to help you plan and plant some native plants on the Grace Chapel Inn grounds. For free, of course."

"Of course," Jane said, smiling.

Chapter Twenty

Louise and Alice were glad to welcome Jane home Sunday afternoon, each giving her a big hug. "We enjoyed each other's company, but it was lonely without you," Louise said.

"We missed your cooking," Alice said pointedly.

Jane grinned. "That's what I like to hear. I'm loved only for my culinary skills. Let me put my bags away. Then let's meet in the library. You fill me in on the weekend, and I'll tell you all about the garden show."

Thirty minutes later that's just what they did. Alice brought in a tray of drinks, lemonade for her and Jane, and a tall glass of yellow-specked, white liquid for Louise. Jane eyed it suspiciously. "That's not what I think it is, is it?"

"Yes, it is," Louise said calmly. "Buttermilk. *Mmm mmm.* And heavenly. Thank you, Alice."

"You're welcome," she said, settling in an adjacent chair. She clinked her glass with Louise's and they each sipped contentedly.

Jane set down her own glass. "All right, what went *on* around here while I was gone?"

"What do you mean?" Louise said with an innocent tone.

"Alice?" Jane crossed her arms.

"I don't know what you mean either," Alice said, feigning ignorance.

"The buttermilk? You know how we've always teased Louie."

"Oh, that," Alice said, pretending sudden recall. "Weren't we silly about that all these years?"

Jane looked hurt. "I thought it was kind of fun. I mean . . . buttermilk? Who drinks buttermilk except old ladies?"

Louise thumped down her glass. "Jane Howard, I am *not* old."

"Louise, I'm sorry," Alice said. "I shouldn't have agreed with you to tease Jane. I wanted this to be a happy time when she came home. Of course you're not old, dear."

"No, of course not," Jane said soothingly, then smiled. "I guess I see why the joking has gotten out of hand over the years." She looked at the buttermilk glass, then at Louise. "Do you *really* like that stuff? Because if you do, I promise to lay off teasing you."

"I really do," Louise said, still sounding miffed. "I always have."

"Then I'll be sure to buy more," Jane said, holding her glass toward Louise. "Truce?"

Louise wavered a moment, then touched her glass to Jane's. "Truce."

Alice sighed audibly. "Now tell us about Philadelphia, Jane."

Jane announced to her sisters more than once that she was glad to be back at Grace Chapel Inn and especially glad to be back in her own kitchen. That night she whipped up fluffy omelets for dinner, while Alice and Louise sat at the kitchen table and chatted with her.

"I like an occasional meal out as much as the next woman," Jane said, "but not all weekend. I couldn't wait to cook something at home." She withdrew eggs from the refrigerator, then peered inside. "Are we out of milk?" she said to no one in particular.

Louise removed a piece of paper from her pocket. "You can look forward to cooking more of your Texas breakfasts next weekend. Guess what? The Havertys are returning."

"So soon?" Alice asked. "Did they say why?"

Louise shook her head. "No, they didn't. As a matter of fact, neither one of them booked the room. It was a woman who identified herself as the secretary for Walter's country-western band."

"Ah, here's the milk. Way at the back." Jane set the milk and eggs on the counter and retrieved a bowl from the cupboard. "Maybe they're coming back because they got a gig around here. Walter seemed to be interested in that possibility," she said.

"That may be the reason," Louise said, placing the reservation on the table and pressing the folds out thoughtfully. "I doubt I'll see much of them though. I'll be busy with the fund-raiser next weekend." She watched Jane pour milk from the carton, then leaped from her chair and snatched it from Jane's hands.

"Louise!" Jane stepped back, startled. "What on earth are you doing?"

Louise sniffed the carton, studied the small content already in the bowl, then handed the carton to Jane. She took a whiff, then made a face. "Whew. This milk's gone bad. But how did you know?"

"It's not that the milk has soured," Louise said sheepishly. "It's buttermilk. When you were out of town, I put it in that carton to hide it from you."

"Why, how very devious of you, Louie." Jane laughed. "But I'm glad you stopped me from using it in the omelets. Although who knows? It might be a new taste sensation for the Grace Chapel Inn menu."

Alice glanced at Jane. Jane glanced at Alice. In unison, they wrinkled their noses and said, "*Eeeww.*"

∽

Jane went to bed early that night, promising herself that she could sleep late the next morning. Although she had enjoyed herself at the garden show during the weekend, she had tired herself out in helping Craig. She hadn't realized *how* tired she was until she nodded off several times during the hour's drive home from Philadelphia.

Nevertheless, she awoke Monday morning at her normal hour and, try as she might, she could not sleep any later. She finally got out of bed and put on her jogging clothes, deciding that what she needed was a good run.

The fresh air and exercise worked wonders to clear her head and reinvigorate her body. The muscles that she had worked lifting plants all weekend stretched with pleasant pain as she jogged away from the inn, past Grace Chapel, and beyond.

She had to acknowledge that as much as she liked to travel, it was always good to be back in Acorn Hill. The summer grass sprang under her step, and the air felt crisp and clean. By the time she had run her course and arrived, panting, back at Grace Chapel Inn, she felt ready to face a new week.

Louise was hanging up the phone when Jane entered through the front door. "There you are," Louise said. "Craig Tracy just phoned, and he wants you to call him back as soon as possible. He says it's urgent."

"Did he say what was wrong?" Jane asked, alarmed.

Louise shook her head. "He just said to call him at the shop."

Jane wiped sweat from her brow with the terry cloth bands around her wrists. She had run hard, and her clothes stuck to her skin, but a shower would have to wait.

Craig answered on the first ring. "Jane! I'm so glad you called me back so quickly," he said after she had greeted him.

"What's up?" she asked.

"It's Kaylie. Trevor called me last night, after we got

back. She was all right after Trevor's dad brought them home, but she started developing symptoms of a concussion, so they took her to Potterston Hospital."

"Oh no," Jane said, gripping the phone. "Is she all right?"

"They kept her in the hospital the rest of the weekend, and they're running some tests. I was hoping that you'd go with me to visit her."

"Of course I will," she said. "I just got back from a run, and if you'll give me thirty minutes to shower and change clothes, I'll be ready to go."

"I'll pick you up in the van," Craig said.

Jane hung up the phone and found Louise standing in the doorway. "I'm sorry if I was eavesdropping," Louise said, "but I couldn't help overhearing as I passed by. Is everything all right with Kaylie?"

"I don't know. Craig said that she's in the hospital."

"Oh my," Louise said.

"Craig's going to pick me up, and we're going to see how she's doing."

"Is there anything I can do to help?" Louise asked.

Jane shook her head. "I don't think so, but I'll let you know."

Craig picked her up in almost exactly thirty minutes. They spoke little during the drive, each one concerned about Kaylie. When they got to the hospital, Craig parked, then retrieved a potted lily from the back of the van.

"It's a native lily," he said. "It seemed appropriate."

"It's beautiful," Jane said.

They hurried to the information desk, where an elderly, white-haired woman in a pink volunteer smock gave them Kaylie's room number.

"I feel terrible," Craig said as they rode up the elevator. "I feel guilty that we went on to Philadelphia."

"We didn't know she was badly hurt," Jane said, trying to be reassuring. "Don't beat yourself up, Craig. The accident was the fault of that driver in the red sports car, anyway."

Inside Kaylie's room they found the patient with her parents and Trevor. They were all laughing and chatting amiably, so Jane knew right away that Kaylie's injury couldn't be too serious. She looked fine without the wide white gauze wrapped around her head that Jane had somehow expected to see.

"Mr. Tracy! Ms. Howard!" Kaylie said, her face beaming. "This is my mom. You've already met my dad." Mr. and Mrs. McKissack exchanged greetings with the visitors.

"Hi, kiddo," Craig said, holding out the lily. "I brought this for you."

"Oh, thank you. It's beautiful. Mom, would you put it on that shelf over there?"

Mrs. McKissack smiled at Craig. "That was so thoughtful of you."

"Hi, Ms. Howard," Trevor said, getting up from where he sat on the edge of Kaylie's bed. "It's nice to see you and Mr. T."

"How are you, Kaylie?" Jane asked, moving toward the bed.

Craig moved right along with her. "Kaylie, I was so sorry to hear that you weren't doing well. We never would have gone on to Philadelphia if we knew you weren't."

"I was fine when I first got home. Well, a little banged up and shaken, but I didn't feel bad. Then my head began to hurt and I was sleepy all the time."

"Her parents were afraid she might have had a concussion," Trevor said.

"Scared us half to death," Mrs. McKissack said. "So we got her to the emergency room."

"And they admitted her," Trevor said.

"But the good news is that I'm doing fine," she said,

smiling broadly. "The doctor was in here just a moment ago. They ran a bunch of tests yesterday, and they got back the results this morning. The tests don't show any problems."

Craig looked relieved. "I'm so glad to hear that. You must be happy too," he said to Kaylie's parents.

Mr. McKissack nodded. "Indeed we are. They say we can take our girl home this evening, after he and the nurse finish the paperwork."

"That's wonderful," Jane said.

They heard a knock at the door. A young man poked his head into the room. "Kaylie McKissack?"

"Yes?" she said, puzzled.

The tall, sandy-haired man pushed open the door to enter, a bouquet of pink roses in his hand. He coughed as though embarrassed, then held them out. "I brought these for you."

"Thank you," she said, her expression perplexed. "Do I know you?"

His face went solemn. "No. At least . . . we've never met." He drew a deep breath. "I'm Dale Parnell. I'm the one who apparently caused the traffic accident that landed you here in the hospital."

The red sports car! Jane glanced at Craig. He set his jaw and stepped forward. Jane put a hand on his arm and shook her head.

"See here," Mr. McKissack said, moving toward Dale. "You don't have any right—"

"I . . . I know I shouldn't be here," he said, stepping back. "But I wanted to see for myself that you are all right. The police said you didn't leave in an ambulance, but they didn't know how you were doing. I did some checking and found you were here."

"So the police caught up with you?" Jane asked.

"Actually, I came forward when I heard about the accident on the news," he said. "I didn't even know I had caused any trouble. I certainly would have stopped if I had."

"You shouldn't have been driving so fast," Craig said, his jaw still tight.

"I know. My wife said the same thing after I found out what had happened."

"She's right," Jane said. "There was no reason to be tearing up the highway like that."

"I thought there was at the time," Dale said, hanging his head. "You see, my wife had just phoned me that she was going into labor. She's been having a difficult pregnancy, and the baby wasn't due for another four weeks. They'd taken her to the hospital in Philadelphia, and I was rushing to get to her. We live just twenty miles from here."

Everyone in the room seemed to soften. Trevor was the first to step forward. "That's a tough spot, man. How's your wife? How's the baby?"

Dale raised his head, a smile on his face. "We had a daughter, and she and her mother are both fine, thank God. It was a little touch and go with the baby for a day or two, but she seems to be out of the woods. I'm heading home for the first time since Friday, but I wanted to stop by and give you these, Miss McKissack."

"Thank you, Mr. Parnell." Kaylie smiled. "They're lovely. And I'm so glad to hear about your wife and daughter."

Dale cleared his throat. "How are *you*? Are you . . . all right?"

Kaylie beamed. "I'm going to be fine. They thought I might have had a head injury, but apparently not. I'm okay. They're letting me go home this evening."

"That's great," he said. "I'm sure you'll be glad to leave here."

"Look . . . Dale, is it?" Mr. McKissack stepped forward. "It was nice of you to stop by and check on my daughter. Most people wouldn't have done that."

"I would have been here sooner if it hadn't been for my wife's situation," he said. "I'm really sorry for the trouble I've caused."

"We're just glad Kaylie wasn't hurt seriously," Trevor said.

Dale turned. "Was that your truck that she was riding in?" Trevor nodded.

Dale groaned. "I'm sorry about that too. I know what a hassle it is to deal with insurance companies. I have one of the best, though, and they've assured me they'll be in touch with you soon to make everything right."

"Thanks," Trevor said. He held out his hand. Dale shook with him, man to man.

"I'd better go and let you get back to your visit," he said, then handed Trevor a card with his address and phone number on it. "Let me know if either of you need anything," he said to Trevor and Kaylie.

"Thank you," Kaylie said. "Give our regards to your wife and daughter."

Dale nodded and left. Mr. and Mrs. McKissack smiled at each other. "It's nice to know that there are still decent people in the world," Mrs. McKissack said.

"Especially people who are willing to own up to their mistakes," Mr. McKissack added.

Trevor hugged Kaylie. "I'm just glad that you're going to be okay."

Craig and Jane echoed their sentiments, then at Trevor's request, told them all what they had missed at the garden show.

The rest of the week leading up to the fund-raiser moved by faster than Louise would have preferred. With Ethel back in town and at the helm, preparations for the Grace Chapel Harmony Fund-Raiser moved efficiently, but not without a few bumps. Louise and Ethel had already gathered what they privately called their big-ticket items for the silent auction and the raffle, but town members who wanted simply to contribute garage-sale-type items were causing something of a problem.

"Too many of them do not understand why we don't want to raffle their old magazine collections," Louise confided privately to Ethel. "Or why we don't want to auction their souvenir playing cards."

Ethel shook her head. "It's just junk, that's what it is. If it's going to sell at all, it will sell better in one of the individual booths, anyway. Well, I'll be glad to handle any complaints, Louise. I know how to deal with these people. You have enough on your mind with the pipe organ."

"Yes, I do," Louise said. The organ had created its usual raucous noises during Sunday services. Florence Simpson had turned and deliberately glared at Louise in the middle of her solo.

Ethel patted her hand. "Don't worry, dear. Things will go well. You'll see."

"I hope so, Auntie," Louise said, wishing she had Ethel's confidence.

Saturday morning Louise was up early, heading to the Grace Chapel grounds, where dew still sparkled on the grass. Fred and his crew of volunteers were putting the finishing touches on the booths, and Louise was relieved to see that everything appeared to be ready to go for the nine o'clock opening.

"Hi, Louise!" Vera Humbert called down from the top of a booth, where she draped red, white and blue bunting.

Louise had to step back to look up high enough to see her friend. "Hi, Vera. What are you doing?"

Vera took a staple gun and affixed the last edge of the bunting to the wooden structure. "All finished. This is my personal booth, and I saved it for last. I'm selling some of the school's old texts that were going to be disposed of, and I have a lot of history books. I understand we have homeschoolers coming to the fund-raiser today, and they love the opportunity to get textbooks at a good price."

"Wonderful. Thank you for all your help," Louise said.

Vera nodded, then went back to adjusting the bunting.

Louise walked the grounds, concerned even though things seemed to be in complete readiness. What if only a few people came? What if the church did not make enough money to repair the organ?

Rev. Thompson came alongside her, coffee cup in hand. "Feeling nervous, Louise?"

"A bit," she admitted. "I certainly appreciate all the effort that has gone into this fund-raiser. I just hope that it's worthwhile."

Rev. Thompson smiled. "It's always worthwhile to see a community come together with purpose. We all know how important the organ is as well—even people who aren't members of Grace Chapel. Have a good time today, Louise."

"Thank you, Pastor Ken," she said. "I'm sure that I will."

He nodded, then moved off to help Fred cart away the last of the unneeded lumber.

Louise stood in the middle of the grounds, admiring the booths and larger structures. Fred and his workers had created a special stage for the raffle and silent auctions, and she understood that Patsy Ley had volunteered to draw winners for the raffle items every hour, starting late in the afternoon. They would raffle a few smaller items then, leaving the larger items for the next day. They wanted to give people plenty of time to buy more tickets.

"Louise."

She turned at the sound of her name and was delighted to see Kathleen Haverty. Today she wore her normally pinned-up, long, dark braid loose. She tossed it over her shoulder and held out her arms to Louise as though they hadn't recently seen each other.

"Kathleen," Louise said, accepting the embrace. "We were glad to learn you were returning to Grace Chapel Inn. But what are you and Walter doing back in town?"

Kathleen laughed. "It was serendipitous. Our gig in Texas got canceled, but we found a place for our band to play in this area starting Monday night, and Walter has contacted some other places farther north for when we're finished here. We've used the time since we left here to enjoy some sightseeing. The rest of the band will be staying in Potterston, but Walter and I would like to stay at the inn until the new engagement is over . . . if you'll have us."

"Of course we will," Louise said. "And that's exciting news about the band. If you don't have to rehearse today, we hope you'll join us at our fund-raiser here."

"I read the flyer," Kathleen said, nodding at one of the papers tacked strategically around the fund-raiser grounds. "The proceeds are for the organ?"

Louise nodded.

"A most worthy cause then," Kathleen said, patting Louise on the arm. "Well, I'd better find Walter. I have to see if he's getting into trouble. He has a tendency to do that when I'm not around."

Louise smiled. The thought of the good-natured man's getting into trouble was ludicrous. "Good-bye, Kathleen. I'm sure I'll see you later."

"You certainly will," she said, winking.

The fund-raiser went without a hitch on Saturday. Everyone who manned an individual booth reported good sales from garage sale items. Raffle tickets sold well, too, and Patsy Ley reported that the first raffle item, a twenty-dollar lunch at the Coffee Shop, attracted more money than its retail value.

As Louise helped everyone shut down at the end of the

day, Craig Tracy approached her. "It's good to see you," she said. "I've been so busy this week that I haven't had a chance to congratulate you on your success in Philadelphia."

"That's why I wanted to see you," he said, handing her an envelope. "This is the money from the sale of my plants. I wanted you to have it for the organ fund."

"Oh, Craig, Jane told me about this, but it's really much too generous of you."

He smiled and shrugged. "Why? It's my money to contribute as I wish."

"But you worked so hard for this," she said, fingering the envelope.

"Exactly. And *you* work hard enriching church services with the organ. You and Grace Chapel *and* Acorn Hill deserve either a new organ or the original one repaired."

Tears sprang to Louise's eyes. It had been a long day, but she had heard not one word of complaint from anyone. Once again the town had pitched together, and now this. "Thank you, Craig. This means a great deal to me. I appreciate your encouragement as well."

"You're welcome," he said, patting her shoulder. "Use the money as you and the committee see fit, and whether it's a new one or a repair of the old one, I'll make a special floral arrangement for the altar on the day that it's first played."

"That would be wonderful," she said. "I'll take you up on your offer when the time comes."

Back at Grace Chapel Inn, Jane insisted that Louise soak her feet in a warm footbath in the kitchen. "You've been working hard all day," she said. "Let Alice and me pamper you."

"This does feel heavenly," Louise said, leaning back in her chair. "But I feel decadent. You two worked the fund-raiser as well."

"But not as late as you did," Alice said, "so we saved you some dinner."

"I hope it's not cotton candy or hot dogs," Louise said, groaning at the recollection of the fund-raiser's food smells that even now wafted through her memory.

"Nope, it's my special chicken potpie," Jane said, setting a plate in front of her sister. "And your favorite . . . buttermilk."

Louise sat up straighter. Jane grinned at her, and she smiled back. "Thank you."

"You're welcome," Jane said. "And by the way, save room. There's peach sherbert for dessert."

"You're spoiling me," Louise murmured, digging into the potpie.

"I prefer to think of it as buttering you up," Jane said. "I'm hoping that either you or Aunt Ethel will give me some inside information on some of those auction items I bid on today."

"Sorry," Louise said, barely looking up from her plate. "Not a chance."

The next day went equally well, until late in the afternoon. An hour or two before the fund-raiser's conclusion, Louise was making the rounds, and Patsy Ley drew her aside for a quiet consultation.

"I don't know if this is important or not," Patsy whispered, "but I've been keeping track of the bids for the items in the silent auction. Everything's getting good bids, most even exceeding their original price, except for one item, Sylvia's quilt."

"How much is the highest bid?"

"That's just it," Patsy said. "It hasn't received a single bid."

Stunned, Louise thought at first that her weariness had

simply prevented her from hearing correctly. "Not one bid?" she asked.

Patsy shook her head.

"That's Sylvia's special quilt, and she has worked long and hard on it. It's so exquisite that people probably regard it to be beyond their means. She was so kind to donate all her labor, not to mention any profit, to the organ fund. How sad it will be if the quilt does not sell, or, almost worse, if it sells for an embarrassingly low amount."

"I know," Patsy said. "Is there anything we can do?"

Louise thought for a moment. "I will pledge the money myself," she said and named an amount.

"That's quite a lot, Louise," Patsy said, her eyes widening. "Still, it will go toward the organ fund."

"It's not about the organ fund at this point," Louise said. "It's about Sylvia. The Bible says that a worker is worthy of his wages, and since she has graciously donated an extraordinary work, I can at least recognize her efforts."

"Well, I think it's wonderful." Patsy put pen to paper to record Louise's bid.

Louise put a hand on Patsy's arm. "Would you mark it as an anonymous bid?"

Patsy glanced up. "Okay, but why?"

Louise smiled. "It's personal, Patsy. Anyway, someone may bid higher before the day is over, and then she will never know. If not, please set the quilt aside for me, and I'll pick it up after everyone else leaves."

Patsy nodded, recording Louise's instructions, then moved back to her command post at the auction and raffle stage.

As Patsy had hoped, everything raffled and auctioned commanded good prices. Proud winners collected Fred's electric mower and the various gift baskets and certificates. To her surprise, Louise caught a glimpse of the Havertys claiming the cloisonné vase that the Holzmanns had donated. What were Walter and Kathleen doing at the fundraiser for a second day?

Louise wanted to stop and count the money, but she knew that Cyril and Florence, with Rev. Thompson and Henry Ley looking on, would do that early the next morning. "You and Ethel should sleep in," Rev. Thompson advised Louise. "You've done an admirable job in a short amount of time. You deserve a rest."

Louise tried to take his advice, but when she awoke only slightly later than her usual time on Monday, she hurriedly dressed and made her way to Grace Chapel. Rev. Thompson and Henry greeted her at the doorway to the Assembly Room on their way out.

"Well?" she asked. "How much money did we make?"

They quietly led her inside the room. Cyril was carefully setting the money back into the strong box, while Florence finished penciling in figures in the report with a flourish.

Cyril's face was long, and his eyes were sad.

Rev. Thompson took Louise's elbow. "I'm afraid we didn't make enough money to afford repairs to the pipe organ, Louise. We'll have to go with either a new one or, more likely, an electronic one."

Florence looked up with a slight gleam in her eyes, but her smile was kind. "Don't worry, Louise. If we buy an electronic one, we might have enough money left over for some other good cause as well."

Chapter Twenty-One

Louise walked back to the inn, still stunned. Jane and Alice met her at the door, hopeful expressions on their faces. When they saw her look of dismay, however, they ushered her quietly inside. Alice walked with her to the kitchen, and Jane quickly brewed a pot of chamomile tea.

Alice sat beside Louise. She took her sister's hand and rubbed it gently. "I'm so sorry," she finally said. "Is there enough to at least buy a new pipe organ?"

Wordless, Louise shook her head. She would *not* allow herself to cry.

"Here, drink this," Jane said, placing a Japanese teacup in front of Louise. "There's no handle, so you have to put both hands around it."

Louise let go of Alice's hand and did as Jane said. The warmth seeped into her fingers, distracting her momentarily from the disappointment and shock.

"I'm sorry, Louise," Alice said, hugging her.

Jane embraced her from the other side. "Me too. Especially after all your hard work."

Louise steadied herself. "It wasn't only *my* hard work. Think of how many in Acorn Hill helped out. I feel as though I've failed them."

"Oh, Louise, if anything we've failed you," Jane said.

"Maybe we could have done more to raise the needed money."

Louise shook her head. "I'm concerned that people will be discouraged that we didn't meet the goal. They may feel that since our efforts were wasted, they won't be so willing to help out for the next worthwhile cause."

"Pulling together as members of a town *is* a worthwhile cause," Alice said, wrapping her arm tighter around her sister as though to anchor her in love and truth. "And that effort is never wasted. Maybe that was God's will in all the problems with the organ."

She sighed. "Oh, listen to me. I must not have learned anything at the counseling class. Who am I to speak of God's will as a way to assuage your grief? No one has died, but, still, you are grieving."

Louise closed her eyes and seemed to draw totally inward, as though protecting herself. Alice and Jane could feel the pressure building within her. She made a small noise, as though gasping for breath.

"I hate it when you're hurting like this," Jane said.

Louise's shoulders shook. Then a sound bubbled from her throat. Jane and Alice released her and looked at each other, bewildered. The sound increased until they recognized it as laughter. Was Louise going into hysterics?

"Oh, Alice," Louise finally said. "You're absolutely right. No one has died here." She burst into laughter once again. "It's only an organ, after all. I'm being prideful. I've tried to remind myself of that from the beginning, but I foolishly kept believing otherwise. It's not even as though we are losing all musical accompaniment. We will just have a different instrument, but at least it will still be an organ. It will be a new challenge for me."

"You're amazing," Jane said, her face revealing her own mirth.

"You are indeed," Alice chimed in.

Louise smiled. "Florence Simpson also pointed out that we might even have leftover money. That would be a blessing."

"Yes, it would," Alice said. "There are lots of needs right here in Acorn Hill."

Louise cupped her hands around the tea. "I think I'll take Joseph Holzmann up on his offer to have his friend appraise the organ. Perhaps he will even want to buy it or will be able to find a buyer. It would be nice to know that someone else can get some good out of it."

"That's a sensible way to look at it," Alice said.

"That's a lousy way to look at it."

"Jane!"

"Oh, all right, Alice," Jane said, folding her arms. "You two are being mature about this, so I guess I should at least try to act the same."

"It wouldn't hurt," Alice said, giving Jane one last older-sister look.

Jane sighed. "I hate having to act maturely."

Carlene heard the good news about Craig's success at the garden show in Philadelphia, and she interviewed him extensively for an article in the *Nutshell*. He talked at length about native plants, and she was so enthralled that she renewed her offer for him to write a regular column about gardening.

"I have a feeling that he has more than just native-plant information to share with this town," Carlene confided to Alice, during a coffee break on Monday at the Coffee Shop.

Alice sipped from her tea. "I think he does too. Perhaps he could share some tips on floral arrangements."

"That's a great idea," Carlene said, jotting it down in the small notebook that she always carried. When she looked up and saw Alice looking at her, she said, smiling, "I really am trying to work less, but a writer still has to take notes when a great idea comes around, doesn't she?"

"Of course she does," Alice said. "But I do wonder whether you've made any steps to get some help."

"Oh, I'll probably get around to it one of these days," Carlene said cheerfully. "But don't you see that my asking Craig to write a column is a step in the right direction? There's no reason I can't eventually ask other people to write columns too. Jane could write a cooking column, for instance, and share recipes. Rev. Thompson could answer spiritual questions. A mechanic could answer automotive questions. When you get right down to it, everybody has some kind of skill or knowledge they can share with others, and it helps if they can get some publicity or recognition in return."

"How about me?" Alice teased. "What kind of column would you ask me to write?"

"That's easy," Carlene said, winking. "You would write the relationship column. You'd be the Abby of Acorn Hill."

Alice grinned and lifted her teacup to her lips. She took a sip, contemplating. "Hmm. 'Dear Alice.' It has a nice ring to it, doesn't it?"

"It certainly does." Carlene smiled.

When Alice got back to Grace Chapel Inn, she found Louise and Jane filling out the paperwork to check out Theo Dulane. She had been so busy lately that she had nearly forgotten about him. Jane had reported that he hadn't eaten many breakfasts at the inn, so she assumed that he was either hiding in his room again or, more likely, that he had found other interests outside the inn.

But now he was leaving. "I . . . I didn't know," she stammered, feeling that somehow she should have kept up with his schedule.

"I wasn't sure myself," he said, smiling as he signed the necessary checkout papers. "But I've been feeling better, a little bit every day, so I decided it was time to return home."

"I know it will be difficult," Alice said, "but I'm confident that you'll do well."

"I'm sure I will too," Theo said. "I feel ready to face the memories of Laverne in our house. And I'll be ready to deal with all our friends too. That rabbi at the grief counseling session really had it right. Some folks say the stupidest things when you're grieving, but they do mean well."

Alice nodded.

"And anyway, Pastor Ken said that if I ever needed to get away for a few days, he'd always take me fishing again. Yes sir, somehow a man can put things in perspective when he's holding a rod and reel in his hands."

"Not to mention when he lands a whopper," Jane said, winking. She had been known to fish a time or two herself.

Theo smiled. "That's right." He held out his hand to Jane and then to Louise. "Ladies, thank you for your kindness during my stay. Now if you don't mind, I'd like to talk to Alice alone if I may."

Alice nodded, unsure what he wanted to discuss, but feeling her trepidation grow as Louise and Jane left the room.

Oh dear, what could he want? Perhaps I should have asked Jane and Louise to stay.

He took her hand, his expression serious. "I just wanted to thank you, especially, for being so kind to me. Some women would have laughed if I invited them to dinner. I know now that it wasn't the right time or circumstance. I may be a paying guest at Grace Chapel Inn, but I'm still a guest. I had no business trying to arrange a social situation with you."

"I understood. You only wanted someone to talk to. That's natural, Theo."

"I'm glad you had the good sense to lead me to Rev. Thompson. He's been a big help, and I plan to get some more grief counseling when I get home."

"Grief represents a difficult road to travel," Alice said. "I think you're wise to seek guidance along the way."

He smiled, squeezing her hand once more before releasing it. "Thank you again. I wish many blessings and much happiness to you and your sisters."

"Thank you, Theo. And to you, the same," she murmured.

After Theo had left, Louise contacted Joseph Holzmann, who made the necessary arrangements for his friend to evaluate the organ for possible purchase. Barton Bolen lived in a Philadelphia suburb and promised to drive to Acorn Hill on Wednesday.

Resigned to the fate of the pipe organ, Louise also thought about contacting Myron Apodaca. She knew that he didn't purchase organs, only evaluated them; but perhaps he might have a lead, either on an electronic or a pipe model, one that they could acquire for Grace Chapel once the old one was sold.

As inevitable as she knew it was, she didn't like to think about the day when the organ would be sold.

Chapter Twenty-Two

That afternoon Louise was dusting the piano in the parlor when she heard Walter Haverty clear his throat behind her. "I haven't had a chance to tell you how sorry Kathleen and I were to hear about the fund-raiser results . . . there not being enough money to repair the old organ, that is."

"Thank you, Walter. It was kind of you and Kathleen to come to our fund-raiser. I understand that you purchased a vase?"

Walter cleared his throat and shuffled his feet. "Yes'm, we did. I can't rightly say that I'm awful fond of it, but Kathleen sets quite a store by it. I don't think that Chinese decoration will go too well in our Southwestern-style home."

Louise smiled. "How are you set for your . . . er, what is the word . . . *gig*?"

Walter glanced up from his boots, all smiles now. "Right well, I guess. Say, you and your sisters ought to come hear us play tonight."

"I don't know," Louise said, demurring. As much as she liked Walter and Kathleen, she couldn't imagine visiting a country-western club.

"Come on, Miz Louise. I bet it would lift your spirits. I know you're down in the dumps."

Wiping her hands on a dishtowel, Jane appeared from the

kitchen. "Who's begging whom to do what? It sounds like there's an adventure hatching."

Walter turned toward her. "Why, I was just trying to get Miz Louise and you gals to come hear me and my band play tonight."

Louise tried to signal behind Walter's back that Jane should drop the topic, but her youngest sister ignored her. "That sounds like fun, Walter. Where will you be playing?"

"At a honky tonk called The County Line."

Jane grinned. "I can guess where it's located."

"The name does say it all," Walter said, smiling back at her. "It's a nice place. Reminds me of the clubs back in Texas."

Perhaps they have a mechanical bull. I cannot see either my sisters or me frequenting such a place. "Thank you, Walter," Louise said, "but my sisters and I—"

"—Would love to go," Jane finished. "We've worked hard all weekend on the fund-raiser, and we could use a little fun."

"But that's just it," Louise said, seeing another out. "We're all so tired and—"

"Nonsense," Jane said, waving her hand. "We would love to hear your band play. Er, by the way, what's the name of your band?"

"The Boot Scooters," he said proudly.

"I like it," Jane said. "We'd love to see you perform. You and Kathleen are two of our favorite guests. Aren't they, Louise?"

With two pairs of eyes trained on her, Louise lost her resolve. How could she ignore Walter's kindness about her own music, not to mention the fact that he and Kathleen had obviously purchased a vase they didn't really want at the fund-raiser just to help with the pipe organ? "What if Alice doesn't want to go?" she asked weakly.

"She'll be tickled pink," Jane said with assurance. "Maybe we can even ask some other people to go with us. I bet Craig would like to check it out. Maybe even Pastor Ken."

"Oh my." Louise felt unsettled. *A minister in a honky tonk?*

Walter beamed. "The more the merrier. Bring as many folks as you can corral. If any of you don't know how to boot scoot, why Kathleen would be glad to teach you."

Louise sat down on the piano bench, feeling dazed. *What have I agreed to? Help me, Lord.*

Alice agreed that a trip to The County Line sounded like fun. She invited Carlene to go with them, Jane invited Craig and Pastor Ken, and suddenly they had a troop of people heading for the dance club.

Jane hung up the kitchen phone. "Trevor and Kaylie are going to meet us there. Kaylie's feeling just fine. Do you think Ethel and Lloyd would like to go?" Jane asked.

"I'll call them and see," Alice said, catching Jane's enthusiasm.

"What do we wear to this . . . event?" Louise asked.

"I checked with Kathleen," Jane said, moving out of the way while Alice used the phone to call Ethel, "and she said that blue jeans or a denim skirt or a square dance outfit would be best."

"I don't believe that I own the latter," Louise said, "but I think I have a denim skirt tucked at the back of my closet."

"I remember that one. You wore it when the grammar school had Western Days and everyone in town dressed up." Jane snapped her fingers. "I just remembered that I have a pair of cowboy boots that I haven't worn since then. I bought them in California but have only worn them one time."

"I'm afraid that I'll have to make do with a pair of low-heeled shoes," Louise said. "Not that I plan to do any dancing," she added hastily.

Jane winked at her. "Are you sure? We could probably locate boots for you if you're interested."

"Heavens, no!"

Alice hung up the phone. "Ethel and Lloyd want to go too," she said. "I have to admit, Jane, that this sounds like such fun. I'm looking forward to hearing Walter play."

"I'm eager to hear him play as well," Louise admitted, "even if it is"—she shuddered slightly—"country-western music."

"Oh, come on, Louie," Jane said, edging an elbow into her sister's ribs. "Music is music. It's good to hear what other people appreciate."

"Perhaps," Louise said, with a shade of doubt in her voice. "But I have a feeling that I will be ready for a staid symphony in the near future."

The sisters inspected each other before they left the inn. Louise wore her straight denim skirt, a red-plaid, button-down shirt and low-heeled pumps. Alice wore a flared, dark denim skirt; a light-blue, denim button-down with a red bandana around the collar; and flats. Jane wore blue jeans, red cowboy boots and a red-and white checked western shirt. "I wish I had a cowboy hat," she said mournfully. "Maybe Walter can tell me where I can order one so that I'll be ready for the next opportunity."

"I still cannot believe that you asked Pastor Ken to go with us," Louise said.

"Why not?" Jane said, shrugging. "Just because he's a preacher, you think he's not allowed to have fun? Besides, he offered to drive."

"Oh, I think it might have been more appropriate to offer to drive him."

"I'm just kidding, Louie. Craig said he'd pick us up in his van. He's put the passenger seats back in. That's the only way all eight of us will fit in one vehicle. Otherwise, we'd have to take two cars."

"I'm glad Lloyd and Ethel are going," Alice said. "It will be good for them to have some fun."

"Do you think they *will* have a good time?" Jane asked. "I mean, how much fun could they have at a dance club?"

"Why, they can sit back and listen to the music, just as I plan to do," Louise said. "Don't tell me, Jane Howard, that you plan to take part in country dancing."

She grinned mischievously. "I just might."

"Count me out," Alice said. "I'll sit with Louise and enjoy the music."

"Thank you, Alice. I'm glad that at least one other Howard sister is showing some decorum."

"That kind of decorum might well lead to boredom," Jane muttered under her breath.

"What?" Louise asked.

Jane smiled sweetly. "Nothing."

Craig arrived for them on schedule. After he picked up Ethel, Lloyd, Rev. Thompson and Carlene, he headed for The County Line. "I used to do some country dancing in college," he said, "but I probably don't remember any of the steps."

"I've never been much of a dancer," Rev. Thompson admitted, smiling.

"Me either," Carlene said.

Craig glanced in the rearview mirror at Ethel and Lloyd. "How about you two?"

They looked at each other and laughed, as though the notion was ridiculous.

Craig found the club without trouble, for Walter had given him detailed instructions. It was out in the middle of nowhere, but a huge, red-and-blue, guitar-shaped neon sign flashed like a beacon above its entrance. Before they even got out of the van, they could hear loud music pouring from behind the doors.

"You certainly can't miss this place," Jane said as they trooped toward the entrance.

"Sure," Craig laughed, "once you find the right road out of town. How did Walter and his band ever get a gig here?"

Jane shrugged.

The interior was dark. A man in Western wear met them at the entrance to a long hall that obviously led to the dance floor. Over the din from the band, which Louise couldn't yet see, he shouted, "There's a cover charge of six dollars a head." Then he held out his hand for payment.

"Six dollars?" Louise looked incredulous.

"It's for the Boot Scooters, Louie," Jane said.

"What?"

"It's for the band," Jane said louder, leaning closer. "It's how they make their living."

"I'm so glad you all came." Kathleen Haverty appeared beside the admissions man. "It's all right, Bob. They're friends. Walter wouldn't want them to pay to get in."

"Hold on," Rev. Thompson said, reaching for his wallet. "A worker is worthy of his wages." He smiled, holding out the required bills.

"Pastor Thompson," Kathleen said, squinting in the darkness at the assembled group, "Ethel, Lloyd . . . I didn't know that so many of you would come. Don't worry about the cover charge."

"No way," Jane said, handing over money in addition to the minister's. The others followed her example. "Pastor Ken's right. Walter and his band deserve the money. I can already hear how good they are."

Kathleen smiled. "I'll at least find you tables up front. Right this way."

They followed her down the dark hall. Just as their eyes adjusted to the gloom, they turned a corner and were assailed by bright stage lights trained on the dance floor. The Boot Scooters were finishing their song with a flourish, and as she took a seat at a table, Louise spotted Walter playing his fiddle with gusto. When the song concluded, the band members bowed, sweaty but laughing. Walter glanced their way and caught Louise's eye as she politely applauded. He grinned, gestured at her with his bow, then launched into another song. How he had seen her past the stage lights, she had no idea.

Kathleen was deep in conversation with Jane, but when the band started up the new tune, Jane said abruptly, "I love this song."

Kathleen smiled. "Do you know how to do the two-step?"

"I think *I* could remember how, ladies," Craig said, holding out his hand. "Would you do me the honor, Jane?"

"I'd love to," she said, hopping down from a high stool. Craig led her to the dance floor. Louise saw them bump into a dancing Trevor and Kaylie, decked out in jeans, Western shirts and cowboy hats. The four exchanged greetings, and Trevor and Kaylie danced away. Craig took a while to show Jane a few steps. Then they, too, moved out of sight on the dance floor.

Seated at the same table as Louise, Ethel sighed. "Don't they look nice together? Come on, Lloyd. Let's show them how it's done," Ethel said, rising from her chair.

"You bet!"

To Louise's shock, Lloyd led Ethel to the dance floor, where they proceeded to move with practiced rhythm. Louise stared, covering her mouth with her hand. *Who knew that Lloyd and Ethel could country-western dance?*

Louise sat alone at the small table, marveling, squinting for a glimpse of Craig and Jane or Ethel and Lloyd. While she watched, someone bumped her shoulder, spilling cold liquid on her arm. Even in the dim light, she could tell that the elderly "cowboy" with a half-full mug in one hand and a tipped hat in the other was slightly inebriated. "Wouldja like to dance, ma'am?"

Louise stiffened. "No, thank you."

He shrugged and moved on to the next table where Alice sat, but Rev. Thompson quickly interceded. "We're listeners only," he said, smiling. "We're friends of the band."

Again, the old fellow shrugged, heading for the other side of the room and, possibly, better prospects. Louise turned to Rev. Thompson with a smile. "Thank you."

"You're welcome," he said, handing her some napkins from a chrome dispenser. "I don't think he even noticed he spilled beer on you."

"I believe that you're right," she said, wiping at the spot on her sleeve. "I have to confess that I've never understood the allure of liquor. Other than an occasional glass of wine, that is."

"Jesus certainly drank that," Rev. Thompson said, smiling.

"To be honest, I'm embarrassed for you," Louise said, blotting furiously to remove the beer stain. "Should you be in a place like this?"

"Why? Because I'm a pastor?" He glanced around the room. "Quite possibly, Jesus would have felt right at home in a place like this."

Louise stopped mopping her sleeve for a moment. She glanced at the other patrons, those on the dance floor and those, like themselves, sitting at tables. Many of them were decked out in what appeared to be their finest Western clothes, trying to impress. Some sipped beer, some laughed, and a few looked somewhat sad. But each person, she reminded herself, was one of God's children and deserved to be loved. Jesus laid down His life because He loved them, just as He had done because He loved her.

Louise smiled. "You're probably right, Pastor."

Alice sat down next to Louise. "I was sitting with Craig and Jane, but they took off. Have you seen them dance? Aren't they marvelous?"

Louise watched the couple twirl on the dance floor, Jane's red boots flashing as she and Craig passed by. "They do look like they are having fun," she admitted.

Rev. Thompson joined the sisters, nodding at the band. "Walter can really play that fiddle."

"Sawing away at it," Kathleen agreed, taking the last seat. "He dearly loves his music." She smiled at Louise. "I'm so glad you all came. I know he's delighted, as well."

Louise watched him closely. He dipped and swayed as he played in a most undignified manner, at least according to her classical music training. His performance ran contrary to everything she thought she knew about violin playing, but he did seem not only to be enjoying himself but also to be making wonderful ... could she really call it *music*?

Carlene pulled up a stool, and the others inched over to make room. "I headed for the ladies' room, and when I returned, everyone at my table was gone."

"Sorry, Carlene," Alice said. "If you look out on the dance floor, you'll see where four of our members are."

Carlene watched as Jane and Craig went by, then Ethel and Lloyd. Her mouth dropped open. "Oh my. I knew Lloyd and Ethel had taken some dance lessons together a year or two ago, but I had no idea they had learned how to country-western dance. If only I had my camera."

Alice smiled. "I sense a future story in the *Nutshell*."

"You bet!" Carlene nodded. "Who knew about those two?"

The Boot Scooters finished their song, and everyone applauded. Walter stepped up to the microphone. "Thank you, thank you. Now, with your indulgence, we're going to play a special little tune." He pointed the tip of his bow from one end of the room to the next, as though singling out each person. "And we want to see all of y'all out on the dance floor. It's the Cotton-Eyed Joe, and we play it Texas style."

He started playing, his fiddle providing the leadoff to the song. Kathleen grinned. "Come on, everybody. Even if you don't know how to dance, you can follow this one."

"But, but ..." Louise tried to protest as Kathleen took her arm.

"I'm game," Alice said. "How about you, Pastor Ken?"

"Sure," he said, taking Carlene's hand. "I think I can manage."

"It's easy," Kathleen assured Louise as they headed for the dance floor. "You see, we all link arms like this . . ."

Louise found herself in a line with her good friends and family, watching as Kathleen showed them how to place their hands on each other's shoulders and waists. She showed them how to cross, kick, straighten, then back up three short steps for eight counts. Just when Louise got the hang of that, Kathleen had them two-step forward for eight counts.

"Right, left, right. Left, right, left," Louise muttered to herself, staring down at her feet as though willing them to obey. When they did, and she managed to keep up with the other dancers in the line, she looked up, smiling. "Why, it's just keeping time, that's all," she said to Kathleen.

She nodded. "It's not so bad, is it?"

"No," Louise said. She caught Jane's eye and smiled. Jane laughed, throwing her head back at the sight of Louise dancing. Jane and Craig had linked arms with Trevor and Kaylie, who were obviously pros at the dance.

All too soon the song was over. Louise tried to break ranks, but Kathleen kept her in place. "Wait. It's time for the Schottische. It always follows the Cotton-Eyed Joe."

Soon they were step-step-step-hopping in a different rhythm from the previous dance. Louise had to pay a bit more attention, but she gradually got the hang of it. By the time the tune was over, they were all laughing as they returned to their seats.

"That was so much fun," Alice said, as they gathered around their table, trying to catch their breath.

Carlene agreed, fanning herself good-naturedly to cool down.

"What did you think, Louise?" Kathleen asked.

Louise smiled. "I wouldn't want to do it every day, but it was quite enjoyable."

Tired from their dancing, they all agreed that they were thirsty. Rev. Thompson went to the bar and ordered a tray of sodas, which they gratefully drank as they recovered from their exertion. Jane and Craig stayed on the dance floor, as did Ethel and Lloyd.

At last the Boot Scooters took a break, and Walter appeared at their table, a mug of root beer in his hand. "Hi, everybody," he said. "Are you enjoying the music?"

"It's wonderful," Alice said.

"We're having such a good time," Carlene said. "I haven't danced in years."

Walter winked. "I saw you all out there doing the Cotton-Eyed Joe. Even you, Parson," he said to Rev. Thompson. He turned. "And you, too, Miz Louise. You looked like you were kicking up your heels just fine."

"I had a wonderful teacher," Louise said, smiling in Kathleen's direction.

Walter's expression went serious. "And the music?" he asked hesitantly. "What do you think about that?"

Louise thought for a moment before she spoke. Country-western would never be her music of choice, but it *was* quite lively and tuneful. Most importantly, Walter brought a passion to his playing that energized the band, the songs they played and everyone in the audience. After all, wasn't that what music was all about?

"I think it's wonderful," she said with all honesty.

Walter beamed.

Chapter Twenty-Three

Having recovered from the fun of the night before at The County Line, on Tuesday morning Jane sat at the kitchen table to prepare a special menu. She had decided to cook a celebratory feast for those who had helped Craig in Philadelphia. As was clear at the dance the previous night, Kaylie had completely mended, and Trevor had returned to helping Craig at the store and the nursery. When she phoned the three of them, they said that they would love to attend a dinner.

She also tried to phone Ethel and Lloyd, but couldn't reach either of them. By dinnertime she had plans for the evening, so extending the invitations to those two would have to wait.

Wednesday morning, Jane managed to find them together at Town Hall, where Lloyd's offices were located. He was back at work, but taking it easier than usual, having learned to delegate more responsibilities and to accept more of Ethel's capable assistance.

After polite chitchat and a few Philadelphia reminiscences, Jane broached the subject of the dinner, which she had planned for that Friday night at Grace Chapel Inn. "You'll come, won't you?" she asked. "You two saved the day for Craig."

"Of course we will," Ethel said.

"Wouldn't miss it for the world," Lloyd added. "Will your sisters be there? Ethel and I have been concerned about Louise, especially since we got the news about the organ situation."

"Alice and Louise are invited. Louise was upset about the organ at first, but she's all right now," Jane said. "I suppose she could use a little cheering, though."

"All of us could use that, right, Lloyd?" Ethel said, squeezing his shoulder playfully.

"Right you are." Lloyd smiled. "I tell you, Jane, that trip to Philadelphia did me a world of good. I had slowed down my working habits as my doctor demanded, but I just didn't feel useful. Ethel and I were so glad to be of service that weekend."

"And I'm glad to host a dinner in your . . . and Trevor and Kaylie's . . . honor," Jane said. "So be there or—"

"Don't worry," Lloyd said, winking at her. "We won't be square."

Wednesday afternoon Louise walked in somber mood to Grace Chapel. Barton Bolen, who would appraise and offer the church a price for the organ, was to meet her there. She had known that this day would come, but it was still difficult to face.

Arriving earlier than Mr. Bolen, she headed straight for the organ and launched into "How Great Thou Art," wondering if it would be the last song that she ever played on the old instrument. If Barton Bolen was interested in a purchase, he might want to cart the organ away as soon as possible.

The organ hissed as usual, but it seemed to try to keep up. Louise smiled, for every discordant sound was suddenly sweet to her ears. It was as though the organ had come to life and was trying to sing along with her. The instrument truly seemed to have a soul of its own.

"I really will miss this," Sylvia Songer said, beside the console.

Surprised, Louise removed her hands. "When did you get here?"

"Just now," Sylvia said. "I took some time off because I wanted to be with you when the organ man comes. I thought you might need some company at such a moment."

"Thank you," Louise said. "I suppose it might make things easier at that."

Sylvia smiled. "I know you probably think I was foolish for lobbying for a new organ. The truth is, well, I'm sorry about that now. This organ is a part of Grace Chapel as much as any member. More so, perhaps."

"That's kind of you to say," Louise said, "but in the end, it didn't make a difference what any of us wanted."

"I wanted my quilt," Sylvia said quietly, "and lo and behold, after the auction it came back to me. Purchased and then returned 'to its rightful owner,' I believe the anonymous note said."

"I heard about that, and I'm glad to hear that you're pleased," Louise said, trying not to betray any emotion.

"I am," Sylvia said. "I worked long and hard on that quilt, and it meant a lot to me."

"It was especially kind of you to contribute it to the auction then," Louise said.

"I wanted to help. Whether it meant a new organ or repairing the old one, I just wanted to help." She paused. "You bought the quilt, didn't you, Louise?"

Louise wavered. How could she tell a lie?

"I know it didn't get any bids," said Sylvia. "I watched Patsy as she collected them, and I could tell by the way she kept looking at my quilt that she was worried."

Louise's resistance gave way. "How did you know it was me?"

Sylvia smiled. "I didn't until just now."

Louise blinked, opened her mouth to speak, then closed it again. When she had recovered, she said, "I didn't want you to know, Sylvia."

"Why?" Sylvia leaned against the organ. "That was one of the kindest things anyone has ever done for me. Especially since we were sort of at odds over plans for the organ."

Louise felt remorse. She should never have let her emotions for an instrument cloud a relationship with a friend. Perhaps, along with Acorn Hill's pulling together for another worthy project, this was why God had chosen not to answer her prayer for the organ's repair.

"If we were at odds," Louise said, "I am sorry, Sylvia. You mean more to me than this," she said, touching the instrument. "Much more."

Sylvia smiled. "Thanks, Louise."

They heard a throat clear and looked up to see a middle-aged man in work clothes and a baseball cap standing at the chapel door. "Is one of you ladies Louise Smith? She called me to appraise an organ."

Louise moved toward the door. "You must be Mr. Bolen. Yes, I'm Louise Smith. Thank you for coming today."

He smiled, removed his cap and walked straight to the organ. "This little lady is a beauty," he said reverentially. He gestured at the console. "I heard you playing earlier. She's a bit elderly, but there's still a little life left in her, I believe."

Louise steadied herself. "I know you'll want to play it and see for yourself."

"I wish," he said distractedly, running his hands along the console and the keys. "But I'd really rather see if you ladies know any burly men that can help me pull the console out from the wall. I'd like to have a peek at what's back there. That's why I always wear my working duds when I do appraisals."

"I think some of the men who helped Fred with the fund-raiser booths are helping with a project at his store today," Sylvia said. "I'll get Pastor Ken to call them." She hurried off as Barton studied the old instrument and played it awhile.

Louise sighed. It would be so much easier if the appraisal would go faster. If Barton wanted to do a thorough job, then so be it. But this waiting around was making her heart ache all over again.

Sylvia finally came back and said that Fred and a couple of helpers would be right over. Rev. Thompson had volunteered to help too, and Sylvia had agreed to help him finish up some paperwork later on so that he wouldn't fall behind in his schedule.

Meanwhile, Louise and Barton discussed organs. Although Barton didn't play the organ, or any other musical instrument, he had worked at an organ-rebuilding shop when he was a teen and eventually worked his way up to appraising the beautiful instruments. He was also quite knowledgeable about organ music. He and Louise were deep in discussion about the merits of various organists and composers when Fred and his workers arrived.

Rev. Thompson and Sylvia were right behind them. "Everything all right, Louise?" Rev. Thompson asked, laying a hand on her shoulder.

She nodded wordlessly, watching as the men discussed the best way to tackle the project.

Carefully, they worked the console free from its mooring. Barton helped as much as the others, giving detailed instructions so that they wouldn't damage anything. At last the console was free, and Barton stepped around to the back. "Well, I'll be," he said. "Mrs. Smith, you might want to see this."

"What?" she said, walking around to the dusty back side of the organ, which she had never seen.

He pointed at a name. "Hook and Hastings. Does that ring a bell?"

She shook her head. "I don't believe so."

"It was an organ-building company in Boston in the early twentieth century." He whistled low and long. "This is a valuable organ, Mrs. Smith. Did you know about this?"

She shook her head. "As far as I know, there are no records at Grace Chapel of the organ's history."

"Are you sure you want to sell it?" Barton asked.

Louise glanced at the gathered group, from Sylvia, whose face beamed with delight at the news of the famous organ, to Fred and his workers, then finally to Rev. Thompson. He smiled as if understanding her hesitation, and said, "Mr. Bolen, why don't you finish your appraisal? Perhaps Louise and I should discuss this."

"I'd be delighted," Barton said. He turned to Fred and his workers. "Thank you, gentlemen, for your help with the physical labor."

"Just call us if you need any more help," Fred said cheerfully. He turned to go, but Rev. Thompson touched his arm.

"Don't go too far, too quickly, Fred," he said. "We may need you. You too, Sylvia."

They seemed puzzled, but nodded.

Rev. Thompson led Louise to the basement, where they could talk in the vesting room in private. "I don't see how we can sell this organ," he said.

"But we cannot afford to repair it," she said. "Even if it's a famous organ. Besides, by selling it to Mr. Bolen, we are likely to get more money than we had expected. We can always find a good use for the money if it should be more than is needed for the purchase of a new organ."

Rev. Thompson smiled. "Since Mr. Bolen drove all the way from Philadelphia and is willing to take the organ off our hands today, I think we should contact the members of the church board for an impromptu meeting to consider his offer as soon as possible."

"Right now?"

He nodded. "We already have two members in the sanctuary. We should be able to round up the rest."

Louise smiled. "If you'll telephone Cyril and Florence from here, I'll call Lloyd and the others from over at the inn."

Jane and Alice were excited to hear her news. She had found them in the kitchen, and their voices rose. "Oh, if only the organ could be repaired," Alice said.

"There's still not enough money," Louise reminded her. "It might even cost more now that we know it's a valuable organ."

"Still," Jane said thoughtfully, "you never know what the board might say. Maybe there's some way to make it work."

Louise shook her head. "Barring a miracle, I don't think so. But we do still need to meet so that we can discuss this matter."

Fortunately, all of the board members except for June Carter were able to drop what they were doing to meet at Grace Chapel. While they met in the Assembly Room, Fred's workers put the organ back in place, and Barton Bolen proceeded in his cheerful way to conduct his appraisal. Occasionally the members heard the sound of the organ.

Florence winced at a particularly noisy hiss. "That thing *has* to go," she said.

"But it's a valuable instrument," Cyril argued. "Who would have guessed?"

"I'm surprised that the church didn't have a record of its purchase," Rev. Thompson said. "Especially since it must have cost a great deal of money when it was purchased years ago."

"Several thousand dollars, Barton guesses," Louise told the board. "The members must have made a lot of sacrifices to purchase such a wonderful organ."

"Just as the members of Grace Chapel *and* Acorn Hill

made a lot of sacrifices to raise money to replace it," Sylvia said thoughtfully. "It seems a shame."

"What's a shame?" Florence asked.

Sylvia shifted uneasily. Where once she had been an ally of Florence's in replacing the organ, she now had altered her position. "I don't want to get rid of it now, knowing what we do about its history."

"We don't have a choice," Florence said.

Jane rushed into the room, holding an envelope. "I say we do. You won't believe this, but I got an anonymous phone call at the inn. Someone said to check the mailbox right away for a donation for the organ, and when I did, I found this envelope. Look at all this dough!"

Everyone clustered around while she held out the money. She counted the large denomination bills out loud, and Louise looked on in wonder. "Do you think it's enough to cover repairs?" she whispered.

"Let me get Barton Bolen, and we can ask him," Jane said cheerfully.

When she returned with the organ appraiser in tow, he read them his estimate for repairing the organ. Unfortunately, it was close to the one provided by Myron Apodaca.

"You mean repairs will cost about the same, even though we now know it's a famous organ?" Jane asked.

Barton shook his head. "In this case, repairs are repairs no matter who the organ builder was. I'm not surprised your first appraiser didn't know you had a special organ here at Grace Chapel. I wouldn't have known it myself if I hadn't seen the builder's name."

Everyone turned to Cyril and Florence, who were rapidly adding the total content from the mysterious envelope to the previous amount in the organ fund. The room seemed to hold its breath as one. "Do we have enough?"

Cyril set down his pencil with a *smack*. "We do."

"Hooray!" Everyone hugged and cheered, except for

Florence, who curled her lip and glanced away. Louise sat down on a chair, stunned.

"This is fantastic." Jane beamed.

"Yes," Louise said, trying to smile.

Jane sat down beside her. "But . . ."

The room quieted. Rev. Thompson sat alongside Louise, waiting.

She felt a tear sting her eyes. How could she make them understand, particularly since she had been the one who wanted to save the organ in the first place?

"Please go ahead, Louise," Rev. Thompson prompted.

She cleared her throat. "What I wanted more than anything was to have the organ sound the way it used to when I was much younger. I wanted it repaired, rather than to have Grace Chapel buy an electronic organ or even a new pipe organ. You all knew that."

They nodded. "Go on," Jane said.

"And finding out this organ is historical and valuable makes this even more difficult."

Florence turned to face her. "What are you trying to say, Louise Smith?"

She drew a deep breath. "Despite this bounteous windfall, I don't think we should have the organ repaired."

Chapter Twenty-Four

*W*hat?"
    No one could believe his ears. "What do you mean
we shouldn't have it repaired?" Jane asked. "I know I'm not
a board member, but you just got this big fat donation from
someone who doesn't want his or her identity known. Are
you just going to let it sit?"

Louise smiled. "I know it doesn't sound logical."

"Not at all," Florence grumbled, "though I can't say I
disagree."

"The truth is that just as the early members of Grace
Chapel must have sacrificed to pay for this organ, so have we.
I know that members of this church, not to mention so many
other residents of Acorn Hill, worked hard at the fund-raiser.
And didn't we have fun while we were working so hard?"

All nodded, still wondering what Louise was talking
about. "What are you trying to say?" Cyril asked.

"Even though the purpose of our holding the Harmony
Fund-Raiser was for the organ, somehow that now seems,
well, frivolous. Nobody loves the organ music in Grace
Chapel more than I do, but I wonder if there aren't greater
needs in Acorn Hill, Potterston or elsewhere that could benefit from all our hard work and money."

The room went silent. "Where did you come up with this idea?" Florence asked.

Louise smiled gently. "From you, when you counted the money after the fund-raiser. You said that maybe after buying an electronic organ, there would be some money left over for a good cause. I think we should vote now on what we want to do."

"And how would you vote, Louise?" Rev. Thompson asked softly.

She glanced around the room at each face, settling at last on Barton Bolen's. She nodded toward him. "It's a beautiful organ," he said. "I'm not a member of this congregation, Mrs. Smith, but I'd certainly vote to hang on to it. There aren't many like it left in the world."

"But it would take all the money for repairs," Florence said. "Every last dime, including those from the anonymous donor."

Louise thought for a moment. "Barton, would it be possible to make *some* repairs to the existing organ? Enough so that it wouldn't make quite so much noise during use?"

A slow grin spread across his face. "I think so, ma'am. She'd still hiss a little, but I think we could make that less noticeable, so to speak."

Louise turned to the committee. "Then that's how I vote. Repair only what is necessary and use the rest of the money for whatever charity the committee sees fit."

Fred smiled. "Louise, there's a lot of truth in what you've said. You have the wisdom of Solomon. What do the rest of you say?"

Lloyd got to his feet. "I think it's a jim-dandy idea."

"W-wonderful," said Pastor Ley.

"I guess it will do," Florence said, sniffing.

Sylvia squeezed Louise's hand, not saying anything. Fred slapped his hands on his knees and said, "Well, there's nothing left to do but vote. All in favor of Louise's suggestion that we make only some repairs and save the rest for charity, say aye."

"Aye!" they said as one, then erupted into applause.

After the decision had been made, Barton and the committee discussed repair plans, and they agreed upon a date several weeks away as a deadline for the repairs to be finished.

"You may have to use a piano for a while," he cautioned.

Louise smiled. "I think everyone will tolerate a small change for a short time. Especially knowing that we will soon be enjoying our improved organ."

As Jane and Louise walked back to the inn, they talked about how well everything had turned out. "Will the board take a vote on what to do with the remainder of the funds?" Jane asked.

"In time they surely will," Louise said.

"I just wonder who donated the money," Jane said. "It was the strangest thing, Louise. I was at the inn and got the phone call, and the person sounded like he was deliberately disguising his voice. To be honest, I couldn't even tell whether it was a man or a woman."

"Yes, it's curious that the caller didn't want to be acknowledged," Louise said. "But I'm certainly thankful for such generosity. It enabled us all to make the right decision."

Friday night Jane prepared a wonderful feast for Craig, Ethel, Lloyd, Trevor and Kaylie at the inn. Louise and Alice were invited to participate, but they politely declined as they hadn't been a part of the garden show.

After they had eaten, Craig rose, a glass of lemonade in hand, and proposed a toast. "My business is booming, but more importantly, I know that I have the support of some dear friends. Trevor, Kaylie, thank you for all your hard work. I'm sorry you weren't able to share the fruits of victory in Philadelphia, but we are all thankful that you're all right."

"Hear! Hear!" Jane said.

Trevor grinned. "My truck's totaled, but I can always get another one." He put his arm around Kaylie. "I can't say the same for my girl here."

"We were mighty worried about you, young lady," Lloyd said. Ethel nodded her agreement.

"Thank you all for including me in your trip, even though it didn't work out for me. I'm thankful to be healthy too," Kaylie said.

"If you ever need some part-time work, I probably have some for you," Craig said. "You may not be interested in horticulture, like Trevor is, but I would be glad to teach you floral arrangement."

"Or deliveries," Trevor said, nudging her playfully. "I wouldn't mind giving up that job."

Kaylie laughed. "I'd rather not do anything that involves driving. The wreck was scary enough."

They all laughed lightly, able to see the humor in her words because everything had turned out all right. "If an accident had to happen, I'm glad that the person responsible was so honest," Craig said.

"And that he had a happy ending too," Kaylie said, reminding them of his wife and baby.

"The trip ended successfully," Jane said, "and, Craig, we're happy for your success."

"I think we made a pretty good team," he said.

They held out their glasses and touched them together, each person smiling.

Sunday Louise played the organ as usual, rejoicing this time in the noises that it made. Walter and Kathleen Haverty attended services with the sisters and commented afterward that they had been impressed with Louise's playing.

"I think it's because the organ issue is finally settled," Jane said.

"Perhaps," Walter said. "Whatever the reason, your sister has a great deal of talent."

After church the sisters invited the Havertys to join them for dinner. Jane fixed apricot beef with sesame noodles, and after the main meal, she invited everyone to have dessert in the library. "Alice, Louise, perhaps you'll help me to carry the plates in there," she said, "Walter and Kathleen, go ahead and make yourselves at home."

"Thank you," they said, excusing themselves.

Alice and Louise followed Jane to the kitchen, where she poured coffee and tea. Then she sliced almond praline cheesecake for dessert. "This looks wonderful, Jane," Louise said. "Did the Good Apple make it?"

"Please!" Jane said, feigning hurt. "I made it myself. Would you mind taking those plates to the Havertys? Alice and I can bring the rest and the beverages on a tray."

Balancing two full dessert plates, Louise headed toward the library. She hesitated at the doorway, however, not wanting to intrude when she heard the Havertys speaking in low tones.

"Now, Walter, I think they've done the right thing," Kathleen said.

"But we wanted that money to go for the organ, Kathleen. They're only going to half fix it."

"A gift is a gift, not an edict. You cannot stipulate what its use will be, particularly if you prefer to remain anonymous." Kathleen paused. "Perhaps you should just tell her who you are and why this means so much to you, Walter."

The Havertys gave the money for the organ? And what other kind of subterfuge has been going on here?

Louise's hands shook, and the plates rattled. The Havertys turned, then rose from their seats, startled.

"You two donated the money?" Louise said, her hands still shaking.

"Yes, dear," Kathleen said, taking the plates from her hands.

"We didn't want you to know," Walter added.

Louise almost began to sputter but stopped herself in time. "You have been so complimentary regarding the organ, but I never would have expected you to do this." She shook her head. "It's a kindness that cannot be repaid."

Walter looked at Kathleen, who nodded in encouragement. Sighing, Walter smiled and took Louise's hands. "It's a kindness that *is* repayment." He smiled. "You don't remember me, but I've been in your debt for a long time."

Louise shook her head, confused.

"A young man once attended a conservatory in Philadelphia. His mama had always forced him to play the violin, but what he really loved was country-western music. He got so discouraged while he was studying that he almost quit. His money ran low too. Then his mama died suddenly. He didn't see any reason to stay with his musical studies.

"But he had a professor who took a real interest in him. Gave him some small chores for pay so that the youngster would have some spending money. But more importantly, that professor instilled a love for music in that young man that never left."

Louise felt her throat tighten. "Was that . . . Eliot?"

Walter nodded. "Yes ma'am. Your husband has more to do with my musical career today than anyone else."

"But when did you learn that Eliot was my husband?"

"The last time we came through this way, we talked more than we had in the past," he said.

"We put two and two together and realized who you were," Kathleen said.

"But why didn't you tell me?" Louise asked.

Walter scuffed the toe of his boot against the rug. "Aww, Miz Louise. I was afraid your husband might have told you what a country boy I was, a hick. I didn't want you to remember me that way. I'm kinda pleased you don't remember me at all, truth be told."

"That's why we didn't want to do an interview with your town paper awhile back," Kathleen said. "Walter was adamant about your not finding out about his past."

"I'm sorry that I don't remember you, Walter," Louise said. "But I would never have thought poorly of you or of any other of Eliot's students. I only remember them as earnest, talented young people." She smiled. "He cared for each one and wanted them to do well."

"And now we want to care for you by helping out with your organ situation," Walter said, "to repay a debt, so to speak."

"And, oh, now we have decided not to use all the money that we raised and you donated for the organ," Louise said. "I'm so sorry if you're offended. But we decided—"

Walter waved a hand. "Don't you even worry about it. As Kathleen was just admonishing me when you brought in dessert, it was a gift. The money is yours to do with as you wish. Have you thought about what you'll do with the extra money?"

Louise smiled. "No one has asked, but since I know the source of the anonymous donation, I think that the extra money should go toward helping someone else with a musical career. It would make a wonderful contribution toward prize money or a scholarship that could be awarded at the Pine Valley Music Festival."

Kathleen beamed. "I think that sounds like a splendid

plan," Walter said, then lowered his voice. "Can you do us a favor, though, and keep this donation thing a secret?"

"But why? It's a generosity that should be recognized." Louise said.

Walter looked uncomfortable. "Kathleen and I tithe, of course, as the Good Book says to do, but we made a pact when we married that every year we would also donate a separate part of our income to charity. We decided to do that without our names being attached. This is our donation for the year. Will you keep our secret?"

"How can I say no?" Louise smiled. "Eliot would be very proud of you, today and always." She paused. "And so, I am certain, would your mother."

Walter grinned. "Thank you, ma'am. That does this country boy's heart good."

Chapter Twenty-Five

L ouise sat at the pipe organ, her hands hovering over the keys. Repaired under Barton Bolen's direction, it still hissed occasionally but sounded much improved. She had played it several times, alone or for a few listeners, but it hadn't been officially rededicated.

Tonight it seemed that everyone in Acorn Hill had turned out to do just that at Grace Chapel. Every seat in the chapel was taken. In the sanctuary a magnificent floral arrangement of red and white flowers complemented by gold ribbon signaled the special nature of the occasion.

Louise stretched her hands nervously.

"Are you ready?" Alice whispered. "If so, I'll tell Walter."

Louise nodded, first adjusting her sheet music, then her glasses.

Resplendent in a finely tailored Western-cut suit, Walter rose at the front of the sanctuary, violin in hand. "Folks," he said, "Louise Smith asked me to perform with her because she knows my love of music. She also now knows that her husband Eliot Smith was a great teacher of mine. I wouldn't be playing today if it weren't for Dr. Smith. So Louise, if you don't mind, I'd like to dedicate my part in this performance to him."

Tears in her eyes, Louise nodded.

Walter smiled and tuned his violin for a moment. Then, eyes closed, he launched into a beautiful medley of hymns.

Louise listened to him, spellbound. She and Walter had chosen the selections because they were some of Eliot's favorites. Listening to them now reminded her of how much love her husband had brought into her life, and also into the lives of his students by nurturing their talent and appreciation for music. She had known that Walter Haverty was a fine fiddle player, but she hadn't known the depths of his classical-music training.

As she entered into the duet with her own musical ability, she reflected, too, that the organ was also a symbol of talent and appreciation. Many people had worked hard to save it as a piece of Grace Chapel history.

She threw herself into the duet with Walter, rejoicing in the sweetness of life, which somehow seemed to renew itself again and again.

Later the sisters met with the Havertys and other guests back in the inn's library for a private reception. Exhausted, but pleased, Louise and Walter accepted congratulations all around for their wonderful performance. Henry and Patsy Ley kept up a lively conversation with Fred and Vera Humbert, while Sylvia and Alice discussed craft ideas. Ethel and Lloyd talked about local politics with Cyril Overstreet.

Florence Simpson sat alone until Rev. Thompson sat down beside her, engaging her in conversation. Kathleen Haverty took photos of the entire group, insisting on several shots of Louise and Walter together. "I'll send prints to you," she said to Louise, "and maybe you'll find a place for them in your home."

"They will be most welcome," Louise said, smiling.

Jane served small dishes of peach mousse, leaning over Louise at one point to whisper, "We never would have known how good that old organ was until we tried to replace it. And to think we owe it in large part to a mysterious donor."

Love has a way of coming full circle, Louise thought. "Yes," she said, casting a sideways glance at Walter. She smiled wisely. "Very mysterious indeed."

Huevos Rancheros

1 tomato
6 green chiles
1 onion
4 teaspoons oil (divided)
6 corn tortillas
6 eggs
2 cups grated cheese

Seed and de-stem tomato and green chiles. Dice onion, tomato and chiles. Sauté lightly in one teaspoon oil.

Sauté corn tortillas in a separate, large skillet in three teaspoons oil. When soft, overlap tortillas to cover bottom of pan.

Cover tortillas with half of the sautéed vegetables.

Break eggs sunny side up on top of the tortillas. Put the rest of the vegetables among eggs. Cover and cook on medium until eggs begin to firm up and are cooked thoroughly—the yokes should not be runny.

Cover with cheese, re-cover and cook until cheese has blended. Remove from heat and let sit for five minutes.

Slice and serve. Serve with a teaspoon of sour cream, avocado slices and your favorite salsa.

About the Author

Best-selling author Jane Orcutt has written eight novels and novellas. *The Fugitive Heart* and *The Hidden Heart* were both finalists for Romance Writers of America's prestigious RITA award. She enjoys writing relationship-oriented books and loves a happy ending.

A native Texan, Jane lives in her home state with her husband and their two teenaged sons. They have four four-legged pets—a German shepherd mix, a Pembroke Welsh corgi, and two lazy but mischievous cats.

In addition to writing, Jane homeschools, works outside the home and occasionally does freelance editing. Her interests are trivia, history, current events, reading and any games that involve letters and words. When she wants to be thoroughly humbled, she attempts to work the Sunday *New York Times* crossword puzzle. Jane is also an avid baseball fan, but still has trouble understanding the infield fly rule and how to calculate the magic number.

An Invitation

Now you can visit Grace Chapel Inn online at

www.guidepostsbooks.com/gracechapelinn

Spend some time with other Grace Chapel Inn readers by joining our chat room. Life in Acorn Hill is never dull, and neither is our online community! You can discuss your favorite characters, talk about your favorite stories and maybe even make some new friends. You'll find a place that celebrates the blessings of family and friendship, and rejoices in faith-filled fun along the way.

You can visit www.guidepostsbooks.com to learn about other Guideposts Books. We'd love to see you!